Christine,
Thank you —
SAIL. May you enjoy
the book + have fun
with Sunday, 1st
Renne'

The Last Payload:
The MECS Experiment

~

Susan Renné Fletcher

Susan Renné Fletcher Siewes

PublishAmerica
Baltimore

ISBN: 1-60563-024-1
PUBLISHED BY PUBLISHAMERICA, LLLP
www.publishamerica.com
Baltimore

Printed in the United States of America

The Last Payload: The MECS Experiment is dedicated to my loving husband, Jon Siewers, and my dad, Bill Fletcher, who encouraged me to publish my book and recommended PublishAmerica.

"Thank You!" to my GREAT mom, Bonnie Allen, and the best stepmom, Wilma, for having confidence in my ability; and to my children, Shannon, Erik and Cami, and my grandchildren, Zaley, Payton and Josie, and all my loving family and friends.

Acknowledgment

Dennis Morrison, Ph.D., for the experience,
Alex Van Keuren, Ken Wood and Karen Bauszus for all the support.

To all the dedicated Aerospace Personnel who make Space Exploration a reality.

Table of Contents

Preface - The Introduction

I remember going down the sailboat's companionway for a glass of Chardonnay, when I noticed a Galveston Bay Chart lying on the navigation table. I picked up the chart to check our heading and current location when a piece of paper fell to the floor. Picked it up, but couldn't help reading the note.

It read, *"Dr. Dalton Masters keep the MECS formula safe. This may be the beginning of life and death not as we know it. The future is in your hands. Your life may be in danger. Be careful."*
Yours truly,
Dr. Jon Keller.

I thought to myself, "I wonder what this means?"

Chapter 1
The Meeting

Lying in bed, I, Susan, couldn't believe how much pleasure and mystery had woven through my life the day before. The familiar memories of yesterday began to flow as I stretched, snuggling contented in my secure and luxuriously comfortable bed, nestling between my silk sheets, remembering all the intriguing details.

It all began as I walked briskly from my car to the marina boat docks in the well sheltered harbor. As always, I was mesmerized by the hypnotic sound of loose halyards, moving in the soft breeze, striking the tall masts, and the gentle pinging sound of the resulting metal against metal, as though the entire marina was filled with incredibly expensive wind chimes. Stately palm fronds waved at me as I walked along the rustic wood-planked docks, carrying me away from the intensity of the previous week. I needed the waiting cradle of comfort I find in my love of sailing to deal with the stressful National Administration Space Avionics (NASA) aerospace work environment.

I would enthusiastically follow my sailing passion, facing the fear of a perfect storm, unrelenting heat, or the strength of the sea, which could merciless swallow up an ill-fated sailor. I've experienced the sea's ravenous appetite, challenging physical strength, but always bringing my soul an indescribable calmness and peace.

But just yesterday, I happened to be on another challenging mission. I was meeting a stranger, a prospective new mate for sailing adventures.

I reside in the upper reaches of Galveston Bay—a picturesque community with a seascape of privately owned marinas nestled in the coastal area of Texas known more for its' off-shore oil platforms and refineries, than sailboats, cigarette boats, and impressive yachts. Nevertheless, boats flow daily in a steady stream from neighboring marinas, crossing under the Kemah Bay Bridge, carrying a smorgasbord of seafarers. Wealth and social class are unknown in this boating community. Whether it's the challenges of the sea or mechanics of repairing a boat, the expertise of the most experienced sailor usually is offered at little or no cost.

As I strolled through Waterford Marina, I thought of how much the name reminded me of Waterford crystal. Waiters dressed in white starched coats were serving exotic, colorful boat drinks. The Caribbean reggae music in the background with its tropical beat created an uplifting spirit for the most downcast of souls.

I leisurely walked down to pier 18 listening to the music that played with my soul, turning left and continuing out to slip 15. I was anxious, but not afraid to meet this potential new sailing companion. My pace slowed, as I approached the slip that held a sleek "Bristol" clean sail boat. It was quiet except for the swaying movement caused by a yacht passing by. I surveyed the area for any movement on or around the yacht. For a moment I was disturbed he was not there to greet me, but I heard a movement in the water and saw a man's head, bobbing in the murky, gray Galveston Bay water of the marina. He raised his head with water dripping down his face, catching my eye as he peered through his diving mask. He gave a crooked smile as his teeth clenched the rubber mouthpiece of his snorkel.

I returned the contagious smile, thinking he looked liked a mysterious, sleek dolphin riding the marina waves as he worked a handsaw back and forth on the rudder of the sailboat. "What's he doing"? I asked myself silently.

As if reading my curious mind, he spat out the snorkel's mouthpiece, saying, "Well, the rudder was hitting against the hull, and it hasn't been turning well. So I'm fixing it. The sooner it's done, the faster we will be on the water. My name is Dalton. You must be Susan."

He was still smiling, trying not to ingest too much saltwater. I still couldn't see what he looked like.

I sat on the hot dock box, with the torrid sun beating on my back. I answered, watching this fish in the water, "Yes, my name is Susan. It looks like you are having a lot of fun." I said in a teasing tone.

He was the notorious Dr. Dalton Masters, Bio-Medical PH.D., whom my girlfriend insisted I meet. I finally agreed. Why not, my luck in men was the least to be desired. Being single was difficult to say the least at any age, especially at the ripe old age of 40. Playing the dating game was a challenge in every way. Frankly for me, it had been a series of mistakes. The last one had cost big money, but the other men cost me emotional baggage.

So, as always if my heart strings pulled a little, my internal tape played the same old song. I'm too trusting, too gullible, and too naïve. Do not trust this one, or the last one, or anyone.

As I stared at him I thought to myself, he was not the regular type of guy I was normally attracted to. He certainly didn't look cute in a snorkel mask, with his few strains of hair left floating on the top of the water.

There was something in his smile, the way he looked up at me. It was a mischievous smile that lit up his face like a child who was opening up his first Christmas present.

Karen, my longtime girlfriend, had often recommended Dalton as a potential beau during the past 2 years. I could hear her say, "Susan, Dalton has been a close devoted friend of my boyfriend, Jackson, for the past 20 years. They share many life experiences, including the old NASA parties that were known for being wild and crazy during the Apollo days. The stories are still being told today by the aged rocket scientists with fond youthful memories." Jackson still had pictures to prove their promiscuous lifestyle, which Karen had shown me.

I was thinking in the back of my mind, Dalton's relationship with Jackson and Karen is a positive point. Not like the last rogue boyfriend, who couldn't locate a 'so-called' friend for miles? Oh well, enough of old scorched flames that had long since burned out. I need to stay focused on today and perhaps bring new beginnings. I felt I already knew him from all the legends and pictures Karen had shared over the years. He looked different today than he did with long hair and flowered shirts that were the rage of the '80s.

I debated inwardly, too early in a relationship to be doing such a thing, but as usual I'm moving too fast, putting false hopes in men I don't even know. I'll just have fun.

I struggled with deep-seated scars from past relationships. Oh well, I'll at least go sailing on a bright sunny day.

His piercing brown eyes met mine as he removed his mask, hypnotically locking us together. It seemed like an eternity before he spoke: "Yes I'm having fun now that you've shown up. Karen said you were smart, but she didn't say you were so beautiful!"

"Don't believe everything you hear," I giggled to myself not knowing what to think of his statement even though he had just scored 10 points in my book. It seemed I hadn't learned any lessons from the past. I still wanted to believe in true love, and trust in finding my Prince Charming.

Dalton worked intensely on the rudder, not able to speak for fear of drowning. As in a trance I fell into a dream world spell with the lines beating against the mast and the exotic reggae music from the swimming pool in the background. The sun beat down on my body. I felt sweat trickling down between my breasts hidden playfully beneath my bathing suit. Even the purple sundress, printed with tiny little fish, was clinging to me.

It must be 105 degrees, what seemed like the hottest summer ever in Houston. It's miserable in the hot torrid heat, but soon I'll be sailing with the precious wind brushing against my body like an artist delicately painting a canvass.

The music at the pool reminded me of the Caribbean, at Foxy's, in the British Virgin Islands (BVI) on Josh Van Dyke. There, I swayed to the erotic music, I filled my body with tropical magical drinks. The combination made me do wild and crazy things only to be seen by the full moon, which could tell no tales. These secrets were only seen by the full moon, such pleasurable memories.* [1]

---

[1] The poem "Caribbean Music" is located in the Poetry section.

Two strangers arrived, breaking into my tranquil surroundings and interrupting a whimsical dream. An immediate introduction was in order, "I'm Leona." I saw a rather plain-looking young woman in her thirties with a strikingly beautiful body.

My evaluation of her was broken by a brusque voice saying "Hi! I'm Ken."

I pulled away from my thoughts and politely said, "I'm Susan, another passenger for an afternoon sail on the Texas Riviera."

Dalton began introductions, "Leona does Quality Control for my Payload hardware experiments. Interestingly enough, you two have a lot in common. Susan does Software Quality Assurance for the Space Shuttle Software. Ken is my payload developer for the Micro-Encapsulation Crystallization hardware. He's a good sailor and owns a coastal cruising sailboat in Annapolis, Maryland."

Stocky built, Ken towered over me, measuring at least six feet tall. At first impression, he seemed congenial and a nice guy, but as I observed him, he seemed nervous, as though he needed the next cigarette like an addicted drug user. I kept waiting to see if he would pull out a cigarette and light up. He didn't. Thank goodness.

Leona was ardently mesmerized with Dalton's every move. It was obvious to me that Leona liked this water fish, Dalton, more than just as a business acquaintance. Instinctively, I knew the look. A woman always knows intuitively. Leona's behavior toward him was very familiar, just too familiar. Maybe it was my imagination. I had plenty of experience with women, who would cut your throat for the attention of a man. For one thing she acted like a little puppy waiting for his attention.

I observed their body language. It seemed these co-workers had more than a casual relationship. This would not happen at SEC, the Space Exploration Corporation, where I work. Interesting enough, I kept wondering what was actually going on between them. Leona reminded me of a teenager rolling her eyes at Ken. Ken eyes squinted at her. It was obvious they had their own secret language.

I thought, perhaps Ken was having an affair with Leona. Who knows? It really didn't matter. I just needed the instant gratification of a sailing fix.

Ken went below and came back with a handful of pictures. He showed me pictures of his other mistress. "There she is my comfortable live-aboard home-away-from-home. She is a pristine, center cockpit, ketch-rigged, 37' Irwin. I keep it in a marina in Annapolis close to my land home. When Dalton comes for business trips we go sailing and he stays aboard. It gives me an excuse to spend more time at the marina away from my land-lover wife."

I commented, "I've a sister ship, just like yours, the "La Dulce Vida", but mine is a sloop. No one ever told me that I would have a mistress, but there is no doubt, she is my mistress. She takes all of my time, energy and money. I guess just like a woman or, possibly, some men I've dated. My repayment from her is one day she will take me cruising to exotic places around the world."

My thoughts of future adventures in faraway passages brought chills to my skin.

Ken continued speaking but was rudely interrupted, "I love sailing on the…" He never finished his sentence.

Leona abruptly ordered, "Ken we have to return the rental car now. Let's get out of here, so we can go sailing." Leona began walking toward the parking lot with Ken following obediently behind her.

Contented from the warmth of the sun, I began focusing on this guy who certainly didn't act like a rocket scientist. He was still feverishly working on the rudder. I could tell he was in good spirits, intermittently sneaking a peak over his snorkel and mask, "Susan, I've almost got the job done. Hopefully the rudder won't rub against the boat anymore and will navigate us through the water. I heard you were an experienced sailor. I can't wait to see you behind the wheel. She actually steers like a dream. She's been in the family for 10 years, when my kids were just…" his words trailed off.

Woman's intuition told me not to pry about his children. Divorces were always messy. I acted like nothing had been said, and questioned, "Shouldn't you patch the rudder with epoxy? When my boat was surveyed it had to be hauled out to inspect the hull. Water had seeped into the rudder. It smelled dreadful from the rotten wood. Yuk. You wouldn't want that to happen. Unfortunately, I had to replace it, at great expense."

He pulled himself effortlessly onto the dock. Like an excited little boy he said, "No time left to epoxy the rudder, my dear, we have to go sailing. I'll fix it another day. Right now I can feel a breeze coming. I hear the wind calling me from afar."

This was the first time I had seen all of Dalton, the picture of a graceful dolphin, out of the water. My eyes consumed his appearance. Surprisingly he had the stunning body of a thirty year old with rippling muscles glistening from the drops of water falling from his youthful body. He must have been in his fifties, but still had the agility of a teenager with his bodily motions.

I thanked God, yes, oh yes. No spare tire around the waist with layers of fat like most men my age, who are out of shape waiting for a heart attack.

"Susan, let's prepare to shove off." No sooner were the words out of Dalton's mouth, Leona and Ken appeared, just in time to board the "Lady Naia", a beautiful 34-foot O'Day, in Bristol condition, with playful dolphins painted on the stern.

I questioned the meaning of the boat's name painted on the stern, "What does Naia mean"?

"Naia means dolphin in Hawaiian," Dalton explained proudly. "I painted the dolphins on the side of the boat when she was out of the water having a bottom job. I restored this boat myself. I got it at a great price after it had been sunk and was a total mess. Now it's a total rebuild, the best of everything."

Enthusiastically, I thought this man can fix boats and mine needs a lot of work. "Yeah, he may be a keeper."

"It's a gorgeous boat. I like a boat without much wood to varnish. What a great job you've done restoring it! Oh, and how talented an artist you are, the dolphins look almost real. I like the way it is laid out for cruising. She even has a large wheel, not like the small wheel on mine. Why do sailors always want big wheels"?

Dalton laughed teasingly, "You really don't know, do you? I guess I'll have to let you get behind the helm and show you."

Even though it was hotter than hot, it was a lovely day in July, with wispy clouds scattered across the big blue Texas sky. I stood up from my dock-box perch feeling a gust of wind blowing across my face.

"Let's go sailing." Dalton said enthusiastically as everyone boarded the boat.

Captain Dalton commanded the wheel, I felt at home, helping release the dock lines. The impromptu crew set sail, navigating through the Kemah channel. We passed marinas majestically displaying hundreds of wood and aluminum masts that created a forest of boats. As we rounded the corner passing the Sundance Grill restaurant I remembered an embarrassing sailing memory.

I bared my secret to these strangers, "Once, as we were returning from sailing, I stopped at Sundance with my crew to eat dinner on their patio and listen to some great tropical music. Of course, as a true pirate I had indulged in way too much sailor's brew. As I made my way toward the dock, everyone at the restaurant watched. I certainly put on a show for the patrons. Somehow I navigated into a piling on the dock. I heard a loud noise and realized the barbeque grill had fallen off. Fortunately it had fallen on the pier and not in the water. A frantic waiter ran down the dock rescuing the grill. He picked it up and handed it to my crew as we were pulling away from the dock. Everyone on the patio clapped. I almost died of embarrassment. Luckily it was retrieved intact, since it was a gift from my girlfriend, Karen."

The crew began laughing at my awkward incident. I laughed, but didn't mention one of the people clapping included an old suitor, who must have found great joy in my mishap.

Ken began singing in a baritone voice, "What do you do with a drunken sailor? What do you do with a drunken sailor, early in the morning"?

The boat meandered slowly behind several boats parading in front of the Kemah Boardwalk (locally known as restaurant row). A cigarette boat with two young women lying on the deck in their thong bikinis drove slowly in front of us.

I asked everyone, "Why do the rich old gentlemen have sexy gorgeous women, young enough to be their daughters, on their go-fast boats"?

No one answered. I responded, "It's because these gentleman don't have to talk to these young ladies, who don't have anything in common with them. Their high performance engines are so loud no one can hear a thing. They have absolutely nothing to say to each other. The young pretty girls don't even remember the Beatles? They are just trophies, just like their owner's boats."

Ken grinned, "Oh that's not true. They do have redeeming characteristics. I can see many of them right now."

Dalton chimed in, "I can see their most redeeming features right now." I pretended to hit both Dalton and Ken.

Soon we passed the Kemah Boardwalk, restaurant row, which is a vacation delight. It has casual-to-formal dining, and the atmosphere of a carnival, with amusement rides and games. Locals dub it the Boat Parade.

The delectable aromas from the restaurants made me hungry, almost famished. Darn, I had forgotten to eat in my excitement of going sailing. To take my mind off of my stomach, I waived back to the people waving and smiling at us, as I leaned against the life lines. Perhaps they wished they were going sailing out into the Bay. Possibly they couldn't afford to go. If it was me I wouldn't spend my money on food. I would buy a ticket and go sailing. It was only $25.00 per person on the charter pirate boat, Captain Kidd.

Two excited children ran toward the boat after getting off the Ferris wheel shouting, "Hey Sailors, can we go"?

I majestically gave them my best Princes Diana wave with a big grin, "Sorry, next time. We can't stop the boat for fear of running aground."

I drifted back to my dream world, safe from reality.

The water soon became confused and choppy at the end of Restaurant Row, where the entrance of channel intersects Galveston Bay. This is a temporary situation at the mouth of the bay, when the current is forced into a small opening resulting from the outgoing current from the channel meets the incoming tide from the bay.

Dalton commanded, "Hold on while we get through this mess. It will only take a couple of minutes. Don't want to lose any of my crew overboard. My first rule of thumb is to keep water out of the boat and my crew in."

"Aye, Aye, Captain," I held tightly onto the rail and secured myself from the tossing of the boat. The crew was silent until they reached the mouth of the channel.

Upon reaching Marker 5 Dalton said to me, "Please man the wheel, and turn the boat directly into the wind."

Dalton directed by pointing in the direction he wanted the boat to go, "Come up into the wind, Susan." I turned the wheel, aligning the bow with the prevailing breeze allowing Dalton and Ken to hoist the mainsail up the mast and unfurl the jib. The sails began to luff.

"Fall off," Dalton yelled. I immediately turned the wheel and the boat began falling away from the wind and soon the Lady NAIA began sailing, her sails filled with air.

As I looked up, the sails looked majestic against the fluffy white clouds covering the deep cobalt blue Texas sky. Dalton masterfully trimmed each sail as the wind filled the jib and main sail. They were as smooth and rounded like a beautiful woman's body. The boat sailed effortlessly, flawlessly, under his skillful effort.

I realized, I could release the wheel and she would almost sail the bay waters herself, unattended. The sails were full of wind and the telltales streamed perfectly horizontal. The warm breeze softly caressed my hair, gently as if being touched by a lover. This quickly brought a smile to my face and contentment to my soul. The sensations made me passionate, truly a passionate sailor. Sailing was fascinating, sexual, an addiction embracing my whole body.

I thought, at least if this blind date was a failure, I would have another sailing buddy. Yes, you can't have too many sailing friends, especially ones that can work on boats. You always need to know your resources.

I gazed at Dalton. He was much older, but his face portrayed compassion with a mischievous boyish smile and a deep soothing voice. His voice was hypnotic and comforting, causing me to relax to it's now familiar sound.

Sailing brought tranquility and peace during my retreat from dating: safe from men who took advantage of my kindness. Every muscle began to relax in my tense body with the rhythm of the sea. This is my therapy, my escape from the real world and its challenges.

Dalton asked, "How did you become such a good sailor? You handle the helm exceptionally well."

"You make it easy. It's effortless to helm your boat since you trimmed it perfectly. You made it simple for me." I said excitedly. "I just love the tempo of the wind, boat, and sea. It's like music lulling me to a place of serenity and peace."

I continued explaining. "Sailing comes naturally to me. This is what I love to do best. It's my passion. It's just like the aerospace industry, my other obsession. Ironically the word Astronaut is derived from the Greek word meaning "space sailor". I guess I'm a sailor on the sea and in space. Just like you." A grin filled my face from ear to ear, as I watched another sailboat pass on the port side waving at us.

Dalton returned my smile melting me. "You certainly do look passionate. A real natural sailor behind the wheel, I mean the 'big' wheel. You space sailor."

He was a charmer, a real laid-back sailor. Dalton could be a possible candidate to go cruising in the Caribbean making many passages to seek adventure. Suddenly I had the desire to reach out and touch him. I restrained myself, I didn't know what was coming over me.

Abruptly, Ken walked up and intruded into my world. He asked, "How are you guys doing"?

Before we could answer he began telling his boat story, "Remember Dalton when I brought the Irwin to Annapolis from Florida. My wife, then my girlfriend, was very interested in the boat she seemed to love sailing, or least pretended to be. Now I know she hasn't the slightest interest in anything to do with sailing? I feel she trapped me under false pretense just to get married. I feel cheated from my other love, my Irwin."

Sad, I thought. At least I won't even date anyone who couldn't be interested in sailing. Ken's wife must have faked it to land a prosperous man. I had heard this unfortunate story time and time again in the sailing world. It must be lonely for him to have an avid hobby and not be able to enjoy it with the person he loved. No it was more than a hobby, it was a life style.

I just couldn't choose someone who wasn't a sailor. No, I would not do that, ever, no not ever. Why should I, life was too short. I must choose wisely from now on. My list for a mate was getting longer, successful, intelligent, spiritual, honest, and of course an experienced sailor.

I said, sympathetically, "Ken, I'm so sorry. If I get to Annapolis I'll go sailing with you. That would be fun." I didn't know what else to say to make him feel better. There was nothing more to add to his hardship. I could see the sadness in is eyes. He turned and looked into the bay.

Leona, with her stunningly beautifully body strategically placed herself between me and the Captain in the cockpit. I felt like an intruder as I listened to their work conversation, a topic I found unfamiliar. They used acronyms I didn't recognize which sounded like a foreign language. Quietly, I listened to their words and observed their body language.

Instinctively I thought to myself, yes, Leona does like him, but does he like her? Oh well, at least I was not emotionally involved with him. I wondered why he had invited me if that was the case. I remembered Karen saying he wanted to be in a relationship since he was tired of playing the field. If that was so maybe he had already found someone else, Leona. Karen's boyfriend may not have known about their relationship.

Leona was definitely engrossed in his every move, but I kept glancing over at Ken. The whole body language thing was driving me crazy.

Finally, I gave Leona one of those smiles, so as to say, I'm not worried about you, the competition or your possessiveness. He invited me. Actually, it just didn't matter, all I wanted at the moment was to go sailing, no involvement, but have a good time. Who was I kidding? I wanted a sailor partner. Yes, I was having fun as each wave crashed into the boat. It felt like we were speeding but the GPS only read 5.5 knots.

Ecstatically, I saw two dolphins playing in the bow waves. They dove in and out with perfect rhythm to the boat's water music. I shouted, "Look at the dolphins. What a wonderful dance they're performing. It reminds me of ballerinas gracefully jumping in and out of the water. I'm so happy to see them. It's unusual to see dolphins back in the bay after the chemicals from the refineries have polluted the water. The water must be getting much cleaner from the

Environmentalists putting controls on the refineries. The dolphins, our little friends, are returning back to the bay."

I thought silently, this must be a positive sign.

Dalton said, "So am I, Susan. Dolphins are such frisky, inquisitive creatures with beauty and grace that compares to yours. I believe they follow the dolphins painted on the stern of my boat finding their way back playing in the bow waves. Look at them jumping. I thought at one time they would never return to Galveston Bay. Thank goodness."

The three dolphins only visited for a short while, giving everyone a show to remember our day of sailing before disappearing into the murky Galveston bay. As always the water creatures were gone just as fast as they came.

I wished out loud, "Why couldn't they have stayed longer? One day I would like to swim with the dolphins, even if it meant being in the muddy bay."

I continued to watch the water for some time, waiting for their return. But they had vanished.

I said, "Please come back. Come back and play for a little while longer. Why would they want to hide from us"?

Dalton smiled at me, "They'll come again some other day, and we will see them soon, together. Susan, dolphins are always attracted to the Lady NAIA. I think they come up to the boat to look at the dolphins I painted on the stern. They want the painted dolphins to join them in their play. Almost every time I go out sailing the dolphins find me and the Lady Naia."

Another sign, I reflected.

"Not only are you a scientist, but an artist as well. Your drawings are excellent and they capture the true essence of the intelligent dolphins. It's almost like you can see into their souls." Another plus, yes he was spiritual.

I remorsefully watched for the dolphins to return. "The water is not like in the Caribbean so crystal blue. I can still visualize the beautiful aquamarine sea with visibility down beneath the ocean for miles. The playful dolphins can't hide in the translucent sea. I hate the fact I can't see anything in the bay."

Dalton said, "But the payoff of this muddy water is that it supplies most of the United States with mouth-watering shrimp and oysters. The other good part is, from the Gulf, you can go anywhere in the entire world through the international gateway jetties at Galveston Bay. Yes it's a strategic outlet to go cruising for upcoming adventures."

I said, "Oh my dream is to cruise the islands, or cruise up the eastern coastline. Stay as long as you want, wake up, with the only decision to make would be, should I move on, or should I stay a little longer? Should I go swimming or take a nap? Should I write poetry or paint beautiful pictures of the places I've seen and the things I've done"?

My creative juices filled my mind. To journal in poetry had become another obsession for me. It had been my life saver releasing anger toward unscrupulous men, the men who lied about their love and faithfulness. Hopefully, I would find a man that would be different, someday. Would this be a start of a new beginning? The only question for me is who will be the lucky sailor companion?

I contemplated men and this man, oh this new man, this man asking me questions, about myself. My pal Karen had been telling me about this rocket scientist man, Dalton, for the past two years.

I explained to her, "I can't. I'm living with someone else. This someone turned into a no good user. I finally got rid of him lock, stock and barrel, but not without a monetary penalty of about $20,000. The only redeeming factor was that he was an excellent chef"

I've tried to forget about the past, but it kept creeping into my thoughts. Standing in front of me, Dalton was smiling. I must admit he's cute, but certainly a geek, a real NASA nerd. He is a real dyed-in-the wool rocket scientist. At least you can communicate with this one.

I'm a geek too, at least my kids always called me that. His body language exhibited youth and zeal. His laughter was contagious, his voice relaxing. Yes, I like his voice, a deep, commanding voice that illuminated his presence. Deliberate, he is the 'Confident Man', so poised in every way, poised and so sure of everything he did. What's the catch? When does the bad stuff come and in what disguise?[2]

---

[2] The poem "The Confident Man" is located in the Poetry section.

This group seemed to be comfortable with each other. Dalton kept bringing me into their work conversation, but I felt like an outsider. Leona made sure of that—it was obvious she wanted me to disappear. We sailed most of the day. The torrid heat didn't diminish the soft stroking breeze across our bodies. Slowly I removed my cover-up to catch Dalton's attention. As soon as he was watching I could see he was pleased to see the low cut leopard two piece covering my breasts. I knew both Leona and Ken were watching him as he watched me.

Dalton said playfully, "Nice bathing suit. Those go-fast boat girls don't have anything on you. You too have redeeming qualities."

Again I pretended to hit him. "Oh Dalton, now do you want to tell a blond joke."

The day was fun, and laughter came naturally with this newfound sailing partner. Dalton was very attentive and placed his hand on my shoulder as I sailed. I felt comfortable with his touch and attention.

I finally asked Captain Dalton what he did for a living. Dalton explained, "I'm an NASA research scientist, a biomedical Ph.D. My last years have been concentrating on experiments aboard the Shuttle."

"How intriguing, I want to hear all about it," I said, noticing Leona and Ken leaning closer to hear the conversation.

"I do cancer research and I'm working on the M.E.C.S. Experiment. MECS stands for Micro-Encapsulation Crystallization of Drugs Delivery System (M.E.C.S.)", Dalton explained. "It's like a pill that is grown in an anti-gravity environment and inserted into the arteries that leads to the cancerous tumor. It's a small microscopic capsule-shaped pill that will destroy the tumor and not affect the rest of your body. It's unlike using radiation or chemotherapy which destroys your good cells. In the future, microcapsules injected directly into human tissue may be the drug delivery system of choice for cancer treatment and other diseases. My Micro-Encapsulation Crystallization experiments have been flown on the previous eight shuttle flights and soon will be the next payload on Shuttle Launch 195. Congressman Dan Fletcher, the famous ex-Astronaut, will be part of the payload."

"This sounds too good to be true. I've known many friends who died because they had inoperable cancer. You could have saved them." I said sadly.

He looked directly into my eyes, "It will be successful and it will happen and possibly do much more, something that even you can't imagine, it will possibly change life for mankind."

About that time Leona rudely interrupted, "Dalton, where do you want to go to dinner? Let's go get crawfish, Cajun style."

I wanted to ask more questions to learn more, but before I could speak Leona monopolized the conversation. They began making their dinner plans that didn't include me. No invitation came my way. Apparently I didn't fit into their dinner arrangements.

I hinted, "Dalton, I do not want the day to end so soon. Please take the helm so I can get something to drink."

"Aye, aye Captain Susan, I'll hold down the ship while you are gone. Don't be too long, my lovely lady."

I turned facing Dalton and gave him a big smile before going down the companion way. Looking for the head I noticed a Galveston Bay Chart lying on the navigation table. I picked up the chart to see our position and heading. Accidentally, a piece of paper fell to the floor. Picking it up, I read a short note:

Dr. Masters,
Keep the M.E.C.S. formula safe. This may be the beginning of life and death not as we know it. The future is in your hands. Your life may be in danger. Be careful.
Yours truly,
Dr. Jon Keller

Curiosity seized me, I was frozen. What was the significance of Dr. Keller's words? I wonder what this note means.

I quickly put the note back under the chart as Ken touched my shoulder. Nervously, I jumped as the massive Ken stared coldly at me.

"Did he see me reading the note?" I thought to myself. I shivered but quickly composed myself, "Ken, can I fix you a drink?"

He snapped, "No, but I'm sure you'll get what you want."

"Excuse me," I inquired.

"Oh nothing" he said. How strangely he was behaving. He must have seen me putting the note back. Suddenly, I really wanted to get off the Lady NAIA fast. Something suspicious was going on.

Dr. Captain Dalton called down below, "Susan, did you get lost? Do you still want to helm the boat?"

"I'll be right up." I fixed my drink and went to the head as quickly as I could. Uneasily I climbed up the stairs.

My hands were shaking as I commanded the wheel of the boat. I gripped the wheel tightly, trying to calm down. I felt I was in the middle of a mystery movie. It was an uncomfortable feeling.

Ken now gave me the creeps. Sweat began running down my face from fear of the suspicious note and its implications.

As I looked across the bay the sunset painted a beautiful picture with vibrant colors of orange, red and blues on the horizon. It produced a calmness distracting me enough to temporarily forget about the ominous note. The waterfront scenery kept me sailing in the bay every chance I had. The same exquisite captivating sunset can be found anywhere in the world, but I was enjoying it in the Galveston Bay in the outskirts of Houston, Texas.

The crew headed back through the entrance channel marked with red and green buoys (Red Right Return) toward the Ferris wheel at the Kemah Boardwalk. I continued manning the wheel sailing through Restaurant Row. As we turned the bend bearing briskly toward Sundance Grill, I headed into the wind so Ken and Dalton could lower the sails and put on the sail covers. The smell of food permeated the air. My stomach growled.

Leona asked, "Where are we going to dinner, I'm starved?"

Dalton said, "We will do just as planned, I've got delicious lobsters at the house."

Leona screamed with delight, "Sounds great to me. I can't wait."

The Lady Naia knew the way to the channel toward home, Waterford Marina. Dalton complimented me on my sailing ability, "You certainly are an accomplished sailor and the view. You look beautiful with the sunset as a backdrop with the wind playing in your hair. Excuse me my dear, we're near the marina. I'll take the helm."

He brushed up against my sweaty body causing the body heat to rise. I thought either this reaction from the sun or his closeness but most likely from my sexual attraction to him.

Dalton said, "I'll take the wheel from here. I've my own special way to dock the boat."

I smiled, "Aye, Aye Captain. It has been a pleasure sailing your boat."

Frankly I was relieved when Dalton took the helm. I didn't want the responsibility, but was amazed as I watched him maneuver the boat stern first into the slip, "Dalton, it's amazing how you backed the boat into the slip effortlessly. Wow. I would never attempt to do that. I would take out the dock. I had heard in Europe this is a preference but not here. Now that was a perfect docking, a magnificent sail and best of all no one got hurt." As my own captain, safety first and being hurt was the one thing I always feared for myself and crew either on the open seas or in the Galveston bay.

My stomach churned at the mixed feeling created by meeting this fascinating sailor guy. The breathtaking sunset made me forget my fear upon reading the mysterious note. Overall, it had been a wonderful, relaxing day, and the best part was seeing the dolphins. I wondered if he would ask me to have lobsters with them.

Grinning, he can even back the boat into the slip. I would never try to do that—another 5 points, 100 points, he was truly an experienced sailor.

Gathering my sailing bag, I waited for a dinner invitation. Hesitating for a second, I finally said, "Thank you so much for the magnificent day. I appreciate the sail and hope we can do it again. It was nice meeting everyone. Thanks." I turned to Dalton and asked, "Can I help clean up the boat"?

Dalton smiled, "No I'll do that later, my beautiful lady. I'll invite you again to go sailing. It's hard to find good crew."

Disappointed, I jumped onto the dock. Once again I remarked, "Thanks for the great sail." I slowly walked down the dock listening to the reggae music in the background. I kept thinking he would call out to me, but he didn't.

When I reached my car I heard Dalton's voice, "See you soon, Susan." I turned, but the threesome quickly disappeared in the parking lot before I could utter a word.

Chapter 2
To Home

Standing beside my car I felt abandoned. I knew it was irrational, but the past insecurities crept into my present world. Abandonment was a familiar word remembering my father's cheating on my mother, which kept him away from home for days at a time. As a child with tears streaming down my face, I would look out the living room window waiting an eternity for my Daddy to return. He would come home eventually, but the majority of the time I had been tucked into bed by my loving mother a long time before he entered the house. The non-existent attention made my delicate self-esteem crater. I kept praying the emotional scars would be healed along with many years of counseling. This situation had been many years ago, however, I never knew what would trigger my insecurities. The lasting emptiness would not fill even though my Daddy had long since apologized to me. Sadly, I got into my car.

Leaving the parking lot I had learned a survival method by diverting my thoughts in other directions such as the suspicious note from Dr. Jon Keller. What did he mean by danger? Danger is always a part of the aerospace world in flying humans into space but NASA research should not be life threatening situation. Accidents do happen like the incident at the Kennedy Space Center where three unsuspecting men were killed in a pressure chamber. The oxygen they were breathing was accidentally replaced with carbon dioxide. In one last breath they were instantly gone forever. KSC Security takes precaution at certain buildings by taking your badge, so if it explodes they will know who died inside. I had met a guy who was supposed to be with them, however, was at a meeting with his manager when it happened. Timing is everything in life especially for this guy who is still breathing. Space is dangerous and danger is a constant companion throughout the space program.

Meeting this sailing companion felt very different for me, not like the long list of many men who had been disappointments in my love life. This one was intelligent, interesting and to my surprise he is doing cancer research, a payload experiment on the space program. It still didn't add up I thought, why would the life of a research scientist be at risk?

The intriguing note had captured my interest. I needed to solve the mystery: I needed more objective evidence, more information, as we say in the Quality world. Random thoughts ran frantically through my mind organizing a sequence of what I should do first. I wondered who I could ask about Dr. Keller. I really didn't know anyone I could ask, but I could do some research at work. The NASA, Johnson Space Center and KSC Intranet sites were at my finger tips. Searching the web would be easy as my job is to find unanswered problems day after day and analyzing for a solution. If I can do my job, I should be able to research Dr. Keller.

I soon reached the City of Kemah Bridge developing my mental plan of attack. Checking my rearview mirror to change lanes I noticed a navy blue car approaching at a high rate of speed. The car recklessly approached, forcing me to move into the right lane to get out of their way. It sped up but immediately slowed down next to my car maintaining the same speed. In my peripheral vision I saw two men wearing dark glasses staring at me. I didn't recognize either one of them.

I turned my head forward wanting to say, "Take a picture, it will last longer." Spontaneously like a child I stuck my tongue out at them and laughed. They didn't turn away, but continued to stare.

Feeling uncomfortable, I sped up and turned onto NASA Parkway, losing them at the light. This had been a strange day. I couldn't wait to get home, take a bath, and wash off the salty spray. Nothing would feel better than to get this clingy dress and damp bathing suit off my sweaty body.

Immediately arriving home, I filled the Jacuzzi with hot steaming water and poured in the relaxing lavender oil beads. I picked up the cordless telephone from the side of my bed and laid it on the tub. Then I luxuriously slid into the silky soft water which would soon soothe my muscle and emotional pain. I glanced at the reflection of my body in the mirrors surrounding the Jacuzzi. The mirrors revealed that the Galveston sun had tanned my youthful breasts a golden brown along with the rest of my body.

This led my thoughts to making passionate love, which had been a long time ago. My body throbbed with desire. Laying down in the water my blonde hair fell backwards against the bath pillow. My thoughts continued wishing my sailing companions had invited me to dinner.

My thoughts turned to Dalton's explanation of the MECS experiment and to Dr. Keller. A cancer cure had not been found even with the insurmountable cancer research that had taken place over the years. They had made strides during this time but the cure was sometimes a Band-Aid fix lulling the patient into believing this time they had beaten the ugly beast. Unfortunately their cancer would return, attacking an unsuspecting location.

Today something was going on with that Motley crew, but I couldn't put my finger on it. It was none of my business, and I really shouldn't be worrying about it, since I didn't even know Dr. Keller or even my new sailing companions. But something had happened today which made me want to know more. I had to know more.

Closing my eyes I began relaxing my exhausted body and mind. I dreamed of sailing in crystal blue waters in the tropical Caribbean, a life style where people were just laid back and didn't have to rush. I would have peace in the early sunrises with the warmth of the sun coming up in the distance while drinking my first cup of coffee in the cockpit. Then I would end the day with the tranquility of the afternoon sunset. I would trade my coffee in for a glass of wine relaxing to the peaceful blue water hitting the bow of the boat. This would be the life of a sailor, I so much wanted to taste.

The phone rang startling me from my peacefulness. I quickly answered, "Hello. This is Susan."

Surprised, I recognized my new sailor friend, Dalton's hypnotic voice, "How are you doing"?

I sat up, gaining composure, I responded, "Dalton, I'm just relaxing, remembering our delightful sail, I'll always commit to memory the three playful dolphins playing in the bow waves." I said wondering what he would think if he knew I was naked in the bathtub. My hormones tempted me to invite him over. I speculated what kind of lover he would be. He had sensuous lips, and a great body. It had been too long, since I had been with a man. The thoughts aroused me.

He interrupted my naughty feelings, "Susan, it was a great sail today, and I thoroughly enjoyed getting to know you. Thank you so much for coming with us today."

He paused, "What I'm going to say is kind of awkward. I know you'll think I'm crazy, but I was wondering, even with a week's notice, if I'm not being too forward, would you like to vacation with me in the Abacos, Bahamas? Please join me and a group of my friends for a week of paradise. You will be well chaperoned by my best friend. I promise to take good care of you. I can give you references, especially from Jackson and Karen."

He resumed his speech, it seemed almost rehearsed. "We can go diving or snorkeling, and searching for lobsters. It's truly a paradise. This trip has been a tradition the past five years joining my friends in the Abacos. We pack up a 40-foot Sea Ray with twin 600 horsepower engines in Miami and all kinds of supplies. It takes us approximately 5 hours to cross the Straits of Florida in the Gulf Stream to go through customs at West End, Bahamas. My friends have rented a place in Marsh Harbor. It's a small house surrounded by tropical flowers, with a porch full of fans that keeps gentle breezes flowing. The view is captivating of the island with a magnificent view of the ocean. The only downfall is the accommodations may be a little crowded with all the people, but we can make room for one more, especially one as pretty as you are. I know you have only just met me, but I've heard Karen talk about you for years. I've admired Karen's refrigerator picture of the two of you for years. Somehow I feel like I know you already. This will give us the opportunity to really get to know each other. Promise, no strings attached, just friends. Please think about it, but not to put any pressure, I need to have an answer, before we hang up the phone. How's that for no pressure?"

I sat in the now cooling water, stunned. This is truly a confidant man with a truly crazy invitation. I could tell in his voice he assumed I would go. I felt uncomfortable staying with a bunch of strangers. If I went it would be as an independent woman, I had to make other plans.

"This is an unusual invitation. I'm caught off guard, though the invitation is tempting." I thought for a second and said, "You know Dalton, my Dad has a Trawler, named 'Dream Catcher' in Marsh Harbor. If I go I will probably stay on it. I have to find out if it's available and if I can take off from work. Sometimes other relatives or friends visit. Let me check it out and I'll talk with Dad."

I hesitated for a minute thinking about the curious note. I needed to know more information, before I put myself in that position with a person who's life may be in danger.

Regardless, it would be a thrilling adventure. Without thinking any further my hormones answered, not my head. I responded spontaneously, "I'll check tomorrow with Dad, and if I can get off work I'll join you in the Bahamas. You know I must be crazy for accepting, and you must be crazy for asking?"

Detecting excitement in his deep voice, "This is GREAT. No you are not crazy. All you need to pack are tiny bikinis, sun tan lotion and snorkeling equipment if you own any. I'll buy a ticket for next Saturday morning. I've got to go down tomorrow to help provision the boat in West Palm Beach. I'll make the passage with my long time friend Nick. I'll call you in a couple of days and let you know the details of your flight and where you can get the tickets."

Abruptly he ended his conversation after closing the deal, "Good bye my new friend. We will have fun. See you later, bye." He hung up the phone, before I could even say goodbye.

Laughing to myself, bikinis, I haven't worn one in years, many years. How much weight can I lose in a week? I surveyed my body again with scrutiny? Oh well, this old body will have to do. I hit myself on the hips, and held in my stomach trying to make it flat. That only lasted a minute, and my stomach poked back out.

Chapter 3
The Research

Then reality hit. The memories faded as the Monday morning sun rose too early to return to my tedious auditing work. Being employed in the aerospace industry had been a long time dream, since I was a little girl. The space program was exciting and dynamic and everyone talked about what was happening. President JF Kennedy had brought the space program into everyone's home. All of my friends wanted to be Astronauts to fly high above in a tiny rocket, become famous and drive around in a fast extreme machine Corvette. I remember as though it were yesterday, when Astronaut Dan Fletcher first circled the earth in a claustrophobic tiny capsule. William Kronite's famous words are etched in my mind forever: 'God Speed, Dan Fletcher, God Speed, each flight'.

Not one day goes by without the ghastly memory of the two space shuttle disasters, each lost, exploding into many pieces along with their unsuspecting crew and passengers. One scattered half way across the vast Texas country side and the other lost deep in the icy blue Atlantic Ocean. I tremble with fear thinking, every time a shuttle launches, possibly I might miss something in my flight audits.

The shuttle software sign off accountability has been an overwhelming responsibility. The stress of auditing for potential errors was too much anymore, just the thought of missing a discrepancy causing another disaster. The Space Software has to be near perfect and if it's not I need to find the problem. The Space Software audit tasks had taken a toll on my body over the years. How could I deal with another disaster? What would happen to the program if another disaster were to occur again? I kept wondering if the software would continue to be as reliable as it had for the past twenty years with all the old timers retiring and leaving with their insurmountable knowledge.

Now, NASA is launching an International group of Astronauts, Canadians, Italians, Japanese, and Russian cosmonauts, and even civilians who have paid $20,000,000 for the ride of their life. Each one desiring to be a space pioneer with expectations of adventures located far away from Earth in the International Space Station.

Many times I've surmised a worldwide space program was just another way to provide international welfare to Russia. Yes, Russia had lost the Cold War, but it was the beginning of a losing proposition for their economy. It helped break Russia's already meager economy by Neil Armstrong making history as the first man to walk on the moon. This one event catapulted the Americans into a technical revolution pouring money and technology into the U.S. economy. Ever since then, the Russians political system just couldn't keep up with the strong American wealth. Now the value of the ruble was weak on the economic market.

As a result the Russians had suffered horrific poverty and senseless long lines waiting for food and products. In comparison, I realize the blessing of being an American citizen and working for the Space Exploration Corporation (SEC).

I sauntered toward my desk filled with piles of paper created by auditing the many inspection packages and documents. Surrounded were the aerospace engineers coding, testing and developing requirements for the complex intricate Space Shuttle Software. I thought, how amazing SEC had attracted so many smart, clever, and intelligent aeronautical engineers for so little money. They did it for the love of the Aerospace Program. In the outside world they would be making double the salary.

I heard them talking, "The navigational guidance should be used on the Avionics Upgrades with the three string Global Positioning System (GPS) for the next flight. We coded the GPS system to make sure the docking with the upcoming International Space Station would be precise and accurate. No errors are allowed or as Gene Krantz would say 'Failure is not an option'."

I knew any collisions in space would end my career and my fellow workers who were devoted to their work.

Sitting down at my desk I looked discouragingly at the masses of piled up papers, sighing. I must check first things first. I checked my calendar for any AM meetings. Fortunately none were scheduled, so I could do my undisclosed research on this mysterious MECS experiment's note from Dr. Keller.

I signed onto my computer and linked to the NASA web site at Johnson Space Center Web. In the search area I entered MECS. Miraculously 10 hits came up.

The first hit came up with Space Transportation System Payload information. Let me start with what is happening on the Space Transportation System (STS) flight Shuttle Launch 999. It's the next flight.

Interestingly, my favorite and the most awesome Astronaut, now Congressman Dan Fletcher, will make the trip again. He was the same one who was a founder of the space program, who made history by being the first man to circle the earth. Wow, now he has volunteered to be a guinea pig on the geriatrics experiment.

The honorable and renowned Congressman Dan Fletcher is participating in the Micro-Encapsulation Crystallization Encapsulating experiment. It's a drug delivery system for multiple medicine applications. He will be instrumental in the laboratory exercises to prove the effectiveness of the application. It's a great honor that Congressman Dan Fletcher will return to space participating with an International aeronautic crew in the International Space Station payload experiment. Fletcher originally was assigned to the Aeronautical (NASA) Space Task Group at Aeronautical Research Center, Huntsville, Alabama, in October 1955 after his selection as a Project Jupiter Astronaut. The Space Task Group was moved to Houston and became part of the NASA Manned Spacecraft Center in 1964. Fletcher flew on Jupiter-6 Independence Flight logging over 300 space flight hours. Prior to his first flight, Fletcher served as backup pilot for Astronaut's Smith and Green. When Astronauts were given special assignments to ensure pilot input into the design and development of spacecraft, Fletcher specialized in cockpit layout and control functioning, including some of the early designs for the Jupiter Project. Fletcher resigned from the Manned Spacecraft Center and was promoted to the rank of Captain, US Navy and retired from the military in 1970. He ran for and was elected to the United States Congress. Fletcher retired from the U.S. Congress in January 1998 serving 28 honorable years.

Fletcher piloted the Jupiter-Adam 6 "Independence Flight" spacecraft on the first manned orbital mission of the United States. Launched from Kennedy Space Center, Florida, he completed a successful three-orbit mission around the earth, reaching a maximum altitude (apogee) of approximately 162 statute miles and an orbital velocity of approximately 17,500 miles per hour. Fletcher 's "Independence Flight" Jupiter, space craft landed approximately 800 miles southeast of KSC in the vicinity of Grand Turk Island. Mission duration from launch to impact was 4 hours, 55 minutes, and 23 seconds.

SHUTTLE LAUNCH 195 Discovery (October 29 to November 7, 2002) was an 11-day mission during which the crew supported a variety of research payloads including deployment of the Stern solar-observing spacecraft, the Hubble Space Telescope Orbital Systems Test Platform, and investigations on space flight and the aging process. The mission was accomplished in 134 Earth orbits, traveling 3.6 million miles in 213 hours and 44 minutes.

I thought, "This seemed odd for NASA to put a qualified, elderly pilot on such an important mission." The article continued,

Along with Congressman Fletcher will be a French cosmonaut from the Russian Space Program, Pierre Duvall, the Mission Specialist. He had flown on the Russian Space Station, *Mirage*, for six months. His duties consisted of ensuring the payload equipment and process would run smoothly. He had been selected by NASA, December 1994. At that time he reported to the Johnson Space Center, March 1995, as an

Astronaut candidate in the 15th Group of Astronauts. After completing a year of training and evaluation, he was assigned as crew representative functioning as the catalyst to resolve technical issues for the Astronaut Office EVA/Robotics and Computer Branches. His assignments included development of Robotic Situational Awareness Displays. He tested space shuttle control software and hardware in the Space Avionics Integration Laboratory. In November, 1996, he was assigned as mission specialist and prime robotic arm operator on SHUTTLE LAUNCH 87. In January 1998, his duties as crew representative for shuttle and station flight crew equipment, and subsequently served as lead for Astronaut Office's Crew Systems and Habitability section. He flew on SHUTTLE LAUNCH 287 (1997) and SHUTTLE LAUNCH 312 (2003) and has logged 30 days, 14 hours and 54 minutes in space.

I remembered the Russians, along with the French, had negotiated exceptionally hard to get him on this flight. A bio was alongside his picture. He had received his undergraduate degree at the Russian University in Moscow. The picture displayed a very masculine gentleman with intense eyes and a stern face. I laughed to myself. They should make everyone smile for these pictures, at least he wouldn't look so frightening and intimidating.

There was one female Astronaut, Chechee Ming, who looked gregarious, energetic with a round happy face. She was a petite Chinese lady whose personality bubbled out from my picture. I continued to read,

Chechee Ming, PhD, Payload Specialist would be observing and providing the quality control of the experiment. She'll be providing quality control as the payload technician ensuring accuracy of the MECS data. Her prior experience included the eighth Shuttle-*Mirage* docking mission on SHUTTLE LAUNCH 189 *Endeavour* (January 22-31, 1998). Their successful mission transferred more than 9,000 pounds of scientific equipment, logistical hardware and water from the Space Shuttle to the *Mirage*. In the fifth and last exchange of a U.S. Astronaut, SHUTTLE LAUNCH 189 delivered Sonny Williams to *Mirage* and returned with Carey Scott who had been on the *Mirage* for three long months. The mission duration was 8 days, 19 hours and 47 seconds, traveling 3.6 million miles in 138 orbits of the Earth.

The Commander, Bob Rankin's picture exuded self-confidence. He had friendly twinkling eyes surrounded by dark shiny hair. You could tell he was a leader. Commander Bob Rankin was commissioned a second lieutenant in the USAF and attended pilot training at Randolph Air Force Base (RFB), San Antonio, Texas. He attended F-4 Instructor School and was assigned as an F-15 instructor pilot and academic instructor in December, 1990. He was later assigned to the combined forces Post Graduate School, where he earned his masters degree in Astrophysics, graduating number one in his class. From there he was assigned to the USAF Test Pilot School. Upon completion of Test Pilot School, Rankin served as a test pilot where he flew the entire inventory of Air Force fighter and bomber class aircraft. Included were the F-111 and all five models of the B2 Stealth Bomber. Rankin was appointed to the Aircraft and Armament Evaluation Establishment at Boscombe Down, England, as an exchange test pilot with the Royal Air Force. He served as a test pilot in the Hawk, Hunter, Buccaneer, Jet Provost, Tucano, and Harvard. He logged over 3,800 hours of flight time in more than 40 different types of aircraft. He was highly decorated in Desert Storm which promoted him to Colonel. Commander Bob Rankin participated on one previous mission: accomplishing the first docking with the International Station and delivering 4 tons of logistics and supplies in preparation for the first crew to live on the space station early next year. The mission was accomplished in 153 Earth orbits, traveling 4 million miles in 9 days, 19 hours and 13 minutes.

I saw another crewmember, Mission Specialist Daryl McKnight, M.D., had sandy blond hair and eyes of blue. He had a California surfer boy appearance. I smiled, he definitely was the best looking Astronaut in the bunch. I remembered his reputation of enjoying fast women and very fast sport cars.

Dr. McKnight, the renowned Astronaut Flight Surgeon, Payload Specialist, specializing in physical medicine will monitor the

Honorable Congressman Dan Fletcher's vital signs. The experiment's results will be logged and analyzed daily.

During medical school, Dr. McKnight performed his active duty training at the Naval Hospital in Bethesda, Maryland. After completing medical school, he continued his postgraduate education at The University of Texas, MD Anderson Cancer Research Center from 1987-1988. He underwent 6 months of aero-medical training at the Naval Aerospace Medical Institute and received his flight training at NAS Pensacola, Florida where he was designated as a Naval Flight Surgeon. From there he was stationed at MCAS Yuma, Arizona and assigned as Flight Surgeon for a Marine Corps AV-8B Night Attack Harrier Squadron (VMA 211). He made numerous deployments, including one overseas to the Western Pacific, practicing medicine in austere environments. He was then assigned as the Group Flight Surgeon for the Marine Aircraft Group (MAG 13). Prior to his selection as an Astronaut candidate he served as a Flight Surgeon for the Naval Flight Officer advanced training squadron (VT-86) in Pensacola, Florida. Commander McKnight is Board Certified by the National Board of Medical Examiners and holds a Texas Medical License.

This flight's payload mission is dedicated to the life sciences projects, with particular focus in geriatric studies.

Soon I stumbled on another payload article explaining that Fletcher had consented to have chemicals from the Micro-Encapsulation Crystallization system injected into his aging body. I wondered what they had omitted with him being a laboratory experiment. It sounded dangerous. Poor Dan, what is the price of glory?

I reflected, after Dan's historic flight, he was elected Congressman. Being a politician or an Astronaut are very similar, both were in the public view bringing attention to them at all times. He fit perfect in both worlds.

It further described a self-contained capsule attached to the International Space Station where he would enter into an atmospheric of pure oxygen triggering chemicals from the MECS experiment.

The environment reminded me of the "bubble boy" who had to be protected against germs. This condition, Severe Combined Immunodeficiency (SCID) caused by a single mutated gene, meant the bubble boy had to live in sterile conditions or risk picking up a life-threatening infection. Fletcher would be in a similar atmosphere while he remained in the solitary capsule.

To Susan, it was claustrophobic comparable to being buried alive in a coffin. At least if he was in a bubble he could move around. He will be far away in space, and isolated in an experimental capsule, but why? How frightening!

The article continued. The chemicals would be administered intravenously in this completely controlled environment.

I became distressed thinking of my lifelong hero incarcerated in an isolated capsule. I visualized him being used as a space guinea pig, sticking him with painful needles, probing him with multiple medical examinations and tests. I just didn't understand why he would have agreed to such a dangerous treacherous experiment.

I was sure Dan took the assignment as a NASA Astronaut, because he was devoted to the Space Program. It has to be the most rewarding, challenging and satisfying job anyone could ever imagine. It was evident all the Astronauts and Cosmonauts would sacrifice their lives and souls for the most elite program in the world, or should the truth be known, universe.

Now, once again, Dan would ride the Solid Rocket Boosters, roman candles, into the dark, challenging outer space.

I tried to read the next article to find out more valuable information. It was called the "Space Software Development of the MECS experiment". I clicked on the file icon, it would not let me enter. Again I clicked and this time the whole screen lit up.

Immediately a flashing warning appeared flickering across the screen **'THIS IS CONFIDENTIAL. PLEASE LOG OFF IMMEDIATELY. Top Secret Clearance, Need to know ONLY TO VIEW THIS FILE'.**

I almost jumped out of my skin with a cold sweat trickling down my forehead. Frozen with fear I couldn't budge from my chair. Trying to calm down I took a deep breathe. What should I do? I had to think, "Wonder who's responsible for sensitive information in the Space Software organization?"

Chapter 4
The Audit

Only one Space Software employee had a high clearance designation that could aid to my secret investigation. It was James Torry a conscientious FWY Systems Engineer who went by the book, strictly by the book.

Whispering, "I've got to use my head. Think rationally. I need to create a check list to ask the pertinent questions. I need to understand the MECS experiment and to locate any confidential files." I had a revelation. "I'm an auditor and as an auditor, I'm permitted to audit anything and everything. I can verify the security clearance ranking. The security clearance ranking would give me access to the MECS data. Yes, the plan sounds doable, sort of, but right now it's all I got. I'll audit James."

I sent an electronic message to him announcing the audit, "Do you have any available time I can audit the Security Clearance process?"

He promptly responded, "Tuesday at one o'clock would be fine?"

I mused, "Yes, that will work for me. Thank you for your promptness and availability for this audit."

I got out the Security Clearance procedures and began quickly developing a comprehensive checklist. I'll get him to show me the Top Security Clearance MECS Experiment files being developed by Space Software. The Top Security documentation is kept in a Black Area accessed by certain personnel who have top security clearance. The information is kept well guarded and under top security.

"Yes, I'm very satisfied with my plan. You must have objective evidence to prove James has Top Security Clearance," I whispered.

I felt the secret file would give me insight into the MECS experiment and why Dalton was in danger. The NASA website had given me a lead, but not enough information to understand Dalton and Dr. Keller's research.

It had been a long and hard day. All I wanted to do was go home and get ready for my trip to the tropics.

The next day, I nervously entered James' office. I had never used my job for personal use. I felt it was unethical but I had to find out what was going on. This was an important audit that could give my valuable information. My underarms dripped with perspiration from anticipation realizing the audit was for curiosity sake and not for the program.

I laughed when I saw his messy office. However my office was just as messy or even messier with the piles of inspection paper.

He saw my laughing and responded chuckling, "They say cluttered office, cluttered mind and vacant office, vacant mind."

"I guess you have a lot on your mind James. Look at all the paper." I changed my demeanor and responded. "Sorry for the short audit notice. I hope I'm not interrupting you."

"You are. I've been very busy," he said with his bi-focal glasses on the edge of his nose, "I'm been doing some extra design and coding on the MECS experiment project."

"James, I didn't realize we had a new software development project. This is odd. I had not been involved in any new planning. I believe you called in MECS experiment project. Is this correct? What is MECS?" I coached James playing the part of naïve and blonde.

Hesitantly he said, "Micro-Encapsulation Crystallization Encapsulation System (MECS) is the software program to monitor the functions in an experimental Space Capsule. They have put this project fully on my shoulders. Yes, I'm the only one in the organization assigned to the project. It's considered part of the black area and you need Top Security Clearance to work on it and unfortunately I've the qualifications. I've been working tirelessly night and day trying to complete the coding and testing of the software on schedule. It's causing me more grief with Pamela Jay than I care to discuss. My wife wants to see me, at least some time during the 24 hours in a day."

"I don't blame you. Hopefully it's temporary. The objective of my audit is to ensure your process is following Top Security requirements. If I find any issues they will be documented on a Noncompliance Report. Any enhancements will be captured on a Space Software Improvement Report. The Space Software Improvement Report is only a recommendation and you do not have to implement it. However it's possible they can become a noncompliance and a serious problem."

"Let's get ready to perform this audit. I promise it won't be long. I know you're busy. Remember, if you don't know the answer, it's OK to say you don't know and point me in another direction. The first question is what security clearance do you have?"

James stated, "Top Secret Clearance in the Black Area."

"Can you show me the approval document, the objective evidence showing proper authorization giving you this type of security clearance?"

He pulled out of a drawer a sheet of paper with the proper signatures. I requested, "Could I make a copy of this Form 2108—Security Clearance Authorization with the proper signatures? This will provide the objective evidence I need for the audit."

James slowly responded to my request, "I guess there is no harm."

Then I slowly asked with in a serious manner, "Since you are working on the MECS project I would like to examine the associated inspection packages and your procedures to ensure that you are following the correct process. A sample of 10 inspection packages would be fine. I would like a mixture preferably of Requirements, Design, Code and Test Inspection packages with a copy of the Software Requirements Specification (SRS) document."

He glared directly into my eyes with a doubtful look twisting his mouth suspiciously, "I don't think this is truly a quality assurance requirement that you need to see all the MECS inspection packages and the SRS."

I held my breath with courage seizing his eyes, "It states in the Shuttle contract NAS 9-25000 that Software Quality Assurance can view any document associated with the Space Software programs to ensure that the process and procedures are being followed per the contract. It's required that the SQA to have objective evidence proof. The Software Quality Assurance shows the proper amount of visibility into the program to the management team. In other words, I'm the eyes and ears of management. Do you disagree?"

James grimaced looking sick to his stomach. I felt he was ready to leave the room at any moment. I fidgeted in the uncomfortable chair, but my large blue green eyes didn't move from his piercing glare.

I again probed with authority, "James." pausing for a couple of minutes. "Should we go right now to discuss this issue with the Program Manager? If it's necessary I'll get his permission to continue the audit. You know I report directly to him. It would not be a problem for me. James, most auditors are suspicious when they discover a situation of the auditee not wanting to share information. The majority of the time a cover up is at hand. I would never want to accuse you of hiding information. James, you realize it's my job to audit Top Secret Clearance records for compliance."

My dilated eyes didn't flinch. I could see in his body language he didn't like conflict. Agitated, he squirmed and backed down from their direct eye contact.

Reluctantly and frustrated said, "Alright, you can continue." He pulled out some listings that were created by the Space Software Application Tool.

I intently studied the code, "This demonstrates the software downloads bodily statistics. This is odd, we have never developed code to download Astronauts' medical data to this extent. Of course we now monitor their pulse, but not their bodily fluids and photographing vital organs using CAT Scan. The Space Software has never developed an application performing complex medical functions."

Wanting to know more I asked, "Do you have any additional requirements?"

"Sure, since you have top security clearance, I don't see what harm it would be to show you the rest." Then he got excited. His voice was elevated. "Susan, this has been a very interesting project. It's GREAT receiving a new development job." He leaned back in his chair, "To think I had a part of this experiment, the MECS experiment. How I enjoy doing innovative programming. It has been a long time."

Studying the requirements it confirmed my suspicions, "The software application downloads bodily functions. It performs a comparison showing any changes to the bodily functions graphing any modifications. Not only does it calculate the differences, but it records the bodily functions categorizing it by age selection. It charts a 6-month vital statistics matrix comparing the norm statistics. All had been programmed in the software application. Written in the footer of the MECS requirement documents was a disclaimer, "Any questions concerning the requirements notify Dr. Keller." Still, there was no address or number.

"James, the requirements document was authored by a Dr. Keller. Have you ever met him?"

James looked troubled, "No," he said quickly darting his eyes away from me. Then despondently he said, "It's heartbreaking, he died in a fire. Dead were his two cute little boys and a beautiful sweet wife gone. They were such nice people and it was such a shock to hear they had died in such a tragic way."

Trying not to show how upset I was, I composed myself. I only thought of the note on the boat. Then reality hit. Oh my God, if Dr. Keller and his family were in danger, Dalton must be also.

I wondered if the mysterious note had anything to do with the fire. "James that is so sad. I'm so sorry to hear about the tragic accident, how alarming!"

James stared away, "Who said it was an accident?"

Shocked I continued with the audit, "One last question, please show me the MECS Experiment file, the "Top Security Clearance file" on the Johnson Space Center Internet. This will prove you have Top Security Clearance." I gave him my reassuring smile, though still nervous from the shock of Dr. Keller's death. I wondered, reluctantly, if I could actually pull this off.

"James, please print it off. I'll go make copies of the printed MECS documents." I quickly retrieved the documents from the classified printer and rushed to his office. I wanted to get this over as promptly as possible. I walked into his office with a smile.

"James, congratulations you have passed the audit with flying colors. You're in compliance. It states that you have followed the process explicitly and that everything is in accordance to your standards and procedures. You have received no non-conformances nor do I have any improvements for your process. I'll have an Audit Report to your manager. If you would like to attend the debriefing meeting, you are more than welcome. Thanks for your time and have a good day. I'm going to sign out the material and take it home with me. Unfortunately I don't have enough time to thoroughly analyze the information today." I said professionally.

James said, "You know the rules better than any of us."

I trembled as I made my way back to my office. Inside I closed the door, barely making it to my chair. I was full of anxiety with my stomach tied up in knots feeling nauseas. I had retrieved the top secret information, but at what cost would it be to me?

I laid out all my objective evidence on my desk to analyze. The requirements state that the downloaded information shall be encrypted. "Whoa."

I had never seen requirements with mandatory encryption. Why would the code be encrypted? This is just too strange. I wondered if I could locate Dr. Keller on the Intranet. Maybe the Intranet phone directory lists Dr. Keller in either Johnson Space Center (JSC) or Kennedy Space Center (KSC). The search had no hits.

He had never worked for NASA or they have all the files hidden. Suddenly a knock on the office door vibrated through my heart, I froze.

Surprisingly James entered with another piece of evidence. He looked concerned, "Susan, I know it's your job to audit, but I think you should not dig too deeply into this MECS experiment. I don't have a good feeling. You are just doing your job, but take my advice, write your report and forget about what you have seen here. OK?" He said as he laid the last report down on my desk.

I glanced up at James convincingly, "I'll do that."

Looking at the final objective evidence there were bold letter written on the top of the paper, **TOP SECRET - MICRO-ENCAPSULATION CRYSTALLIZATION SYSTEM (MECS) EXPERIMENT.**

This is only for Top Secret Security Clearance MECS staff. Anyone without the Top Security Clearance can't work, perform any of the experiments or have knowledge of the design, formulas or results of the MECS project. Please notify Dr. Keller immediately if any information is misdirected or missing. His number is 281-5000 and Internet ID is drkeller@jsc.space.gov.

Without reading any further I immediately picked up the phone and dialed the number. It had voice activation, "Please enter your security clearance code."

I immediately hung up. It was too late since tracing a call was not a problem for NASA. They only had seven law enforcement agencies on campus. Nervously, I thought, "What am I doing? This is way over my head. It doesn't make sense Dr. Keller's number wasn't in the NASA Phone Directory. I don't know why I dialed the number? What purpose did it serve? Maybe I want to get in trouble. I know Dr. Keller is deceased and his number was probably was removed from the directory. They probably don't have a new person in charge yet or possibly never will. I must get back to work and forget this nonsense."

Still agonizing over the situation, I thought. "Maybe I shouldn't go to the Bahamas. I don't even know this guy, except what my friend Karen has told me."

Trying to convince myself otherwise, "I do want to get to know this new man. What could happen far away in the Bahamas? I'm not part of the MECS's team. I should be safe and, boy, rest and relaxation sounds wonderful. Yes, some fun in the sun."

Rationalizing any situation was my greatest trick. Houdini couldn't do it better. Oh yes, this was my pattern, staying with men who had broken my heart with their cheating and lying.

I gathered the MECS's information together along with the security policy and the letter of agreement. I signed the letter of agreement along with the proper authorization allowing the top secret document removal from the premises. Again I read the confidentiality policy knowing full well I should not be doing this at all.

I whispered, "Tonight at home I'll decipher this information in peace and quiet." An irritating thought kept gnawing at me. The Lead SQA was removing Top Security Clearance information from the building. I assured myself, first thing in the morning all the documents would be returned safely and then I would shred them in tiny little pieces.

Preoccupied with thoughts, the drive home seemed very short. I began analyzing the data as soon as I walked into the door. I sat down at the kitchen and spread the piles of papers organizing them by their authorizations. I was intrigued with the information describing a new software application which downloaded vital statistics from a CT scan being performed at the International Space Station, along with blood samples, hearing tests, vision and much more. Technology certainly had changed and to think, I was previewing the future.

It was late in the night when I finished studying the data. Exhausted I hid the MECS package in my lingerie drawer for safe keeping. "It will be out of harm's way here with my undergarments."

Extremely tired I finished entering the audit report on my lap top planning my next move, "I'll take a quick trip back to the office and sign the Top Secret documents back into the Black Area. Next the audit report will be sent to management and everyone will be happy. No one will ever know. Or will they?"

I didn't want to be in deep trouble with management or worse lose my job and over what? The curiosity of who was Dr. Keller had caused a violation of my personal ethics and a fine line of the business ethics. This was not a good thing to do and to a questionable end. What is the old saying, curiosity and yes curiosity did kill the cat?

Yes, I felt like that curious cat falling into a deep sleep dreaming of the upcoming adventure. My eyes squinted as the morning sun shown down onto my sleepy face. The luggage was filled with sexy play clothes suited for a tropical paradise. Included was the thong bikini, definitely suited for pleasure. I couldn't forget this since it was the only clothing request from the new found sailor friend Dalton.

Soon to be going on the desperately needed vacation I anticipated the upcoming exotic Bahamas adventure.

Chapter 5
The Provisioning

Dalton arrived in the humid Miami heat to outfit Nick's boat. As he walked through the airport Dalton reflected back the number of years he had known Nick. Friendship between the two continued to be an adventure with each crossing. Nick had not changed over the years with his Greek God appearance coupled in the company of his bronzed muscular body. Nick was waiting for Dalton at the baggage claim. He slowly surveyed Nicks' sculptured body glistening with sweat trickling down his muscle definition. Physical labor had never been a problem for the strong masculine friend as he effortlessly loaded Dalton's suitcases in his trunk.

Dalton said, "Thanks for picking me up my friend. I've missed seeing you." They rode to the marina making small talk. The two were like brothers who shared all their secrets. They were comfortable with each other and in tune to each other's feelings. The two men provisioned the boat as soon as they arrived at the marina. These supplies were extremely important due to the food shortage in the Bahamas. The only product not scarce in the islands is Mount Gay Rum, which flows as deep as the ocean. The comparison of the economic situation in the Bahamas and the U.S. is similar to the difference of the two friends, Dalton and Nick. Distinguished small frame Dalton was dwarfed standing next to the massive Adonis, Nick. The contrast between them is as large as the respect between the two.

Nick questioned, "Dalton do you want anything special to eat or drink? We can stop at the store before heading out."

Dalton laughed, "Nick, the lobster, fish and rum are plentiful in the Abacos. That's all I need for substance except for my new friend Susan. Anyway we need to put money into the economy to help pay for their high importation taxes. We do want to make the Bahamian government richer not poorer."

Dalton changed the subject in midstream, "Nick how I love crossing the Gulf Stream except for the emerald ocean's challenges. Remember the last crossing the sea was smooth as glass, then the next minute it was raging and ready to swallow us up in one big gulp. The provisions came undone and began to fall overboard. Luckily I caught the food and rum before they both sank in Davies Jones locker and before the sharks got me and our food. I really moved fast. The sharks weren't getting our food, but boy they almost got me. You can never predict what will happen off shore."

Nick grinned, "Yeah but next time I'll let the sharks get you since you taste better than me or at least that's what all the women shark think."

Dalton laughed contagiously, "Yes I agree they would spit you out, that's for sure."

Dalton changed his mood and became serious, "Life has been damn stressful these days, Nick. The MECS experiment demands are politically ridden. It has been too much, I need this vacation. I hope I can relax with my good buddy and my new friend Susan."

Nick inquired, "Tell me about this new friend. I haven't heard you mention a girl in years."

Dalton stared at Nick, he felt naked wearing his emotions on his shoulder, even though his best friend knew all his secrets. He was vulnerable from the past and he knew it. Nervously he finally said, "Nick, I've not wanted anyone but my work for the past two years. The long nights and lonely years have made me tired of being isolated from female relationship. Even now I'm not forgetting about my sweet Linda and the kids. They are in my heart and on my mind in everything I do. I miss them desperately every day. I've tried to fill the emptiness with a lot of one-night stands. Funny not one caught my fancy nor did I want to talk to them in the morning. Nick, they were beautiful women with great bodies, but I need more than a beautiful body, I require intelligence. Now I've found the sweetest woman who has brainpower behind beautiful, electrifying eyes. She has caught my interest and boy do we have chemistry."

Nick encouraged Dalton, "Whoa, tell me more about this electrifying woman."

That's all the encouragement Dalton needed, "I'm not sure, I've only met her once, but I've heard stories about her from our friend Jackson for years. You probably think I'm crazy, but gazing into her large beautiful eyes, I get lost. It touches places that have long been dead. A warm feeling comes all over me when I just look at her. It's an indescribable sensation which glows inside me with excitement. It brings back my desire to go on sailing adventures again. I can see myself going up on deck enjoying her gorgeous nude body, basking in the sun on deck, swimming in the warm salty turquoise water, and kissing in the early morning sun. After a full day of sailing we could have the perfect ending making love with the rhythm of the waves. It would be paradise or possibly heaven on earth, my friend."

Dalton drifted into a dream world. Nick shouted, "I can see you are more than smitten, but you are beginning to scare me. You sound like a romance novel. Actually you are making me sick so please come back to reality. Let's get to work. I need your full attention to load the boat. Work first Dalton, women later. We will have plenty of time on our crossing to discuss all the intimate details and I believe me I do want to hear them. I can give you some pointers."

"Point this." Dalton said as he threw his duffle bag at Nick. He smiled and started helping Nick. He surveyed the abundant food, medical supplies, flares, wine and beer that were enough for a small army. Yes, only the staples in life. He had even thought of extra fuel needed to make the passage. Nick was well prepared, remembering everything.

Nick said, "Our first stop is West End, 100 miles off the coast of West Palm Beach, Florida where we can check in customs at the open roof building. The local custom's officer will charge us a nominal fee for permission to cruise the Bahamas.

Dalton chided, "Don't want to over shoot West End like we did last time. I forgot to account for the continuous fight against the 3 knot current. Let me see your calculations Captain." Dalton gave an infectious laugh, which made Nick laugh.

"Nick, I have to call her before we shove off. Wait until you meet the prettiest girl with blond curly hair, big blue grey eyes with a smile that can go on forever, and a cute butt. I can already imagine her in a bikini. If she doesn't bring one, I've already bought her one which will fit her perfectly. The saleslady was about the same size of Susan and I made her try it on. Not too bad. Excuse me while I make a very important phone call." Dalton retrieved his cell phone from his sailing shorts quickly dialing Susan.

"I hope she will answer the phone," he said to Nick.

As he listened to the phone ring he visualized her in the clingy purple sun dress as she sat on the dock box.

I answered the phone. "Hi, this is Susan, your friendly sailor."

"Hello Susan. Dalton speaking, it's your new Bahamian sailor. I'm still in Miami but I wanted to call you while I'm still in the States, since I'll lose reception on the high seas. Did I tell you how to retrieve your airline tickets?"

"No, you didn't, but I was wondering," the excitement was in my voice. Needless to say I had begun to worry about the whole trip.

"I'm sorry I haven't called before now, but I've been overwhelmed and over-worked by Nick, who is a real slave driver. I had tickets delivered to my friend and neighbor Nancy. They're at her house along with a package I would like you to bring with you, if you don't mind. Nancy is the greatest neighbor who lives across from my Cove Glenn house. Give her a call at 555-2200 and make arrangements to pick up the tickets and package."

Dalton's voice hesitated for a moment and he slowly said, "Susan, I'm looking forward to your visit and sharing the tropical romantic sunsets and sunrises. This vacation will be special with you by my side."

How romantic, I was taken back, "You certainly know how to charm a woman. I too am looking forward to sunsets, sunrises, having my own personal tour guide and scuba instructor. I want to have fun and forget about work. Do you think you can accommodate me? Do I need anything other than lots of bathing suits and sun tan oil?"

"Just your contagious smile, your delightful sense of humor, and of course your gorgeous body. I'm here just to accommodate you Susan," said Dalton.

I teased, "Boy you certainly are forward to someone you don't even know."

"Yes I am. The cell phones in Bahamas do not work so you will not be able to reach me. I'll be picking you up at the airport wearing a straw hat, sandals and a big grin on my face with a sign that reads Desperately seeking Susan."

I laughed, "Is that all you'll be wearing?"

Dalton was caught happily off guard, and replied, "Hmm, maybe not. I don't want to get arrested and ruin our plans by spending it in jail."

I chuckled, "I'll come visit you every day my dear after I play all day. I'm looking forward to our adventure." I thought to myself he acted very comfortable with me.

"Dalton, I'll be dressed in red. See you Saturday."

Cheerfully he said, "I'll be looking for you, lady in red. Please be safe."

The tone of his voice made me feel warm inside and out. I mumbled to myself, "How could I feel like this? I don't even know the man!"

I continued mumbling, "At least I'm going to be staying on Dad's trawler, Dream Catcher. I'll be safe there. This entire situation about Dr. Keller and his family gives me the creeps."

Chapter 6
The Ticket

I mumbled to myself as I dialed Nancy's number, "I must get the airline ticket, time is growing short."

A cheerful voice answered the phone, "Hello."

I responded, "Hi, I'm Susan, a friend of Dalton Masters. He asked me to give you a call for the tickets to the Bahamas and a package."

"Oh yes I do. It's on my kitchen counter. You can come over anytime, I do not have any plans this evening. I can't wait to get together with Dalton's friend."

"I'm looking forward to meeting you. I certainly appreciate you handling this for Dalton. Thank you Nancy."

"That's no problem at all. I'm just glad he's going on with his life. Hope you two have a wonderful time and remind him to bring back delicious lobsters and conch for our usual feast. Susan, Dalton is such a nice man with a big heart. I don't know if you know this, but he has been a very lonely man, since his wife and kids were killed in a car accident seven years ago. Since the incident he just hasn't been the same. Truthfully, you are the first woman he has shown an interest in or at least share his vacation. He has become a recluse for the longest time, not much interest in anyone or anything."

Now his silence about his kids made perfect sense. Nancy was filling in the missing pieces and his pain. I shivered thinking of the resemblance between Dr. Keller and Dalton, both loosing their families. The difference, Dr. Keller lost his life.

"He was the best father." Nancy continued, "You should have seen him with his kids, two beautiful precious girls. Both as pretty as can be—looked like their mother but had their father's intelligence. Do you know how smart that man is?"

I smiled inwardly as I agreed over the phone, "Yes, I've gotten a small glance into his brainpower. He is so versatile, a real renaissance man."

Nancy continued, "He amazes me with his fortitude and endurance working all the time. He asked me to send another bag with you with some clothes and a package which I repacked into one bag. . I'm glad he is vacationing and hope you two have a good time."

"Thanks for your trouble," I responded, "I'm thrilled to have a vacation, which I need terribly."

As though Nancy had not heard a word, she continued, "It will be great if you two hook up together. Ah, am I being too forward? I don't mean to be, but I'm so excited that he is showing an interest in life again. When can you come over? I work at home doing my husband's books, so I'm here all the time."

I couldn't get a word in edgewise. I felt like I had to breathe for Nancy. I finally broke in, "Would after work be OK?"

Nancy said, "Of course, Darling. Hope you don't mind me calling you Darling. I call everyone Darling, even my cat. I'll see you at 3 o'clock."

"I'll be there," I hung up the phone before getting directions. "Oh well, I know the vicinity. I can call on my cell phone when I get close to her home." No wonder I had forgotten, Nancy had given me a piece of the Dalton puzzle. Interesting Dalton's family died in an auto accident and Dr. Keller and his family died in a fire. Both scenarios are sad, such losses, both accidents. No wonder he had buried himself in his work avoiding his great loss.

My stomach growled. I made a turkey sandwich covering the bread with mustard and mayonnaise as Under the Boardwalk played on a music video. The Golden Oldies took me back to my childhood at Myrtle Beach when life existed without responsibilities.

The music played as I washed the food down with a cold glass of milk. I laid back in my recliner closing my tired heavy eyes with a full stomach. The Top Secret documentation laid heavy on my mind. Even so, my eyes closed, and soon I was in a deep sleep dreaming of swimming with the dolphins.

A sudden crash startled me, I jumped up from the recliner cautiously making my way toward the noise in the kitchen. I found the sandwich plate lying on the floor broken into a million pieces. Fear gripped seeing the back door standing wide open and the chimes clinking. I froze from the sound realizing there was no wind and wondered how the back door got opened. Chills ran up my spine.

I heard my voice screaming, "Who's there? Take anything you want! I'm calling the police." I waited, but no response. "Maybe it's a blessing that I'm leaving town."

I yelled again, "I've called the police. Do you hear me?" Still I heard no sound. As usual I immediately began rationalizing the situation. Yes, I must have left the door open. What would the police say if I called? I could imagine their interrogation. "What happened here, Ma'am?"

"Officer a plate broke in my kitchen." I would admit.

Then their next question, "Did you leave the plate near the edge of the counter? It must have been an accident. This thing happens all the time to lonely women who live alone and have active imagination."

I would meekly answer, "Well, officer, I do have a cat that walks on my counter. I guess she could have knocked the plate off. But officer I'm not lonely, it's just I haven't found my Prince Charming, although I'm getting close."

The officer would surmise, "Case closed."

It must be my imagination as I convinced myself going into the living room. "What would anyone want in my house?" I stopped in my tracks remembering the Top Secret documents hidden in my lingerie drawer.

I slowly made my way into my bedroom. Carefully I surveyed the room for any movement. Not seeing anything or anyone I opened the lingerie drawer. Frantically I emptied the drawer throwing all my lacy lingerie onto the floor. No documents fell out of the empty drawer. The top secret documentation is gone? I put my hand inside the drawer in disbelief. Suddenly I realized the culprit could still be in the house. Frightened I grabbed my keys and cell phone from my chest of drawer and ran outside.

My hands were shaking as I began dialing the police. I stopped dialing, remembering I must notify James Torry immediately of the stolen documents. Would I get fired for the disappearance? What should I do? I didn't want to enter the house again. I felt violated. This was not good. My heart felt heavy as I stood outside shaking. Why had I removed the papers from the office? Why had I violated my personal ethics and for what, curiosity sake? I dreaded the call to James. It was a real possibility I would lose my job, along with my reputation. No longer would I be considered the SQA expert with high integrity. My shoulders sunk as I held back the tears.

Thoughts ran through my mind. How did anyone know I had taken the documentation home? How did they find it? The scary thing was I had been in the house. Why had I gotten so tired? Whoever did this may want to harm me? Doubtful if the other deaths were accidents? I remembered what James had said about Keller and his family. They were all dead and so was Dalton's family. Was this a coincidence?

Reluctantly I called James. I knew it was the right thing to do. I had to alert the company of what had happened. The papers were missing and delaying telling them would be the wrong thing to do.

I dialed his number very slowly with shaking hands standing in the middle of the yard. My fingers trembled as I dialed the number.

James answered the phone, "Good morning. James Torry, Space Exploration Corporation."

My voice quivered, "James I've bad news. The MECS papers I signed out yesterday have been stolen from my house. It happened while I was asleep in the house. What should I do? I'm very frightened. Why would anyone steal the documents?"

James firmly cautioned Susan, "Please calm down. You must take control of yourself. I warned you about this program and you should have listened to me. Are you safe?"

I said softly, "Yes, but I'm scared. Should I call the police?"

Surprisingly James said decisively, "No, do not involve the police.

I'll alert NASA authorities to take care of the situation. The paper work will be momentous and horrendous. Go on your vacation and get lost for awhile. Do not return to the office before leaving. I'll talk with you upon your return. When are you leaving?"

"Saturday, James. Please don't be mad at me."

Suspiciously, James questioned, "Why should I?" he hesitated, "You were only doing your job. Unfortunately you took your work home after I advised you about the program's sensitivity. It's partly my fault. I should have said absolutely not. I'm the one who gave you permission."

"I know you warned me, however it's my fault I took the papers home. I'm so sorry this happened. Hopefully you will find who did this. I'll see you when I return. Goodbye."

James staunchly said, "Goodbye Susan. Have a wonderful trip."

My nerves were shot as I held my hands in front of me. I felt guilty not telling James about Dalton, the Payload Owner of the software he had created, who was soon to be my Bahamian escort. I began calming down thinking going out of town would be a good thing and I would be far away from all the mystery.

Still mumbling, "I'm having a difficult time with this situation, new guy, same old problems. Something always has to go wrong with me and men. It's already 9:30 AM. I'd better get going to Nancy's."

I locked the front door from the outside not wanting to go back inside. I felt violated. Frantically I jumped into my car heading toward Dalton's home in Glen Cove Development.

Remembering my telephone conversation with Nancy, I knew she would talk my head off. All I want to do is get out of town as quickly as I can. I muttered as tears began filling my eyes.

As I drove into the older neighborhood, I noticed the gigantic majestic oak trees making a tunnel like an awning over the street. It reminded me of Gone With The Wind traveling the southern plantation road. Just like Scarlet I must have strength, tomorrow is another day and tomorrow things will change.

I wonder which house belonged to Dalton. I thought, trying to forget about the stolen papers. His house was at the end of the street, but I really didn't know for sure. I had heard it was on the water front with a beautiful view of the lake. Karen had said it needed a lot of work, but I'm sure Dalton never has any time left over with his busy schedule.

Sleeping in my boat with the comforting water crashing against the bow and hearing the seagulls laughing over head is pure luxury. Each morning paradise is captured watching the fiery red and orange sunrise glistening on the blue Crystal Lake. This world of boaters captures heaven in the liquid backyard. This memory made me momentarily forget the fear of the mystery, thief and suspense.

Leisurely driving through the older neighborhood Glenview Cove I fumbled for the cell phone to dial Nancy's number. It took a minute before the phone only rang once, when a raspy voice woman answered. I did not recognize the voice, instantly I knew it was not Nancy.

"Hi, I'm Nancy's sister. To whom am I speaking?"

"I'm Susan. Is Nancy at home?"

The voice hesitated before saying, "I'm sorry but Nancy had to run out on an errand."

"Nancy is holding tickets and a package for me. I'm in the neighborhood to pick them up." Susan inquired.

"Oh yes, everything is here the tickets and a package." The smoky voice stated.

"Could you tell me where your sister lives? I've never been to her house, but I believe I'm very close. I'm on Glenview Cove Street near the park." I said.

"Yes, go to the end of the street and we're the last yellow house on the right. Pull out front and I'll come out and give you your stuff".

As I pulled up, a tall skinny woman came out from the backyard with the package and tickets held tightly under her right arm. She walked toward me with a crooked smile, "Here is your package, dear. By the way, do you know where Dalton is staying on the island?"

I returned the smile, however feeling very uneasy, "No I don't know. I guess I'll find out though. Why do you ask?"

The woman stared straight in my eyes, "I've always dreamed of going to the tropics and thought he might be staying at a nice place for me to check out."

Politely, I said, "Sorry I can't help you. Thanks for bringing the package and tickets. Please tell Nancy I want to meet her. What's your name?"

"My name is Carol."

I quickly took the package and tickets from her skinny hands. "Thanks again, Carol." I immediately left the scrawny woman standing in the front yard staring at the back of the car as I drove away. Suspiciously wondering if Carol was really her name and wondering where was Nancy? It was all very confusing. Time passed very quickly as I tried to reconstruct what had happened at Nancy's house. I drove very fast not realizing the speed thinking about where was Nancy. Soon I had arrived at the house wondering if I should make a quick get away. I left the motor running as I sat in the car wondering whom or what was waiting for me inside the house. "Dear Lord, Give me the courage to go inside."

I opened the ticket envelope to read the itinerary, it said early morning departure 6:30 AM Sunday from Clear Lake Airport arriving in Marsh Harbor, Bahamas at 2:30pm. Clear Lake Airport was my choice for travel, since it easily provided fast transportation to the main Houston international airport missing the congested Houston traffic. It was generally chosen for its close proximity to NASA, which offered convenience to the Astronauts and aerospace subcontractors living in the area.

Always thinking I would meet an Astronaut, just like the last time, when I met Toy, an ex-Astronaut. He was a legend in his own time, especially with the women, a true womanizer. What a great guy though, always friendly and so sexy even with his bald head. No wonder he had such a passionate following with his smooth personality and moves. Unfortunately he was the oldest Astronaut forced to leave the program when Dalton's new payload began taking formation. Shortly afterwards they selected Congressman Dan Fletcher bringing him back for the geriatrics study.

I wondered if Dalton was like Toy or were they friends. Of course Daddy would say, "Birds of a feather flock together." Heaven knows it would be my luck, another ladies man.

The house looked normal, quiet and serene with the flowers blooming under the window sills. Eventually I climbed out of the car taking the package and tickets with me. I opened the door cautiously calling out, "Anyone there?"

Of course no one answered, the whole scenario made me feel foolish, and of course why would anyone answer if they were hiding. I went through the house looking under the beds, opening the closets, while locking all the windows and doors as I went.

Trying to take my mind off what had happened, I finally called Daddy. Talk about cutting time short getting his trawler in the Bahamas. He would probably give me the second degree about who, when, what, where and how much, nevertheless Dad's are like that even at my ripe age of 40. I definitely would not tell him about the break in, the suspicious note and the deaths. He would forbid me to leave the country ordering me to come home. You know my Daddy was always right.

I dialed the number. The phone rang and Daddy answered, "Hello," he said in a strong southern drawl.

"Hi! Daddy, it's me. I've missed you so. How are you doing?" I asked excitedly trying to cover up my fear.

"I'm fine," he replied, "Why am I honored to hear from my Princess?"

I smiled inwardly knowing he was very perceptive, "Oh Daddy, guess what? A rocket scientist just invited me to Marsh Harbor, the Bahamas. He is a Biomedical Ph.D. research scientist from NASA and responsible for the development of the next payload on the Shuttle with the famous Congressman, Dan Fletcher, the oldest Astronaut in the program. I was wondering if the trawler's available this week, since I've tickets for tomorrow morning. I want to stay on the trawler since I don't feel comfortable staying at his friend's condo. So, what do you think? Is anyone using the trawler? Can I use it? Daddy, pretty please."

Daddy hesitated but finally remarked, "Do you know him well enough? You know what all men want. You really should know that at your age and I know you are old enough. If you must please keep in mind if you stay on the trawler you have to leave the boat in tip-top shape. Young lady I don't want you to go wild down in paradise."

I sighed, he always gave me a lecture even though I'm conservative and needless to say a true geek.

Daddy said, "I guess it's OK since no one is resident on the trawler at the present moment. Let me tell you what to do. Listen carefully. Go to the Marina Office and ask Joe for the boat keys. I'll give him a call and let him know you're coming."

Then he softened which was a surprise, "Just please be safe. The Bahamas are not the United States. I know what can happen in the islands little girl. Things can be dangerous and it concerns me that you really don't know this guy. As always you have never listened to me before, so go and have a good time."

He said hesitating, almost in an afterthought, "I've a funny feeling. I know you think this Dalton guy has good credentials, good job, impeccable intentions but you never know, my precious. He is a man and men will be men. Don't let him take advantage of the situation. Be careful. All I want is the best for you. Please call me when you arrive."

Intently I listened to him to his voice tone which was different. It was a tone of a father who was really concerned, "I will Dad. Thank you so much for all that you have done for me! I'll keep both eyes opened, even when I sleep. I appreciate you letting me stay on the trawler. I will take good care of it. I love you. Tell Mom I love her too."

I heard the cell phone disconnect and held it close to my heart. Yes, Dad was always right. What he didn't know is I'm scared and excited at the same time. I did want Dalton to take advantage of the situation, "Daddy I need affection more than anything. It had been too long since I've had a lover. I can't wait any longer for romance, even if it meant putting my life in danger."

Chapter 7
The Trip

I climbed into my comfortable bed wanting sleep, but instead tossed and turned wondering if anyone was going to set my house on fire or murder me. If I fell asleep would I ever wake-up again. The thoughts would not go away but finally dosed off around 3 AM out of exhaustion. In reality I had only slept a couple of hours when the alarm went off.

Morning came very early, too early. The irritating sound of the alarm made me jump up reaching over to turn it off. The silence was a blessing leaving me alone and alive. Immediately I leaped out of bed to take a bath, locking myself in the bathroom for safety. I thought that the little lock would not keep anyone out. The icy cold water from the shower spout slowly revived me from the long sleepless night.

Desperately I wanted all the chaotic problems to disappear. The danger of all the tension disappeared as I applied delicate soap over my soft slim body in circling motions. The touch felt so good taking me away from the harsh reality of someone invading my privacy.

With each gentle touch I could feel myself losing all concept of time concentrating on my desires. I abruptly stopped, recalling something or someone may still be lurking outside or even be in the house. I thought a security system must be installed and to buy pepper mace for protection.

Finally I turned on the hot water to break the hypnotic spell rinsing the soap from my skin. As always I applied baby oil to every inch of my body making my skin soft and supple. My nipples became aroused and firm from pleasuring myself.

I thought to myself, "No time for such things. Later, I could forget about time and think only of self gratification, rest, and sunshine."

Maybe Dalton could help me fulfill the sexual desires which I keep under control each waking moment. Perhaps I had a problem with sexual addiction, since I enjoyed sex so much. I decided, "No I'm not abnormal. I just enjoy sex and had been a long time."

I laid my bright red sexy sundress with matching beaded sandals on the bed. I quickly put them on and applied the makeup perfectly. Looking in the mirror I saw a 40 year old woman who was off for an adventure. My eyes still showed fear of the unknown. With the bags in hand I peeked out the front door. No one or no cars were seemed at the wee hour of 4:30am. I ran to the car dragging my bags with my keys in hand. Nervously I opened the car doors throwing the bags in the backseat. As soon as I was behind the wheel the car doors were locked. With a sigh of relief I started the car. Driving toward the airport I noticed a navy blue car approaching slowly in the rear view mirror. The car was a Mirage, but the occupants were not familiar. A chill went up my spine remembering the stolen top secret documents and the other navy blue car on the Kemah Bridge. I wondered if it was the same car. I was startled when all of a sudden the mystery car pulled recklessly away, passing at high speed.

The incident scared me, however, I began rationalizing I was not the only person who was traveling so early in the morning and this car was just another traveler. Driving in the Clear Lake Field was tricky for me since it had roads that led to nowhere. Surprisingly, this intelligent woman couldn't navigate through the airport maze. Truly I was a blond even though it came from a box, a box blond.

Clear Lake Field still resembled the former military base converted to a commercial airport. Consequently, so many of the buildings were designed with the same architecture. 'Intra-National Airlines' check-in facility was nestled between identical buildings. One of the buildings had the Shuttle Training Aircraft Simulator located to the right which I audited the simulator software. Once when I was auditing the

Software Shuttle Simulator Flight Engineer allowed me to fly the Shuttle simulator, which I crashed in no time flat. You would think flying the shuttle would be easy to do, but it was not. It required a lot of patience and gentle movements. Then the female Software Shuttle Simulator Flight Engineer, whom I was auditing, took over using the heads up display to land the shuttle flawlessly, and without a glitch.

It was a small aerospace world. She was the wife of a co-worker who developed space software requirements. They were both aerospace enthusiasts, just as nice as they could be. I had often thought the roles were reversed between them, a woman Astronaut and the guy, a computer geek. Yes how great, one point for women even though he was promoted just recently to a leadership position. He was now running the control board and the program technical decisions, a very important position. The space community is very small when everyone is connected through the shuttle. It is a family. I wondered if I would ever learn to fly a plane, much less the simulator for the space shuttle. I turned left heading toward the airport.

The navy blue car was now behind me again. I looked over my shoulder grumbling, "This is giving me the creeps. Who are they? Could these suspicious characters be taking the same flight?"

When I glanced over my shoulder I saw some Astronauts were getting into their T-38 jets preparing for take off. What a wonderful job to be able to fly around in jets and get paid for it. The Astronauts were elite field training at Clear Lake Field. I recognized only a few of the Astronauts in the local stores, from pictures on the walls around the office.

The navy blue car followed close behind me, which distracted me from dreaming about being an Astronaut, traveling all of the country to keep your flight hours current in T-38 jets. At one time the Astronauts could take civilians, but not now the rules had changed. My luck or my bad luck was either too late or too early. This time it was too late.

Nervously I drove through the maze without a glitch checking in my rear view mirror for the mysterious car. There was a parking space close to the Clear Lake terminal. Stopping the car I removed the luggage while watching over my shoulder for the navy blue car. I wished my luggage wasn't so heavy since it made it much harder to move quickly to the terminal. I hated carrying luggage but with modern technology the wheels and handles to ease the pain until luggage fell sideways. Breathless I got up to the airline counter full of anxiety. I waited impatiently to check-in standing behind a loud obnoxious lady. She was dressed in large, bright, pink and black dotted Capri pants with a tight black shirt which displayed her bolt-ons or some people say breast implants.

Then she began talking up a blue streak asking all kinds of questions, "Where are you going? Are you traveling alone? I would never travel alone when I was your age. You are such a brave girl to be traveling alone. You are such a pretty girl with pretty blond curly hair. Is it permanent?"

I ignored her trying to make her disappear, but she would not. Then I realized the talkative lady was on the same flight going to the Bahamas. Why couldn't I be talking to Astronaut Toy? How could I make sure this lady would not sit next to me? Ugh, I don't like this, what can happen next? This woman was ridiculous.

The woman ignored the fact I had not spoken, but continued with her conversation. "I haven't had a vacation in a long time, young lady. What about yourself? Where are you going?"

I hesitated, but eventually answered her question. "I'm going to the Bahamas to relax in the sun." I looked for an escape after I checked-in. I decided to hide in the plane's restroom until the last minute so I could position myself away from her.

When I thought it was safe from the talkative woman I sat down next to a distinguished black man. He wore dark glasses and didn't seem the friendly type, so I figured he would not want to talk. I was right. Exhausted from the lack of sleep I fell asleep before the plane left the runway and didn't wake up until the plane landed in Houston.

As I changed airplanes, I noticed "Chatty Kathy" which I had nicknamed her and immediately sped up my pace finding a secluded seat to wait for the plane. I sat down waiting for the plane when suddenly "Chatty Kathy" was sitting next to me just chattering away. "Well, I can't believe we're on the same flight. I just knew we would see each other again. Who are you meeting in the Bahamas? I'm going to the Bahamas to visit my brother who lives on a boat in Marsh Harbor. He's a retired physicist from Exxon Oil, a smart man but an engineer introvert."

She rambled on, "Can you believe he lives on a boat? How could anyone live on a small smelly boat? I certainly couldn't, not for anything in the world. I'm getting a comfortable clean hotel room. He wanted me to sleep on that nasty boat. I just can't see why anyone would want to live in something that moves, up and down, down and up," as she said moving her arms to the motion. "He will never get me on the boat, no, no, and no not ever. His name is Carey. I'll introduce him, if we run into you at Marsh Harbor, which we will you know. It is a small island." Chatty Kathy said.

I just nodded acknowledgement to her with a blank look not encouraging additional conversation.

Finally I heard the airline personnel call for them to board the flight, they loaded the plane. Hoping I would get rid of this new nuisance, I sat in the back of the plane. "Chatty Kathy" followed and sat down next to me.

I excused myself, "I'm very exhausted and I must get some sleep." I turned my back facing the window and pretended to sleep. My thoughts turned to Dalton and the quest for romance. I realized how little I knew of this man, only the mysterious note and deaths, and his sail boat. Now I was escaping to the Bahamas away from danger in Houston with the catalyst.

It was a terrific opportunity to learn more about him without work or Leona. Wonder what's behind his great mind? Could he be the great love of my life?

The tropical, magical Bahamas islands were waiting, to enjoy somber rest, lazy relaxation basking in the hot torrid sun.

Uneasiness interrupted the needed sleep since I was so nervous, nervous about the break-in, the new exciting man and nervous about the possibility of being intimate with a man again. The flight went by too slowly anticipating the arrival into the stranger arms.

I should have listened to Daddy when he said, "No telling what could happen in the islands?" It certainly had been a strange mysterious last couple of days since I had met this new man. I still thought about the note and Dr. Keller and his family demise?

Well Dalton life certainly is full of mystery which made me tense of the unknown. Maybe I didn't want to tap into the deep dark secrets of his soul. I must be crazy for going on this trip with someone whom I had just met who was surrounded by secrecy and possibly murder. My thoughts were interrupted by the airline attendant, "Welcome to the tropical Bahamas. Please stay seated until the plane comes to a complete stop. Trudy will be passing out the custom pass for you to complete. Remember while you are here you can bring back $500.00 of duty free products and you know rum is everyone's favorite duty free product. Have a wonderful vacation and thank you for traveling the Airline that makes travel fun."

As I left the plane Chatty Kathy followed me, continuously talking. "I can't believe you slept the whole time. You must have been tired. You know you won't sleep tonight."

I smiled and got into the crowded custom's line waiting to present my passport and the completed customs pass good for two weeks. The customs officer reviewed my passport and pointed me to the baggage claim. Taxi cab drivers were hovering around asking everyone if they needed a rid. I retrieved my bulky bags looking around for my escort. No Dalton in sight. No one was waiting for me, had he abandoned me or just forgotten I was coming to the islands. The abandonment feeling intermixed with the excitement of being in the Bahamas. The feeling made me anxious and insecure. Anxiety was gripping my delicate emotional state which turned my thoughts inside out.

Even "Chatty Kathy's" brother Brent was waiting for her. He was just as I thought he would look, thin creepy with beady eyes. He was just nodding his head up and down to the continuous chatter.

I sat down on a bench, swinging my legs back and forth, getting more anxious by the minute. My hands twisted with sweat as if I was wringing out a towel full of water. I thought to myself, I'd better not bite my nails in this make-shift airport. The humid heat was rising in my body. I could feel my face flush with redness and sweat. If I had known he was a no show I could have already been relaxing in Daddy's trawler, Dream Catcher.

Half an hour passed, the waiting was an eternity, and then another hour, forever it seemed. The only people left were me and two dancing Bahamians selling conch shells to the beat of the steel drums.

They kept smiling as I paced back and forth hoping Dalton would show up. How could he be so rude leaving me in this strange place? It seemed out of character for him. Wonder if something had happened to him? He could possibly be in a hospital dying or even captured by the culprits who broke in my home or were responsible for killing Dr. Keller and his family.

Suddenly I felt hot breath softly breathing down my neck which made the hair at the nap of my neck stand at attention. Before I could turn around or scream for help I felt two hands turn me around and there he stood with a big smile covering his face. He softly kissed my lips tenderly.

"Sorry I'm late. I hope you didn't mind waiting my dear. I had a disaster with my water transportation. The prop broke when the dinghy hit a log drifting in sea. I was so anxious to get here to see you my lovely lady I didn't see the damn log. Then I had the challenge to create a makeshift shear pin. Do you know how hard it's to find a shear pin on a boat in the middle of the ocean? Fortunately, I found a bobby pin which did the trick. I feel very lucky or I would be drifting to the open sea, thirsty and hungry, without my beautiful Susan."

I wanted to be upset with him, but his boyish earnest expression on his angelic face made me smile from ear to ear. He looked so adorable, which made the anger magically melted away.

"Well, Dr. Masters I was getting a little nervous about being stranded on this beautiful tropical island. I would have to make friends with the natives. This would hard duty, but I know I could do it." I returned his smile and gave him a hug.

Enthusiastically I said, "I've good news, Dad let me stay in the trawler, since my brother, Sonny is gone this week."

"That's great since Nick's place is crowded. What a wonderful surprise."

I said, "Do you know how to get to the Marsh Harbor marina? We need the trawler key before the Marina office closes."

"Your escort is waiting my lady the dinghy is this way." Dalton said.

I continued, "I've never seen Daddy's yacht but I'm sure it will be in Bristol condition just like everything he touches. Dalton I'm anxious to leave this airport, I have been here too long." Taking huge strides I made tracks out of the airport as fast as my legs would carry me. The fear began to leave my body, but the abandonment feelings lingered.

Dalton whispered, "Wait just a minute, slow down, you're in the Bahamas now and on Bahamas time. Let me look at your red satin sun dress. What a beautiful dress, but the truth is the dress is not what makes you beautiful, you are truly lovely in anything you are wearing my temptress."

He stared lovingly at me making an electric bolt go through my body and my skin tingle. The hairs on my arms stood up with goose bumps covering them. I found myself being drawn emotionally toward this new friend.

Instinctively I felt danger surround me in more than one way, the deaths, the MECS experiment, the stolen documents and Dalton who reeked with charismatic charm. His loving intimacy had a calming affect on me. Then he reached out running his hands across my bare back as he led me to the dinghy. I followed him without saying a word, for the first time my anxiety began to subside.

Chapter 8
The Marina

"Madam next stop, Marsh Harbor Marina," Dalton said in a deep, sensuous voice as we got into the Avon inflatable dinghy. "Hopefully the shear pin will last until we get to Marsh Harbor." He gently took my hand flowing electric energy between them caused mixed feelings. The surge was exciting. Where he ended, I began. What was happening between them? My face became flushed with redness as the heat rose in my cheeks. I was lost for words.

Dalton commented, "You are blushing, my darling."

I gazed into his soft brown eyes giving a demure smile. Still I couldn't say anything, but feel the touch of his hand on my hand. Sweat was dripping from my body with the temperature rising. I was afraid to say anything, afraid I would give away my thoughts, afraid he could read my desire to have wild passionate sex. My lust made me forget the strange happenings back in Houston.

We docked the dinghy in the marina as I grabbed onto the pier tying the line to the dock cleat. Carefully climbing onto the pier I noticed Dalton checking out my legs.

Dalton handed me my luggage. "I'm impressed you didn't bring your entire wardrobe like most women. My philosophy is if you have any clean clothes left over after your vacation then you have brought too much. Then the next time, you have to remove the same amount you didn't use."

"Well I'll make sure I'll wear everything I brought." Teasingly I said, "Only if you say so."

My eyes scanned the bare bones marina which had only a rickety broken down bath house. There were so many sail boats with home ports from around the world. Sailors were living out dreams of cruising the islands, just like I have dreamed of floating through the islands with the man I love, "I want to go cruising?"

Dalton sincere brown eyes met hers, "So do I."

They entered the marina office where a large man was sitting behind a well worn desk. His ratty white shirt was smeared with lipstick on the collar. His thick dirty glasses made it impossible to see his beady eyes, only the twitching muscle under his right eye was visible. His appearance gave me the creeps.

"How can I help you?" He said in a rough manner hacking into a soiled handkerchief.

"I'm Bill Fletcher's daughter. He should have left a message that I'm staying on Dream Catcher for the next two weeks." I watched him as the twitch almost moved his whole face.

His clumsy body maneuvered out of the ripped leather chair to retrieve the boat key. His sweaty hands held it too long as he passed the key. I quickly pulled my hand away gripping the key until it almost cut into my hand. I felt repulsed wanting to wash my hands immediately.

Dalton saw his maneuver and positioned himself between us and said, "Where is Dream Catcher located?"

The marina man answered roughly, "Pier 25, Slip 68."

As we walked out I said, "Dalton, I don't like that man."

"I don't either. Please do not let him know you are staying alone. He is definitely a shady character." Dalton confirmed how I felt.

Off they went holding hands to locate the trawler. They stopped to admire all the boats along the way. I saw three 37 foot Irwin, just like my La Dulce Vida, which meant the sweet life. No wonder they are here with their four foot draft, which makes it perfect for navigating through the shallow waters. Finally they arrived at the Dream Catcher nestled between two stately sailboats. There she was a fine grand ship, beautifully varnished bright work and, as expected, in Daddy's pristine Bristol condition.

Dalton put down the gang plank and we climbed aboard. As I walked onboard each step clanged on the metal reminding me of bells sounding in a distance. "I must change into my boat shoes before I do any scuff up the deck. My Daddy will kill me if I mess his baby up."

Dalton agreed, "I would too if I had something as pretty as this, "as he touched my arm. "and the boat is nice too."

I climbed down the natural wooden companionway admiring at the beautifully decorated furnishings. The honey-gold teak glowed from the soft light in the salon. It was soothing to my eyes with the sea color accessories decoration. My whole tense body began to relax and forget about Houston, NASA, the missing confidential papers, and the disgusting harbor master.

Yes, Dream Catcher had all the comforts of home, a refrigerator, stove, microwave, washer, dryer and an icemaker. Wow, what luxury. Tranquil aqua and purple colors flowed throughout the boat into the aft cabin captain's quarter's comforter.

The entire boat was tastefully done, Daddy's decorator had exquisite taste. I threw myself on the bed feeling the luscious satin comforter which produced chills on my arms, "I'm home Dalton. I may never leave this room. I love it here."

Grimacing with my nose wrinkled, "My boat never looked this good in her best day."

Dalton grinned joining me on the bed, "Well, I love it here too, and if you are staying, so am I. Move over here I come."

Giggling like two little children Dalton barely was audible, "Let's escape from adult responsibilities." He held me tightly in his arms caressing my hair, "Susan, you are my distraction from all that I have to do."

Caringly he reached over kissing me with soft tender kisses. I became lost in his gentle touch as his arms surrounded me. He began embracing me from the tip of my head to the bottom of my feet. I felt the magic in his sensuous hands.

Dalton stared into my big blue grey eyes as if he was looking into my soul. He forced himself to break the hypnotic trance. Breathlessly he said, "Wonderful, just wonderful. I want you to know how much this means to me. Make my dreams come true."

"No, you are the one who is a wonderful dream," I whispered into his ear with a contented smile.

He said sheepishly, "Why are you smiling?"

I responded, "I'm happy, happy to be here and happy to be alive." I turned away so he couldn't see my fear of what had happened at home.

Dalton said, "What more in life could you ask for? We have the best of all worlds, sailing, tropical paradise and each other. Thank you for coming. I was afraid you wouldn't since you didn't know me."

"I couldn't have missed it for the world. We need nothing more for our escape but each other," I confirmed my happiness in coming to the Bahamas.

He pulled me close to his body, kissing my forehead, cheek, nose and eyes. I felt as though I was being put into a spell. He brought my fingertips to his mouth sucking them with tiny kisses. Every moment was more than magical, it was exciting and sensuous. I knew I had to break this trance, before the tenderness went any farther and I couldn't stop my lust or his.

My desires were uncontrollable. I wanted to spend the next 8 hours exploring the newness of his body. With all my strength I pulled away from him blurting out, "Dalton, I'm famished. Feed me. Feed me. Where are we going to eat?"

He looked at me with little boy's eyes, droopy, and disappointed, "I know the perfect place to take you. For your first night, my lady, I've reservations at the finest restaurant on this tropical island. This is a very special occasion for us, our first date. Why don't you freshen up and I'll return to Nicks. I'll be back before you know it. Thank you again my sweet Susan for coming to the islands. Our two weeks will be too short in paradise."

Softly he kissed me on the nose, "Maybe we can stay a month!" Next he kissed my left cheek, "No a whole year!" Then he kissed my right cheek. "How about we stay forever? I promise you'll not regret the time spent with me," he kissed me gently on the mouth. I began to tingle all over as if he had pushed a magical button.

He asked, "Oh yeah, did Nancy send my stuff?"

"Oh Dalton, Nancy wasn't at home, but I got the package and tickets from her sister."

Dalton stared in disbelief. He frowned, "Nancy doesn't have a sister. She is an only child. I don't know who you met. This really concerns me. Wonder where Nancy had gone?"

I handed him the package. He quickly opened it up, "Susan, my belongings are missing. Why would anyone put torn up newspaper inside?"

"I don't know?" I turned my back to him. I considered telling Dalton about what had happened in Houston.

"At least you got the tickets," I could see he was not happy.

I asked, "That's strange, wonder who the mystery woman Carol might be? This is so bizarre!"

Dalton grimaced saying, "Susan, I just don't know anymore. I probably should not have invited you to this place. Things are happening in my life I can't explain."

I thought to myself, "Should I tell him about the dish breaking at my house, the navy blue cars, and the stolen documents. How about the really big question? Who killed Dr. Keller and his entire unsuspecting family?"

I decided not to say anything, after all what would he think of my suspicious snooping behavior. After all I didn't want him to know that I had investigated his MECS project. I determined it would be best if I would be the good listener, "Tell me about these events."

He grinned and laughed, "If I tell you I'll have to kill you."

I said, "That's comforting. Dalton, all the kidding aside, what's going on?"

"I really don't want to talk about it right now. All I want to do is play with you. Susan, would you like to take a shower alone or shower with your new friend, me?"

Dalton smiled. He held me very close while he gave me one more passionate kiss. His tantalizing lips pulled me farther and farther away into a dreamlike state far away from the prior traumatic events.

I listened to my panting and squeaky noise making me dizzy, as if I was on a merry-go-round with my emotions going up and down. His enticing hard muscles rippled across his shoulders, arms, and down the middle of his back.

The magic spell had to be broken and with all my strength I pulled abruptly away, "Now kind sir, pray tell me where you are taking me to dinner, is it some place special?"

He coyly smiled and said, "Yes, I am. Young Lady, I'm taking you to the best place in town, it's a secret, a surprise just for you. So get all prettied up my dear and I'll return in an hour to pick up."

He quickly left leaving me alone, but not lonely. I wasn't even afraid of the unknown, but just in case I locked the hatch securely behind him. The tropical paradise was like an imaginary dream, I thought as I made my way to the head. I filled the circular tub with steaming hot water which was pure luxury, a true condominium on water. I seductively removed my clothing slipping into the delicious silky warm water. I wanted to soak myself forever until all the aching muscles relaxed. It was a pleasure when I turned on the water, it worked, not like my boat, which I sometimes thought had hidden secrets, but then again it's a boat.

The mechanics of each sail boats were different and sometimes I think it required an engineering degree to even operate the head. Thank goodness the luxurious Dream Catcher was different. There was no comparison to my 30 year old sailboat, with its rudimentary plumbing, which smelled of diesel and sulfur.

Time was getting short so I hurried to take my bath, so I would look beautiful when Dalton returned, at least presentable from the long torturous day and the long wait in the humid hot terminal. I must look my best, of course sexy and desirable. The water melted all the tension of the long journey away, smoothing out the accumulated anxiety from the hard day. As I poured the scented shampoo on my hair, it smelled like a bed of lavender. Then my shaven body felt velvety and soft, as I applied silky baby oil to keep my skin supple and moist. I laid my head down on the back in the tub when I heard a loud noise outside on the deck. I laid paralyzed in the water praying it was my imagination. My thoughts raced thinking of the newspaper headlines, "Space Shuttle Executive Murdered in the Bahamas". Possibly "Naked Space Shuttle Executive Murdered in the Bahamas, Bathing, Drinking a glass of chardonnay, looking for Love, of course, in all the wrong places."

I collected my strength, jumped out of the beautiful tub and quickly wrapped myself in a small towel to investigate the suspicious noise. Shadows were moving outside the porthole as I peeped around the corner of the aft cabin. I couldn't make out what or who it was lurking outside. It was probably some Bahamian teenagers playing around at the docks. Bravely I inquired, "Anyone there?" No one answered. I realized my towel was not covering the majority of my body and I was standing partially nude in front of the portholes. Mortified I closed the shades trying to relax again by listening to the soft romantic music, which seductively drifted throughout the entire boat. Then I remembered the refrigerator had oak tasting Cake Bread Cellar California Chardonnay which I poured a full glass. I lifted the crystal wine glass in the mirror for a private toast, "To the best vacation a girl could ever dream about and with a true charming prince. May my fantasy stay alive with life? This is just what the doctor ordered."

That was just enough detraction to make me quit thinking about intruders, since it was probably just my active imagination. Dancing to the tune of "Great Balls of Fire", I searched for my cute outfit to wear in my overly packed suitcase, I found a lacy aqua blue silky sexy lacy halter dress. The dress contoured my body displaying my youthful shapely body and seductive cleavage. Not only did it match the boat's décor, but it made me feel sensuous. My long golden blonde hair fell into beautiful natural curls onto my bare shoulders. I applied a little lipstick and pinched my high cheek bones to have a little color. The dim light made the facial lines disappear from my face. I stood back and looked in the mirror at a youthful vision displaying a picture of happiness and contentment.

My expression immediately changed when a knock on the boat's hull made me jump with fright. I screamed, "Who's there?

No one answered. Again I said, "Anyone there?" Again no one answered. I sat down on the couch looking around and debated to myself whether I should peak out the door. I decided not to go near the door, instead I poured myself another glass of wine, which calmed my nerves.

Chapter 9
The Dinner

A loud thunderous knock echoed throughout Daddy's boat along with noises from topside which sounded like an intruder walking heavily on deck. I listened intently to every deafening foot step. Each step caused my heart to skip a beat. Within 15 minutes my eyes were wide as saucers as I watched the cabin door opened slowly.

"Hi sweetie," there stood Dalton.

Breathe I thought to myself. I finally took a deep gulp of air and frantically said, "Dalton you frightened the wits out of me. I thought the door was locked when you left. Maybe I had a blonde moment and forgot. Didn't I lock the door?" Too many strange things had happened causing a persisted prickly feeling on the back of my neck. I shivered thinking of the intruder in Houston could be the same person who had been walking topside. That mysterious someone could be lurking in the dark shadows.

Ignoring the panic in my voice Dalton said, "I don't remember, but I'm here to take the prettiest lady on the island to the best restaurant in town. Are you ready to go on our first date?"

I excitedly said trying to forget the strange noises, "Yes I am."

Dalton leaned over and kissed me on the cheek squeezing my hand, "Do you shiver all the time or just when I'm with you? You know, this is twice in one day. Let me look at you. You certainly are beautiful. I'll be the proudest guy tonight with the prettiest Bahamian girl on the island. Let's leave before I change my mind and hold you hostage on the Dream Catcher."

I forced a smile trying not to show my fear, "I too could get lost in your charms but my stomach says it's time to feed me. I'm famished. We should leave now before I keep you captive. Can we take Daddy's 19 foot Whaler? Not that I don't like your inflatable dinghy, but we'll stay drier in the larger boat and it's much faster. Daddy said I could use it. Here's the key."

I handed it to Dalton inquiring, "Please tell me, tell me now, what is my surprise, pretty please."

"You will see, my Tempest," answering as they climbed onto the Whaler. Dalton read the name, "Dream Catcher's Carolina Dreamer's. Are you my Carolina Dreamer?" The name was written in English inscription in the colors turquoise and purple located on the stern of the nineteen foot fishing boat. It matched Dream Catcher's interior.

I answered, "You will have to share with Daddy. He has called me Carolina Dreamer, since I was a little girl, his Carolina Dreamer."

Dalton said kidding, "I don't share, even with your father." Dalton turned the key starting the boat immediately. The dock lines were removed as I pushed the boat away from the wobbly slip. The engine purred like a kitten as we idled, but as soon as he backed up it roared like a lion. I barely had time to sit next to Dalton, as we sped away when he kicked the 150-horsepower engine into full throttle. Boys must be boys. We flew across the crystal blue water shimmering in the sun light, as I held on with all my strength.

Dalton slowed the boat down as we watched the sun sinking from the sky illuminating radiant colors of reds, yellows, oranges and blues. "Isn't the sunset magnificent? It looks like a Monet pointillism painting with brilliant colors mixed together. Dalton, I wish I could keep this scene in my mind forever."

"Me too my Carolina Dreamer," Dalton said turning on the navigation bow lights of green/red and the bright white stern light. The glowing lights gave me a feeling of safe and comfort sitting next to Dalton. The bright orange and red sun disappeared leaving the two gazing at the brilliant shore lights below the beautiful twinkling stars.

The boat's LED lights were glowing in the dark making it visible for other boats. The night traffic on the water could be tricky since some boats ran without lights. I cautioned Dalton to slow down, so I could watch for any possible collisions on night water.

The warm sensuous wind blew my hair into the night air as the moonlight silhouetted my body. He glanced over approvingly slowing the engines to dock the boat on a sturdy pier. Two men mysteriously appeared helping with the docking. I almost screamed in fright, but soon realized these locals worked at the restaurant securing boats like Carolina Dreamer for their patrons.

I gazed upward at a brightly lit sign mounted high on the wall of rocks that read Grey Cliff House Restaurant, fine dining with an arrow pointing up. Suddenly I realized why they called it a cliff house. It reminded me of a German castle positioned high on the edge of a cliff. Much to my disbelief the only way to the restaurant was to climb straight up a manmade carved out rock steps.

I held my grimaced face resting between my hands realizing my dilemma of the very, very short skirt. Not only was it short, but I had chosen not to wear any panties. This seems to have been the wrong choice, but at the time it felt right being free from all constraints.

Dalton saw the dismayed look on my face and asked, "What's wrong?"

I blushed, "I'm afraid that I may bare my soul, so to speak," pointing downward to my skirt.

He whistled, "It's not that big of problem, I'll be more than happy to help you climb the rocks."

As they began their ascent up the steep steps, he put both his hands on my smooth, soft bottom, giving me a gentle push forward, "Now I understand your dilemma," he laughed,

Laughing, "Young man, you are getting a little too fresh for our first date."

He ran his hands down my legs, "Is this fresh enough?"

Chills covered my legs making me quiver with excitement, "Quite enough," and began climbing up the rock steps, slowly. By the time we managed to reach the top, I was panting with anticipation. I didn't know if the anticipation was the hike, food or his touch?

The opened air crisp linen restaurant eluded romantic ambience. A three foot rock patio wall was covered with climbing intertwined English ivy. The mild salty breeze from the wicker fan kept everyone comfortable. The gentle wind stroked every inch of my damp body. I noticed the upscale Grey Cliff House restaurant was almost empty. Looking down the steep jutted rocks I had climbed I said, "Dalton, the view is captivating and hearing the sound of the waves hitting the shore is just perfect. The white foam covered the beach in an interesting design. It almost takes the shape of a mermaid."

"Susan, you have captivated me, my mermaid." He studied my face as the moon peaked through the wispy clouds beaming down. "You have a face of an angel with a little bit of mischief."

A waiter dressed in starched white tails approached motioning them to sit near the ivy wall. He lit a tall aroma candle that sparkled in the middle of the crisp table cloth.

I noticed the fire from the candle flickered along with the moonbeams on Dalton's kind face.

The scene reminded me of a poem, I had written long ago, possibly for this very moment. I took Dalton's hand whispering these words, forever in time.

Forever in Time

Crushing waves to shore
As the moon hides behind the cloud
With the wind sounding roar
Hearing a voice faintly so loud
Can you catch the wind?
Can you catch the moonbeams?
Can you see waves blend?
Can you see what I've seen?

Sending shivers to my soul
Taking each inch of my body
A touch that is much like a hold
Speaking softly somewhere in me
Can you catch the wind?
Can you catch the moonbeams?
Can you see the waves blend?
Can you see what I've seen?

Looking through the dead tree
As the moon surrounding rays
This was done before with thee
Saying long ago from today
Can you catch the wind?
Can you catch the moonbeams?
Can you see the waves blend?
Can you see what I redeem?

Reflecting on the time before
Fluttering of my delicate heart
Leaving me desiring much more
Recalling not wanting for us to part
Can you catch the wind?
Can you catch the moonbeams?
Can you see the waves blend?
Can you capture this scene?

Forever in Time

Dalton stared deep into my large sincere eyes, the windows to my heart. He was speechless. He cleared his throat and whispered in my ear so softly, "Not only are you smart and beautiful, but you have captured my heart. Susan, who are you? How could such a fascinating woman be so talented? I love whoever you are."

I was lost for words for a moment, "I'm just me."

He ordered a bottle of expensive Australian Shiraz. The waiter cordially asked in a Jamaican ascent. "Can I get you anything else?"

Dalton answered, "Maybe some Escargot for starters."

The waiter brought back an open bottle of wine allowing time for it to breathe. He poured a small sample for Dalton to taste and offered the cork for him to smell. "The taste is not too dry with a flavor of oak, and very nutty."

"It's an excellent choice. If you wait at least 10 minutes the air will permeate throughout the wine. Excuse me while I retrieve your hors d'oeuvres."

The light of the moonbeams flickering along with the light of the candle across the table made the magical moment enchanting. Dalton's gazed directly into my large dazzling eyes, smiling as a mischievous little boy. He raised the sparkling crystal wine glass in the moonbeams casting a prism on the wall. "To you and to the best vacation ever, you are more intriguing in the moonlight than ever I could imagine."

"Thank you. You say the kindest words, my dear." I genuinely felt he was speaking from his heart, not like the other men.

In the corner of my eye, I noticed another older couple seated across the room. I almost slid under the table when I recognized "Chatty Kathy" from the plane. "Oh no," I thought, "so much for a romantic dinner." I tried to avoid any eye contact, but when she saw me, Chatty Kathy stood up from her table appearing almost instantaneously. Their brief special moment was gone forever.

"Well, well, well, I just knew I would meet you again. Let me introduce you to my brother, Carey," She paused briefly looking toward his way. "Who is this good-looking gentleman you are with? Please, please introduce me. Please do, Susan." Chatty Kathy exclaimed.

I politely said gritting my teeth, "Dalton, I would like you to meet Kathy. We met on the plane in Houston."

Dalton stood up and shook her hand and her brothers. He said, "It's very nice to meet you."

I could tell Dalton wanted her to disappear. This meeting was not included in their evening's plans.

Then she began, "I can't believe how tacky my hotel room is decorated. It's certainly not my standards, so muggy and hot. My clothes even smell like mildew and you should see how they clean the room." On and on Chatty Kathy talked much about nothing, but eventually she sat back down next to her brother Carey.

Dalton gave a sigh of relief when she leisurely returned to her table.

I turned to Dalton and raised my wineglass, making the second toast of the evening. "This is to a special dinner, my surprise vacation, our new friendship, and wherever this adventure takes us. I'm so looking forward to whatever life in the Bahamas brings us. I'm in it for the ride. Thank you Dalton for sharing your vacation with me."

Dalton looked into my eyes and said, "To us." He quickly stood up bending forward kissing my lips tenderly.

The waiters started clapping making my face turn a scarlet crimson blush.

"I would love to take you in my arms and dance with you all night. I've not felt this way, it seems like forever. You make me act like a teenager in love. Whatever happens between us, I'll always remember tonight in my heart forever." Dalton explained.

I smiled, "This warm feeling is so quick, probably too quick, but I can't explain it. How is this possible? When I'm with you I want to crawl inside of you, to hide in a safe place and to be loved forever. Dalton, this is a dangerous sign for me, but I can't stop feeling this way. Tell me it is OK?"

Dalton countered, "It is OK since I feel the same way as you do. Just to be near you makes me content. You are my temptress and certainly a diversion from my work. Let's have the best vacation ever and not worry about tomorrow or any other day. Can you agree to those terms?"

Before I could answer Dalton questioned, "Do you know how to scuba dive?"

I grinned, "No, but I brought my snorkeling gear. I would love to see the beautiful fish, especially the parrotfish, the purple sea fans, pink coral, and the exotic marine life. I've been snorkeling in Hawaii, and the Caribbean but never scuba diving. I've always wanted to learn. I think that would be the best freedom ever, to go below to the ocean floor and become one with the fish."

Then I made a fish face, which made us both laugh. The waiter finally brought over the appetizer, along with a menu. The local Bahamian had a Jamaican ascent, his face was round and jovial. He quoted the specials very fast, "Succulent fresh trout smothered in a butter lobster tail sauce just cooked special for you the lovely lady with blond curly ringlets."

I squealed with pleasure and said, "I don't need the menu I'll have the special."

The juicy butter reminded me of the movie, Tom Jones, which I had seen as a teenager. I had never forgotten one scene when they ate fruit running down their faces and Tom licked the juices from her face. I always wanted to reenact the scene so symbolic of pure pleasure.

I quickly requested, "Also I would like a bowl of fruit for dessert."

Dalton ordered for us lobster and a lighter chardonnay he had seen on the cover of the latest Wine Spectator magazine.

I was beginning to feel tingly from the wine, the music and ambience. Everything was perfect, too perfect. "Dalton, I wished I could put this feeling in a bottle and take the warmness out when things were tense and stressed in my work environment." Then I thought of the stolen confidential papers. Should I tell Dalton now? I should but this certainly was not the place.

"Me too, it is difficult in the aerospace industry for everyone. Let's forget about that now and may I have the pleasure of our first dance." The music was slow and tropical. Dalton took my hand and escorted me to the small dance floor when he slowly wrapped his arms around me. He put his hands on my lower back and pushed my shaking body close to him. As he led my around the floor, his hand gracefully guided me seductively. His movements were smooth and sensual, almost like he was making love to me on the dance floor.

I gasped with excitement. This man was driving me crazy with passion. I thought, "Forget dinner, forget dessert. NO! Go directly to dessert." The unthinkable thought was screaming in my subconscious. My heart was pounding and my body trembling, I just knew he could feel and hear the beating of my heart.

I looked up and smiled happily at Dalton. He returned my smile with a wink. Even his smile was contagious. I wished the evening would never stop. The waiter was putting their entrees on their table as Dalton led me from the floor.

I realized my stomach was grumbling and I was very hungry, I had not eaten a bite all day. The escargot was not enough to hold me even after I soaked up the garlic butter with the rolls. After devouring the scrumptious dinner, the Jamaican waiter delivered the enticing fruit, I picked up a ripe papaya and slowly took a big bite. The juice ran down my chin and to my surprise Dalton leaned over and kissed the liquid off my delicate chin. I couldn't believe that my fantasy was coming true. Then I offered the succulent papaya to Dalton and he took a huge bite. Slowly I bent seductively forward licking the sweet juices around his full lips.

Our eyes met locking the sexual tension between us. He kissed me passionately as if no one was in the restaurant and ignoring the stares from Chatty Kathy and her brother Brent. He tenderly played with a handful of my curly hair which laid on the back of my neck. This sent chills down to my vulnerable open soul.

The happy waiter brought the bill, "I can see you two enjoyed your meal, please have a wonderful evening and come again."

We both broke the trance and said, "Thank you, we will."

We left immediately laughing all the way down the rock steps on the steep cliff. It was more difficult on the way down than their climb up, Dalton held my hand for balance. Finally we arrived at the Carolina Dreamer and Dalton helped me aboard the sturdy Whaler. "Your chariot awaits you, my Princess."

Chapter 10
The Touch

The ocean was smooth as glass with the moon glimmering on the gentle waves. Dalton started the engine, which echoed against the steep cliff with a loud, vibrating noise that penetrated the silence for miles. I covered my ears as the warm sensuous air blew gently pass. Dalton touched my naked back and I leaned back against him. He took me in his arms kissing me with a tenderness of love I had never felt before.

We slowly made our way back to the trawler enjoying the moon and the tranquility of the beautiful Bahamas. Dalton pointed to a beautiful 42 foot cutter rigged Tayana that was anchored in a safe haven near the white sandy shore. As we passed by the boat we heard laughter aboard. I turned round in time to see two lovers toasting to the beautiful moon and to their love.

Before I knew it Carolina Dreamer bounced off the back of Dream Catcher. I caught onto the swim platform climbing out of the whaler and onto the dock as Dalton whistled, "I do like that outfit. You certainly know how to tempt a man."

I growled at him seductively, "A woman has to do what a woman must, especially to tempt a man who tempts himself with lust." I ran toward Dream Catcher with Dalton chasing close behind. Dalton opened the trawler door pinning my heated body to the door. The tropical paradise hypnotized me. He moved his hands from the base of my neck making his way to the softness of my derriere. The stroke was gentle, not like previous lovers, who were rough and possessive, this was a tender love, this felt special. He took my hand and I led him into the aft cabin. He slowly unzipped my dress as he said, "A man has to do what a man must."

He approved of my silhouette against the salon moonbeams, he whispered. "Susan, you are so stunning. I want to taste you, to love you, and to have you." I responded by kissing him passionately. I could feel his hardness making my body tense up with fear.

Dalton noticed my uneasiness, "Are you OK? I don't want to rush you. I have all the time in the world to wait until you are ready."

I looked at him, "Maybe this is just too fast, let's wait until I can get to know you better. It's not that I don't want you, it's just I need time. Making love complicates things, I get so confused when sex plays a part of a relationship. When I make love, it is a serious, but afterwards, emotionally my lover is also my partner. I'm not ready for a commitment this early. Let's just have fun and play."

Dalton grinned, "I'm willing to wait. Sounds like a good plan. My precious, can I tuck you into bed?" He then bent over giving me a tender kiss good night.

No verbal answer was needed just a passionate kiss.

"Tease, are you Susan?" Dalton inquired. I laughed turning over contented knowing tomorrow would bring more happiness. Dalton shouted walking toward the door, "I'll lock the boat up and will see you, my beauty, first thing in the morning." He was gone leaving me sound asleep from exhaustion.

I dreamed of the deceased Dr. Keller. His face had no features as well as his burning children inside their blazing home, screaming desperately for their Mommy and Daddy. They were crying out, "Daddy, Mommy help," trying to hide from the fire under their beds with vacant eyes and mouths gasping one last breath, as the scorching fire closed in on their little vulnerable bodies. Then there was silence.

Twisting and turning in the berth I too struggled for breath, as the oxygen was being robbed from me. It was just like the helpless, innocent children. The nightmare woke me up in a cold sweat. Water dripped from my forehead and my throat parched, needing a cold drink of water.

I sat up in the darkness disoriented asking myself, "What does all this mean? Oh how frightening." I whimpered finally dozing off in the wee hours after tossing and turning trying to forget their lost faces.

Finally the brilliant sun woke me up blinding my eyes as I quickly covered them with the blanket. In the background was the sound of tropical steel drum music. I smelled the aromatic smell of coffee hearing Dalton, "How do you like your coffee my lady?"

"Please with just a little sugar, Sugar." I answered.

"Susan, I'm bringing you a freshly brewed cup. I hope you like cinnamon coffee, since it's my specialty, my dear." Dalton entered the captain's quarters sitting the cups of coffee down beside me. He fluffed the pillows behind me, so he could crawl in beside me. We both picked up our cup of coffee smiling like two little children, who had found pleasure, newness and happiness in their lives.

"Hope you don't mind. I just love having coffee in bed," said Dalton holding his cup up for a toast with a contagious laughter. "To my darling Susan, who has me mesmerized with all the delights of our secret world in the islands?"

We clicked our cups sounding like wind chimes in a soft breeze, "Dalton you're going to spoil me, but go right ahead I deserve to be spoiled." I said with delight throwing back my hair.

Dalton touched my hair lying on the satin pillow. "You have beautiful hair, it reminds me of finely woven threads of exquisite gold. You are certainly a precious gem, a mermaid and so special," I was enchanted.

"Dalton, I love the smell of this coffee and the taste is fantastic. Thank you." I said trying to keep myself grounded.

"Susan, you are more than welcome. Where would you like to explore today, us or the ocean?" Dalton questioned.

My face burned with passion, but I got enough courage to say, "Ocean first, us later."

"Well then, I have scuba tanks in Carolina Dreamer just waiting for us to explore several of the islands. Here's a dive map of the best places. Let's see where our hearts takes us, I mean desire takes us, or maybe just maybe the map." Dalton smiled mischievously.

"Dalton, you certainly are a confident man" I responded and hit him playfully with a pillow.

"Are you saying I'm arrogant?" Dalton questioned.

"No, I'm saying, you are a man who knows what he wants. There is nothing wrong with that. I wish I were more confident, like you." I teased.

Dalton questioned, "You are confident and stunning Susan, now where would you like to go?"

Before I could answer, Dalton suddenly turned to kiss me making the unreserved passion return. The uninhibited passion exploded from the repressed feelings which had long ago been turned off. Now far away from home my emotions had returned for this rocket scientist, this man I did not know. I didn't know what he possessed, but here I was acting like a shameless teenager. Well, maybe being a teenager at heart was just lust, but at last I could feel again.

He took the cup of dark aromatic coffee from my hand placing it down on the end table. He began kissing my lips nibbling on my bottom lip, pulling it gently with his mouth, while he felt my ear lobes with his fingers, causing me to melt. Dalton moved to cradle me in his arms protecting me from the harmful past, and the chaotic relationships.

I was lost in the mystical vibes, when he abruptly sat up handing me my coffee cup.

He hurriedly said, "We better go hunting for lobsters, before the day gets away from us. Let's go now, or I will stay here in your arms, spending the next 24 hours just making mad passionate love. There are some lobsters with our name on them and I'm going to get some just for us."

I said, "First I want to take a quick shower and get my bathing suit on."

"Bikini, of course, but you really don't require a shower. We will spend the day in the ocean," Dalton commented.

I said, "I guess you are right, I'll just get dressed."

Dalton responded, "Well if you didn't bring a bikini, I've a black and gold on with your name on it. This is your first surprise gift and I have many other surprises, but you'll just have to wait for the rest."

I laughed as he held out the bikini in front of me, "I love surprises. It's so small Dalton, I hope it fits."

Dalton responded, "Well that need not be a criteria." They both giggled as he kissed the tip of my nose.

The sexy bikini fit perfectly contouring the shape of my body. It actually was flattering to my figure more than I expected. Looking in the full-length mirror I held my stomach flat, as best I could. I was pleased, hoping he would be too, he seemed much too good to be true. He certainly had an eye for size, I thought. When I walked out of the head, the nautical term for rest room, he gave a wolf whistle.

I turned red, "You make me blush kind sir. Thanks for the bikini, it certainly fits me well. How did you know the size?"

"I just found a perfect bikini for a perfect girl," Dalton said evaluating me from top to bottom.

I gave a huge smile picking up a full bag with my camera, suntan lotion, snorkeling equipment and a towel, "You certainly have a way with words. Are you sure you are not a wolf disguised as a rocket scientist or a rocket scientist in a wolf disguise?" I was thrilled to begin our adventure.

Dalton gave a wolf sound, lifting his head to an imaginary moon, "Wooooooo and you are my little red riding hood."

"What big eyes you have, Grandma." I said climbing in the Whaler laughing with pure joy. I surveyed the scuba equipment, and opened the ice chest, which was full of water, soft brie cheese, green succulent grapes, turkey slices, freshly made French bread, which smelled delightful, and my favorite chardonnay wine. He had planned perfectly for a perfect day. We raced to the first snorkeling spot.

The sun blazed down making my skin hotter than hot. It was time to apply sunscreen all over the exposed delicate places that had not been in the sun. Slowly I applied the silky suntan lotion down my long well-formed legs, over my well-rounded cleavage above the skimpy bikini top. Dalton was in a hypnotic trance staring at my body. I tried not to laugh, and purposely put more suntan lotion on my chest, and stomach making suggestive movements with my hands gently caressing the top of my breasts.

I thought to myself smiling, "What am I going to do with him. He is so corny, romantic, and certainly a geek. Funny I really like him. Chemistry is a funny thing, and boy does he excite me."

I broke his hypnotic trance, "Dalton, would you put some suntan lotion on my back. I don't want to burn on our first day out."

He threw the boat in reverse bringing the boat to an immediate stop, "Your request is my bidding. I'll put suntan lotion anywhere you want it, your back, your legs and anywhere else, my Susan." He covered his head with a ball cap which read, "Sail Slow and Live Fast."

He was wearing a mischievous grin reminding me of a little boy, as he rubbed my back, accidentally dropping his hand to touch my breasts. I stared at the deep tone of aquamarine blue water, as he continued to gently apply the suntan lotion. The enchanting sea was calling me, deeper and deeper into a world of mystery.

I finally broke the thrilling spell asking, "Are we there yet, Daddy?"

Dalton beamed, as he removed his hands, "No little girl, we're not there, but soon. The wait will be well worth it. I know a place where no one will find us, our own private island, where we can find some big bugs. It will be dinner tonight for my lady at Nicks place. I'll cook. It's time you meet my best friend."

I dreamed lazily, "He cooks too, a Renaissance Man." Wonder what his friends will think of me. I was nervous in meeting his best friends.

Excitement pulsed through my veins, almost like an electrical surge. The warm thrill felt sensational. I shivered thinking of what was yet to come.

Dalton asked, "Susan, I know it's not cold. What's the shiver about?"

My face turned blood red, "Never mind young man." I knew he could read my thoughts, my feelings, and my emotions. I felt naked emotionally. This is a scary feeling, which brought back hurtful memories from past lovers. How I wished I could tuck all the baggage in the past. Dalton touched my cheek, "Where have you gone?"

I placed my hands over the side of the boat throwing water in his face, still not saying a word.

He teased, "No fair, wait until we stop. I'm at a disadvantage."

I purposely distracted him to avoid any conversation about the past. It was not what I wanted to talk about in this beautiful romantic place, much less share anything negative about past lovers.

The whaler skimmed across the crystal blue water bouncing my rounded breasts up and down. This felt very uncomfortable, so I put one arm holding the bow line and the other under my breasts. Soon the motor began to slow down.

In the distance was an incredible white sandy beach with white foamy waves beating against the shore. Palm trees lined the beach as if someone had planted them in a row as a protector against the weather. A moderate breeze gently swayed the palm trees as if dancing to a rhythm of a song. It was a perfect day, just a magnificent magical perfect day.

Dalton turned off the engine pulling the propeller out of the water as the Carolina Dreamer drifted to shore. I balanced myself on the side of the boat and jumped playfully into the warm silky water. Dalton tied the Whaler to a palm tree and carried our lunch onto shore while I swam in the clear salty water.

I soon leaned back, floating in the crystal blue water, with my hair streaming around my head making a golden halo.

Dalton soon joined me. "What a beautiful sight. Mermaid, would you like your snorkel, mask and flippers? Susan, are you the mermaid that will tempt me into the deep depths of the sea."

"Certainly I will take you to the depths of the sea and into Neptune's world to experience the marine beauty hidden beneath the enchanted water." Susan said.

Immediately Dalton geared up. "I'm ready if you are." I nodded watching him putting on a purple mask and fins. I laughed at the bright purple combination, he must be a metro guy, as he handed me matching bright yellow snorkels and fins. Silently he took my hand guiding me in the direction of the live reef to the left to a cave. It had huge stalagmites hanging from the ceiling and below the surface was another world, a world of peace and serenity. The sea fans floated back and forth with the grace of ballerinas. Million of tiny silver fish were surrounding me, touching my body delicately as they passed on their way to find food and safety in the reef. I examined the reef, everywhere was a bustle of sea life and beautiful coral.

Dalton gently held my hand, pointing at a sea turtle floating lazily in front of my face. I reached out to touch the shell of the prehistoric reptile, which felt smooth and slippery. Suddenly it turned opening its big mouth trying to frighten me away. I swam as fast as I could, while the turtle effortlessly slipped away into the reef.

The excitement didn't stop with the biting turtle, but Dalton pointed to a menacing moray eel in the reef under a jagged rock. He held his hand out pointing to the ominous eel when it darted out beneath the rock showing his sharp threatening teeth. Dalton quickly pulled his hand away. Again another sea animal opened their jaws warning us away. We were in their territory and were not welcomed. Dalton snatched me back next to him and off we went exploring away from the turtle and eel.

We found the remains of a sunken ship with broken doors, a lost shape of a once fine wooden ship buried on the bottom of the sea. Together we discovered its abandoned anchor outlying from the ruins, long ago forgotten. The image gave me an eerie feeling, wondering what happened to the crew. Were their bones buried deep in the bottom of the ocean by the wrath of King Neptune?

I pretended to be a beautiful mermaid drifting gracefully in my deep-sea kingdom with my prince, protecting me from the demons of the sea. The salt water silkiness caressed my body with sensations making me feel like I was in a dream, a fantasy come true.

Dalton motioned toward the beach, "Let's go back to shore. All this swimming has made me hungry."

We swam leisurely toward the shore to share our gourmet lunch. He served the packed meal first offering me water. I quickly discovered how thirsty I was drinking the cool clear liquid quenching my thirst, but not for his touch.

I smiled at Dalton with glistening lips, smiling from ear to ear. Never had I felt this way, never had I experienced such lust. Dalton reached up and pulled me down into his arms. He caressed me gently pressing his face close to me, rubbing the smoothness of his cheeks against mine, and bringing my chin up kissing me gently, delicately and passionately. The kiss took my breath away while his hands studied my body making me shake with pleasure. Pleasures making me forget I was in the middle of tropical paradise. He removed my bikini top leaning me back, so he could admire my beautiful round firm breasts with erect pink nibbles.

For a moment I blushed with embarrassment at his admiration, "You wear red very well." taking me into his arms giving me another passionate kiss. He slowly removed my bikini bottoms, never did he stop kissing me, first my lips, and then my breasts. I thought I was going to explode with excitement, the heat inside rose matching his passion. Yes I thought, oh yes, oh yes, he fulfilled me in every way.

We made love tirelessly and endlessly. Time seemed to stand still. The touch was unbelievable. Thoughts of his touch…[3]

Dalton followed the rhythm of the rushing waves. As the last one would go to shore, then another one would rise, repeating again and again. The sky was full of brilliant colors: pink, orange, yellow and red as the sun set while we clung to each other. The day, the moment was spectacular in every way.

Dalton gazed deep into my eyes, "Young lady what are you doing to me? I haven't felt this way in a very long time, which seems like another life time, another world. Oh Susan, such a perfect day, with a perfect lady. Thank you for coming and thank you for being with me. I want to stay here forever, but darling it's getting late and we need to return to reality."

I leaned against Dalton feeling safe and comfortable not wanting to leave the seclusion of this tropical island. We finally made our way back to the boat taking off in the direction of the safe harbor.

---

[3] The poem "The Touch" is located in my Poetry section.

Chapter 11
The Confrontation

The peaceful contentment was soon diminished when out of nowhere a black 50-foot cigarette boat, a corvette on water, with five Bahamians aboard sprayed water across the deck of the Whaler.

Dalton exclaimed, "What the hell?"

I yelled, "Let's get out of here."

The pilot, an unsavory threatening character, straight out of the godfather movie seemed to be out for blood—their blood.

We hastily took off as I revved up the 150 horse power Mercury engine pushing the throttle forward at full blast. The whaler charged off lightening fast with me at the wheel. Fear gripped me as they weaved back and forth trying to lose their frightening pursuers.

Screaming over the loud thunderous engine, "Dalton, what is this about? Why are they chasing us?"

Gunshots were firing which sounded like an automatic machine gun. One shot almost hit my hand so I jerked it frantically back toward my chest. My white clenched hand continued to grip the wheel keeping the whaler under control.

The truth suddenly hit me, "Dalton, they are trying to kill us."

Out of the blue Dalton saw an escape route. He shouted, "See the two islands, it's just wide enough to fit the Whaler through. Turn left now to the port side in between their shores."

As I veered to the port side I notice a hidden rock concealed below the surface of the deep blue crystal water. I maneuvered swiftly around the jagged rock immediately leaning on the wheel turning the boat to port, careening wildly in the narrow channel. Praying I wouldn't run the Whaler aground, I grabbed the wheel for support as the accelerating G-forces almost threw us overboard.

The Scarab followed in high-speed pursuit not realizing the danger ahead. Their response was not as quick as mine and they were now committed full speed ahead. It became apparent to us they didn't have local knowledge.

The throttles on the Scarab were full blast in hot pursuit, their engines screamed in the chase. Before the unsuspecting ominous characters knew it, their boat stopped abruptly hitting the concealed rock. We heard the sound of fiberglass crunching and breaking under the shock filling the night air as they rammed into the submerged rock. The whites of our pursuer's eyes were full of surprise as the impact threw the entire crew in the cockpit. The cigarette boat exploded almost immediately, lighting up the sky with a display that would compete with any 4th of July fire works. You could see the explosion for miles, an expensive fire work celebration, only these were much more dangerous. I instinctively ducked as sharp jagged pieces of shrapnel flew by our heads. I looked aft to see if Dalton if he had gotten hit. I was relieved to see he had not.

Fearful of the situation I began shaking, "I'm scared."

Dalton leaned forward in the dinghy as it came to a halt in the water. He reached for me and held me closely, "I'm scared too, let's get back to the trawler and figure out what in the world just happened?"

I wanted to cry, "Who were those mean characters? What in the world happened here?"

Dalton released his hold on me, "I honestly don't know exactly what's going on, but we need to get out of here now and leave the islands as quickly and discreetly as we can. I'm sorry you are getting involved in this situation. "

I gazed at him, this man whom I had quickly grown so attached to inquired, "Tell me now. What is this about? Why would these people want to kill us? Does this have any thing to do with Dr. Keller?" I said hotly. "Damn it…" I yelled. With this moment of insanity, the almost unbelievable desperation, I had unveiled the fact I had read Dr. Keller's note.

Dalton glared angrily, and to say the least, suspiciously, "What do you know about Dr. Keller?" He demanded as he tugged on my arm.

"Dalton you're hurting me. I just saw a note from him on your boat the day we went sailing." I said.

"And what else?" Dalton questioned.

I was afraid to answer, but I knew I should come clean. "I did some investigation work trying to figure the note out. I got curious about why someone would say the world might change as we know it. Surfing the Internet I ironically found Space Software supports a project for Dr. Keller. We had programmed the top security software. I couldn't read the software because of the encryption, so I audited the director heading up the project to get enough information to interpret what it was about. The funny thing is, all it's doing is downloading life signs, but with a twist. Now it's monitoring the chronological age of the vital organs. Why?"

Dalton's expression changed as his level of suspicion changed. He realized he probably was right about his first impression, but could I be trusted? He looked down at me tenderly, shaking his head, "My little Susan, I'm so sorry you have gotten involved in this mess. I must admit you are a bright little thing and full of surprises. It intrigues me that after seeing the note and the software code you still came to the Bahamas."

I laughed nervously, "I enjoy being on the edge and this has certainly been on the edge."

I asked myself if I should tell Dalton about removing the documents from work and the stolen documents. This is the right time to confess, but I couldn't make myself do it. I was too embarrassed and afraid that he would be more suspicious. What could I do?

He wiped the black smut off my face with the back of his hands. "Let's return to the boat. We've got to come up with a plan to get off the islands. Unfortunately we have to leave our vacation too soon. This adventure has become much too dangerous. Our vacation has ended, my love. Now we have to escape this island in one piece."

Dalton scanned the horizon for any other thugs thinking the explosion must have awakened the dead. He turned the wheel, bringing the whaler back in the direction of the trawler. As he turned to parallel the coast, he slowed the boat enough to maintain stability and steerage over the minimal waves.

The bright stars twinkling on the beautiful water calmed me down making my shivering stop. Dalton reached forward and touched my hair, gently playing with my blonde curls. I turned to see if there were any other surprises coming up behind us. When we pulled up to the dock, I returned his touch, "Let's not think about what happened today, let's just think about it tomorrow and being together."

"Ok, Scarlet you don't want to think about today, because tomorrow is another day," using his best Rhett Butler's voice. He gave me a playful pat on the butt as I climbed off the Whaler.

Dalton followed, securing the Whaler to the dock cleats to the back of Dream Catcher's stern. My eyes scanned the harbor one more time which was calm compared to the dangerous chase an hour ago. Finally I could breathe, my heart was returning to normal, but not for long.

Chapter 12
The Escape

A forceful hand covered my mouth, eyes surrounding my body. I couldn't scream, move, nor see anyone. I was terrified. I tried to turn to see Dalton. I couldn't budge. The arms were holding me like an iron vice. "Where is he?" I wondered, as fear mounted. "What were these people going to do with us? What have I gotten myself into?"

I heard a slow, deep calculated voice, "You will not get hurt, if you both just relax. Do not scream and I will let you go! If you agree, nod your head up and down and I'll remove my hand from your mouth."

I nodded my head up and down, indicating my intent not to scream. My trembling body shook with fear. Fear of dying, fear of not fulfilling my dreams, fear that this would be the last time I would see my now beloved Dalton. Slowly the tight grip around my mouth was released.

My eyes searched for Dalton but only three ominous men in navy blue suits, starched white shirts and dark glasses were in sight. Then I saw him standing behind them. I edged nervously over to Dalton, gripping his hand tightly. He felt my hands trembling holding them tightly with both hands.

The leader spoke, "Dr. Masters, we have come to take you back to NASA. Your life is in danger."

This time our life is in danger, what about just a few minutes ago when we were in imminent danger. I couldn't believe my eyes. The scene reminded me of a Bond movie, only I was in it. Certainly not the beautiful sexy heroine who ended up in bed with "Bond, James Bond" but with my luck, I was the dame murdered by the bad guy. This was not a very pleasant thought, so I began wondering what would happen next.

I concentrated on the tall, rough looking character speaking to Dalton, "We have a helicopter to take you, Dr. Masters with us."

"Let me think for a moment," Dalton questioned, "Can you show me some identification? Until then I do not believe you are affiliated with NASA or anyone else?"

He produced his Central Intelligence Agency (CIA) identification badge. Dalton began to relax knowing he was safe. Immediately he turned toward Susan, "What about Susan? She has to come with me or I'm not leaving."

The man growled, "It's against policy, we do not have orders to bring her with us."

"She goes, or I don't. Got it?" Dalton knew he had put his rescuer in a compromising predicament. His orders didn't include Susan but Dalton's did.

The CIA agent remarked angrily, "I'll make accommodations for her to catch the first plane home."

Dalton stared straight into the agent's beady blood shot eyes, "That is not acceptable. I'll not leave her unprotected. We have already been attacked tonight. She'll stay beside me or this is an unsatisfactory solution. Until this treacherous situation is resolved, I'll not allow her out of my sight. Please don't underestimate my resources with the NASA chiefs. I dare you to go against my authority!"

I couldn't believe my ears. This new guy was standing up on my behalf, not like the other lovers who had turned their back and walked away when times got tough. He was truly an honorable man, a kind awesome man, who had won my heart in just a few hours. But then again, this felt different. He was different.

I began packing my bags as quickly as I could. The beady-eyed man grimaced at me, making me feel more uncomfortable. It just wasn't fair to be whisked away from paradise to what? The thought made a shiver go up my spine. If they couldn't go home, then where would they be taken?

Soon a black boat arrived to take them away in a Navy Seals rigid inflatable dinghy just like the movie, GI Jane. I propped myself against the back of the dinghy and held on for dear life as it sped into the darkness of the night. Off into the night we went to an uninhabited island.

I remembered that I had not given the boat keys back to the marina harbor master. My Daddy will be furious. Would he understand my predicament? He had told me to be careful. Again I had not paid attention to his warning. Would I ever learn my lesson?

Dalton whispered, "Please do not be frightened. I don't know what is going on here. All I want is to save humanity from painful deaths by helping patients defeat cancer. Sounds harmless enough, yes, but sometimes things get complicated. My plans were to catch rock lobsters, lie around in the sun, and get to know you better. To learn what makes you so fascinating. Yes, you are my passionate, sensuous Susan. What do you say for yourself, sensuous Susan?"

The conversation seemed strange in light of the immanent chaos and danger. I softly spoke, "I must admit you are not my typical dull date and certainly not boring. Not like my usual date which I want to disappear within an hour. The short time I've spent with you has not been dull at all. What a first date, even though it was a little risky for my health!" I exclaimed, staring into his puppy dog eyes. He looked so sweet and innocent even after all that had happened. I smiled, despite the situation, but I immediately snapped out of the reverie when reality hit.

I glanced at the men, there were five of them dressed as Navy Seals. Their faces were harsh, rigid, displaying a scowl. They obviously had a job to do and they were serious.

I shivered again. I didn't like the idea of them being in control and not me. Dalton said, "Don't worry. I believe they will protect us. They're taking us to Kennedy Space Center. No one can get us there. We will be protected by the government."

"But Dalton, it's our vacation. Tell me what this is about?" I insisted.

"If I could, I would. If I knew why all this was happening, I could better protect us. Frankly I'm as helpless as you are." He said firmly.

I rebutted, "That is not fair. Let me guess, does this have to do with Dr. Keller, or, your last payload? I'm risking my life and I want to know why? I've been shot at, kidnapped and now being taken to a deserted island."

I wanted to scream, hide, or just disappear. Reality was kicking in. My hands began to tremble uncontrollably. I sat on them so no one would notice. My emotions were running wild, from one extreme to another. I had never felt this way before and hated the fact I was not in control of my feelings, my situation, or my future. I had to get control of myself. They approached a deserted island in the Rigid Inflatable Dinghy (RID). Quietly they drifted to the beach as the driver lifted the engine out of the water.

The leader commanded, "Move out of the dinghy immediately. Men, get their bags."

The five men retrieved the bags. The tall, dark headed man reached for my hand but I withdrew it quickly. I turned to Dalton who gently took my hand. He pulled me out of the dinghy pressing his hand into mine. The expression on his face made me feel wanted and safe, "It will be OK, don't worry, I'll take care of you. This web will soon be torn down. I will protect you."

He made me feel warm all over with desire masking my fears. It felt natural for him to protect me.[4]

Suddenly, a loud, whirling noise surprised me with fear. I wanted to climb under Dalton's skin to be safe but I felt tired, really tired. In the distance I saw the source of the deafening noise. It was a Seahawk helicopter, the Navy's dull, metallic grey version of the highly successful Blackhawk helicopter, landing in an area of well packed beach sand. Men put lights in a circle on the hard pack ground. The leader relayed instructions to his men explaining, "This is a special ops, magnum force Seahawk-ST606, Sir. We are the world famous Swamp Foxes out of Navy Jacksonville Florida, Sir."

As the helicopter landed, sand blew into my eyes. I tried to protect them with my hands but they burned from the granular filling my eyes

---

[4] The poem "Safe Inside" is located in my Poetry section.

with tears. This was just enough encouragement for the tears to flow like a violent river breaking through a dam. Where were the tears coming from? Was it the relief of meeting someone who genuinely liked me or the fear of the near death experience? Yes, I was alive and I had met a special guy. Fortunately my body had suffered minor damage, but my emotions had run wild with fear and terror.

Dalton heard the weeping and put his arms around me. "It's OK. Everything will be just fine. I'm here with you."

He kissed my eyes holding my face close to him. His lips soft and tender were removing the burning sensation from my eyes…I kissed him passionately mingling my tears with our now salty kisses. The Navy Seals pretended not to notice our affectionate display.

The rotor blades were not shut down. The sound was thunderous. The forward boarding ladder was lowered from the doorway behind the pilot's seat. I felt minuscule next to the helicopter.

Someone grabbed my arm from behind as I climbed up the ladder. Frightened, I turned quickly seeing Dalton touching me. When I reached the top of the ladder a 50-caliber machine gun was positioned beside the doorway.

My eyes focused on the gun as I maneuvered around it to a row of six seats. I quickly sat down on the hard uncomfortable seat. A crewman came by and tightly buckled my seatbelt securing a shoulder harness which held me against the helicopter's wall. Then he handed out a canvas helmet with ear cups to block out the loud excruciating noise.

Over the roar of the rotor system and engines, I pressed my hand into Dalton. I demanded in a loud voice shouting over the noise, "Tell me Dalton. Please tell me what is going on?"

He inhaled and then exhaled a huge sigh. He leaned toward me, "Remember I told you about my cancer research experiment. I think someone is trying to steal the formula. I'm not sure why? It's flown 6 times before and nothing like this has ever happened. The only thing different is the experiment with Fletcher."

I grimaced, "Dalton, surely you have a patent on the process. Can't someone just figure out the formula? They don't have to kill us for it."

"Possibly," he said. "But they don't have the key for making the crystallized molecules," he yelled over the noise of the aircraft. No one could hear him over the noise. The crew was concentrating on their job which hopefully meant getting them out of there fast.

I peeked out of the upper hatch into the blackness of total darkness. I felt lost in a black mysterious hole captured between the present and the past. I felt misplaced. Then I saw in the distance a sailboat passing through the massive deep blue ocean. It was like a beacon in the night. I pointed to it shouting above the chopping noise of the rotor blades, "I want to be there with you, not with you here. I've a dream of sailing and playing with the dolphins all over the Caribbean. Can you imagine what the maritime couple are doing onboard the sailboat? They probably just had a wonderful dinner and now are laying intertwined in each other arms full from their galley food. I can see them toasting to their nautical love. Love of each other, love of the tranquility of the sea. I feel their calmness. I want to be there."

Dalton squeezed my hand, "We will do everything you wish for darling, please just be patient. We will have our time away from this craziness. I promise that will be us one day."

They lifted off, rotating forward as the helicopter picked up speed and passed through that uncomfortable zone known as the translational lift. As the helicopter quickly picked up speed, both Dalton, I and the helicopter shuttered. A painful cramp worked its way up Dalton's back torturing his neck feeling extremely uncomfortable. I could only imagine how he felt.

It seemed like an eternity until I saw in the far distance the outline of the Space Shuttle on its launch pad. It must have been 34 stories high. It was like a lighthouse beckoning them to safety.

"What a beautiful sight to behold." I said pointing. I remembered thousands of NASA employees were working on the shuttle at that very moment. No one was aware of their treacherous situation. I wanted to be safe on the ground, safe in my lovers arm not far above the ocean in a mechanical bird.

Dalton replied, "I've flown my experiments multiple times and this is my last payload. I want to retire and begin living a normal life, to settle down and have a companion, a sailing partner."

Abruptly he changed the subject, "My heart can't take this chaos. Once we get to KSC, I've to bury myself in research work required for the next flight. Leona and Ken will be arriving to begin the planning and implementing of the training and creating the Micro-Encapsulation Crystallization formula. We are in for the countdown. It's obvious you can't go back to Houston since your life is in danger. I won't let you go back alone. It's not safe. This is my plan I'll have NASA security issue a classified security clearance. You can help me get this payload ready. I'll have my management contact your company requesting a special assignment. Is that okay with you?" he stated not as a question but as a statement.

I said, "Do I really have a choice? First choice, be with my man and second choice, I could go back to Houston and mysteriously die. The funny thing is I don't know why someone would want to murder me? Or is my only option to have an adventure with a mad scientist doctor at KSC."

I prodded Dalton. "How many people are on this special assignment? What will the people at work say or will they even know?"

Dalton ignored my questions, "Our accommodations are at the Astronaut's cottage. It's a lovely bungalow on the beach. It's not the Bahamas, but it's the best we can do at this moment."

I questioned, "Well, my mad scientist, do I get a room with a view, a heart-shaped hot tub and a heart-shaped bed with champagne and fruit waiting?" I came up with enough courage to smile nervously.

He gave a contagious laugh that added warmth to my soul. "Oh you wouldn't say that unless it was so. Unfortunately we're dealing with the bureaucratic politics of NASA. They will not allow us to stay together. They will chaperone our every move. This is good, but this is bad. It's good we will be under surveillance to ensure our safety, but bad from the standpoint we can't be alone. There are cameras everywhere, so behave accordingly. We will have full time surveillance and protection."

I reached over and touched his forehead, both cheeks, and the tip of his nose. I put my hands on each side of his face lovingly, and gazed deeply into his eyes, "Dalton, I trust you, but do they have cameras in the potty?" I began laughing thinking of different ways to protect my modesty. "I can put towels over the camera possibly, do you have any duct tape?"

He laughed back and said, "We'll figure out a way to have some privacy of course. We are not kids. Do you think, for a moment, I would be able to keep my hands from touching your beautiful body? You are an obvious distraction, but I'll try to behave."

I was exhausted. My feet and hands hurt from all the activity. Hopefully this cozy cottage would have a tub, so I can soak my weary body.

From the corner of my peripheral vision another helicopter appeared camouflaged against the moonlit clouds. My heart sank as I screamed, just like I would do in a sailing regatta, "Eleven o'clock! Another helicopter, is it friend or foe?"

Dalton grimaced, "I don't know, it seems to be foe."

I watched the crewmen positioned themselves in the doorway. One grabbed the .50-cal for firing from the gunnery post there. The first shots were fired from the other helicopter. I flinched. I couldn't hear the sound of the other helicopter firing but saw tracers of red phosphorescence leading the operator to the position of their target: their helicopter. I screamed as the pilot immediately dropped the nose of the helicopter, taking evasive action. They dove for the blue crystal water. I gasped for air and tightened the grip on Dalton's hand. "Dalton, are we going to die?"

Dalton screamed, "This is not the way I want to end our vacation."

The shoulder harnesses kept everyone from flying out of their seats. My face grew white as a ghost. My eyes were filled with terror and fear. Now I had no voice to utter one word. The machine gun fire was returned and I could hear the bullet casings hit the side of the aircraft, pinging against the aluminum airframe.

I finally screamed as though in a deep tunnel, "Oh my God!" The helicopter jerked in another direction. The "G-forces" were acting pushing against our bodies, driving them deep down into our seats.

Without warning, the helicopter banked steeply to the right and did an amazing 180 degree turn just in time to make a direct hit on the enemy aircraft with a missile from the port side of the aircraft. The light from the accelerating torch seemed to blind me, but as I blinked to clear my vision, the opposing helicopter went down in flames. The moving parts fell into the ocean creating a sea of fire. I took a breath and Dalton turned, just staring at me. The helicopter circled the wreckage once and turned back toward Cape Canaveral. It streaked across the water until it crossed the beach at the Cape. I felt a sense of relief crossing the white band of beach reflected in the moonlight. We moved at a high rate of speed, not wasting any time. I was surprised, as I had had no sense of real speed in a helicopter. There had been no reference to give me a visual clue of our progress. I could, however, now see the blur of lights going past at a high rate of speed. No one spoke. Everyone on board was consumed with tension.

Finally, as if nothing had ever happened, the Seahawk ST606 began its transition to a hover over the helipad. The nose raised quickly, enough to halt their forward movement. They sat suspended in air for a second before making an effortless landing into the wind. No brakes grinding like on jets, just floating softly to the pavement making a perfect landing.

The commotion outside began as the crewman indicated it was safe to deplane. I unbuckled the harness and safety belt securing me to the bench seat and stood up waiting for directions. Dalton did the same. The crew leader looked at his watch for the first time abruptly motioning me and Dalton to the ladder. Dalton took my hand again, departing the aircraft. "I don't want you to fall, better yet, and I don't want anything to happen to you at all." They ducked to pass safely under the whirling rotor system. Although the maneuver wasn't necessary, it was instinctive. They ran outside of the rotor arc.

I smiled. It took all my strength, and said, "I feel the same way, I don't want anything to happen to you either. All this craziness," I

I screamed out loud, "A girl just needs warm hot water to melt the muscle spasms away." Raising my hands up in the air I said, "I just want to take a bath. Is that so much for a girl to ask for? A girl needs what a girl needs and sometimes that need is just that simple."

Unhappily I would have to settle for a nice, long, hot shower. I felt dirty, sweaty and dog-tired. I glimpsed in the mirror scaring myself with matted hair, smudged makeup with two black circles around my raccoon eyes. My little cute outfit was tattered, dirty, and black, which were ripped into pieces.

Without warning I collapsed crying hysterically. The last 24 hours had been too much. I slowly removed my torn clothes finding the shower more than inviting even though it wasn't a tub. As I turned on the soft water, my only thought was to clean my body from all the events of the day and hopefully with hot water. I got my wish, the hot penetrating water felt good embracing all my aches and pains. The steam surrounded my body lathered with soft beads of lavender body soap. I inspected the black and purple bruises on the top of my thighs and on my bottom which hurt to touch the sensitive areas.

I chanted, "Poor, poor me, I guess I'm just lucky to be alive. I had died a million deaths and at the same time was reborn with a love, my Dalton."

It seemed like an eternity as I stood under the hot water as the soil and dirt floated down from my hurtful body. I found a miserable little rough towel to dry off my damaged body. The white soiled towel was so coarse it scratched every part it touched. I would think they would have had luxurious towels for the Astronauts.

I noticed a movement in the room outside my open bathroom door. I froze, naked. The towel was so small I was unable to wrap myself completely. Who could it be? I dared not call out. Whoever was in the room must have seen me in the shower. Where was Dalton when I need him? I told myself, "Remember I'm at the Cape and protected by NASA." Peeking cautiously out the door, my teeth dropped in surprise. It was Leona, the same girl who lusted after Dalton on his boat. Yes, Leona had arrived.

Leona spoke first as I quickly secured the small towel around the front of my aching body. "Hi. Let me explain. There are no more rooms in the Inn so we have to share."

I didn't want to share a room with Leona and lose my privacy. I had no choice of the matter but to make the best of the situation, "I guess that will work since my last roommate was in college. It might be fun, but she snored. Do you snore?" I said with a sheepish grin on my face.

Leona responded abruptly, "No, but I do want the bed you have your clothes on. I like to be nearest to the rest room since I've a weak bladder and have to go in the middle of the night."

I knew Leona was jerking me around but I played her game. I just wanted control of the situation. I said, "I've to get dressed. It must be that you are getting old and have weak kidneys. I'll remove my purse and luggage off the bed in a minute."

Leona glared, "I'll do it for you." She threw everything over to the next bed scattering my clothes all over the bed.

Angrily I said, "Keep your hands off my stuff or I'll break them. I'm in no mood for your rudeness."

I was furious at this stranger who had disregard to my personnel belongings. I needed to know about this mean person.

I began blurting out questions to Leona. "How long have you known Dalton?

Leona just stared blankly at me.

"What do you do for his projects?" I inquired.

Again Leona didn't respond.

"Has anything happened lately on his research that has been suspicious?" I pursued my questions with no response from Leona. It was like I was performing an audit. This is what I usually does best, but it wasn't working.

Leona's reaction was typical for people who were taking great pains to hide information. Leona acted like a caged tiger, she moved back and forth, her eyes never made contact with me.

Leona finally glared at me, "It's none of your business. I don't want to talk to you about the work I've done with Dalton. I really thought you would be gone by now. How did you end up here?"

The tables were now turned by another auditor. Briefly described what had happened in the Bahamas. No explicit details but just enough information for her not to ask any more questions.

Leona responded coldly, "Dalton asked me to go, but I couldn't. He was so disappointed. I guess that makes you second choice. I've known Dalton for a long time and we are extremely close. You know what I mean and if you don't then let me spell it out to you. One, we have been lovers for years even when I was married. Two, he has asked me to marry him when he retires. Three, keep your hands off of him because he is mine, all mine, alone. You will not get in our way of our happiness. He only took you to the Bahamas because I couldn't go. Understand. I guess I was lucky one though, because if anyone had died it would be you and only you. I was not put in harms way. Yes, that would be your job."

I died inside. I turned away so Leona would not see the tears swelling in my eyes. What a fool I had been. He was a player. The no good, he's just like all the other men. The pain returned remembering all the men that had taken advantage of my good nature, my love. I couldn't believe my ears. It felt like someone had slapped my face without even touching me. It burned deep inside with the realization he was like the rest of the guys who hid behind a mask to just get their way with me. I thought he would be different but no he was not. The emptiness I felt burned deep into my soul taking away a little bit of my heart. All I could think of was he another liar, a no good for nothing liar. Just like all the other men in my life. I was devastated with disappointment.

I turned toward Leona and with all the anger in the world screamed, "You are a liar. That may have been then but this is now. A real woman can tell what a man wants and I know what Dalton wants."

I got under the covers so Leona couldn't see my tears. My heart was broken into tiny pieces. Our bond had been removed from my heart. The Bitch, she knew I couldn't question Dalton. It was perfectly clear he was a woman's man. I had been second choice and to top it off he had not answered my questions. It was all an act. Men, I had learned a long time ago not to trust them. Now this had sealed my hopes and trust in men and my emotions away for a very long time. The wall returned, this time stronger than ever, forever.

Sleep didn't come easy. Tossing and turning with the pins and needles straight through my heart. Again I had trusted and found love full of complications and grief. Would I ever meet a good man who loved me for myself? When would there be no game playing? Sad I thought, but very true in the game of life. I had given myself to him and he had used me, he had worn a mask of deceit. He really wanted Leona, not me. I pulled the sheet over my head so my grief was hidden. I finally fell asleep from exhaustion. The dreams were troubling filled with his pretense and lies. I fell asleep thinking of his mask of lies. [5]

* * *

No sooner had I fallen asleep exhausted, I heard a knock on the door hearing a voice I didn't recognize, "Get up ladies". I glanced toward Leona's bed. Thankfully she was not in it. I was grateful not to see her face.

I thought she must be with Dalton, her Dalton. Leona probably sneaked out of the room as soon as I fell asleep. I called out, "I'll be right there."

Looking in the Mirror I saw an awful sight. My eyes were swollen and red. My curls had matted from twirling my hair as I slept. I said to myself, "I can't go out looking this way. I can't let them see me this way. I've got to put up a good front. She will not get the best of me, the bitch. She is just mean, mean, mean, nothing but mean."

I took another shower to remove the tears leaving no time to dry my hair. Pride made me want to be my best, even though my heart was breaking leaving me miserable.

Remembering my mother telling me, "Susan, before you go out always apply your lip stick. Do your hair and your make-up because you never know who you'll meet. You must look your best at all times."

---

[5] The poem "The Mask" is located in the Poetry section.

Momma had a point, I would fight fire with fire. Maybe Leona was lying about Dalton, but it really didn't matter, in any case I had to protect my heart and myself from her and Dalton. Work needed to be done, which was the most important part of my life at that moment. Duty called. I would not let Leona and Dalton interfere by playing their game of deceit. "Just let them try'".

Since the only clothes I had were my Bahamas wardrobe I threw on a cute short flowery dress with sandals. I put a fake smile on my face and walked proudly out the door. I smelled bacon frying, which signaled my stomach that it needed food. It had been a long time since I had eaten and the hunger pains matched the pains stabbing at my heart.

My smile was painted onto my face as I followed the potent aroma of bacon. Dalton was already sitting at the table with a huge smile on his face when he saw me, coffee in his hand and a large amount of briefings on the table. He reached over and gave me a quick kiss on the cheek.

I thought, how unprofessional and wondered where was Leona? It's difficult having two women in the same laboratory.

I grimaced. Dalton didn't notice, he must be blind or just didn't care. My heart was expendable to him.

He nonchalantly began instructing me on the data analysis process, what data to be captured, what the Astronauts would do, how he would train them and how they would analyze the information.

He explained the whole process feverously. I unexpectedly blurted out, "You look like a mad scientist." I couldn't help but laugh at his hair strands combed across his forehead barely covering his baldness.

Dalton's face didn't change expressions, "This is my life. I've worked hard on the research. Let me explain. This is the last chance to make this experiment work. From the time I started working at NASA I've wanted to help people who have cancer. To make a difference and my real dream was to become an Astronaut. I've had fellow scientist steal my creative ideas, use them as their own, resulting in their promotions and the glory. This is the end of the line, either it will work or not. I love the aerospace program. I do not mean to be hard on you, but I'm serious—dead serious. Study hard because we don't have much time and no room for error."

I told Dalton I had completed my assignment. I watched Dalton's expression, but it didn't change. How could he be with both of us here in one room?

I reflected remembering the short spend time they shared in the Bahamas.

Dalton continued explaining his process. Astronaut Congressman Dan Fletcher will be undergoing a top-secret experiment with my drug delivery experiment. He will enter the capsule that will be attached to the International Space Station. This will provide a controlled environment to administer the tiny molecules developed in space with the anti cancer medicine.

I gasped, "Does Fletcher have cancer? Dalton, it can't be true. He is my hero. I've secretly adored him since I was little."

Dalton said seriously, "Yes he does. He agreed to this experiment since it's his last chance. His cancer is inoperable and if he doesn't try this Fletch will live only 3 more months and at the best 6 months. Actually this was his idea. He had heard of my research and decided he wanted one more chance at life. He loves his wife very much and would do anything to stay with her. I've met her and she is adorable and worships her husband, as he worships her."

Then to my surprise he gave me a very warm smile reaching for my hand and squeezing it gently. Leona saw this display of affection and interrupted, "Dalton, please continue speaking on the MECS process."

Dalton cleared his throat and began speaking, "We will be monitoring his vital statistics. Fletcher has more than cancer. He has high blood pressure, a heart murmur, his hearing has deteriorated, poor eye sight, has a little arthritis, but overall has been in generally good health for a man of his age until now. We will observe his heartbeat, size of the tumor, heart murmur, vision, hearing and body temperature. The one good thing is he has a positive attitude. He is quick as a whip for his age. He's always in good spirits, a man who makes sunshine every day, a true pioneer in space. Listen I don't blame him for wanting to go through with this experiment."

I smiled "I can't wait to meet him," and then I said, "Maybe I'm being presumptuous. Will I get to meet him?"

"More than that we're having dinner with him tonight here at the cottage," Dalton said.

I jumped up and down inside like a little girl, but maintained somewhat a professional attitude, "I'm looking forward to meeting him."

Leona rolled her eyes and said, "You've seen one Astronaut, you've seen them all."

I thought to myself, how could Dalton love such a person? Space was my life and constant motivation. Doing the Software Quality for the Space Software made my life meaningful. It was more than I ever hoped for in a career, thank you God. I retorted, "I feel so fortunate to be a part of the program. Thank you Dalton for giving me another perspective of the space program."

Dalton looked me straight in the eyes and said, "I'm so glad you are a part of my life."

I almost forgot the conversation with Leona last night. Thoughts of Leona being so brutal quickly sobered me up. Straightening up in my seat, I noticed a little hyper Japanese chef. He had a smile engulfing his face with huge teeth dominating every feature of his face. He equally portioned out bacon, scrambled eggs, grits and homemade biscuits, serving breakfast. I inhaled my food in not a very lady like behavior. I forgot about everything, including Leona and Dalton, except the food I was devouring. The food was just what my body needed but it didn't fill the emptiness in my heart.

Chapter 14
The Security

The men in navy arrived to take us to the Payload Laboratory located in the Astronauts building. We all three sat in the back seat with the notorious Dr. Dalton, who was sandwiched between his two blonds. My eyes looked straight ahead without speaking or glimpsing at the other two love bird passengers. My feelings were controlled, always professional, even though an irrepressible anger burned inside. Dalton was cool as a cucumber wedged between his two lovers. Imagine that, he certainly wore his mask well hiding behind his deceit.

The driver spoke to Dalton "How are you doing this morning Dr. Dalton Masters? It's so nice to see you again working at the Payload Laboratory. It's only five days away from launch and you must have many long hours before your experiment will be ready for flight."

He rambled on like his long lost buddy, "Congressman Fletcher is waiting to meet with you. I just took him over to the lab. I certainly enjoy his company. What a nice guy. Just like you, Dr. Masters."

Dalton smiled with his eyes twinkling with excitement, "Thank you. This is going to be a great day, I'm ready for a good day of hard work or is that a hard day of good work? Are my two Quality Assurance ladies ready for some challenging labor of love?"

I sat silently not answering but Leona spoke, "Oh yes Dalton, anything you want my master. I will work hard and good. I'm ready, just give me the instructions. We have done this together many times, our labor of love."

Leona paused as she stared deep into Dalton's eyes whispering, "Haven't we?"

"Yes we have. This is our seventh mission creating Micro-Encapsulation Crystallization molecules. Each time I come closer to having the perfect molecules. It has to work, especially for the next flight." Dalton responded.

My stomach felt nauseated with Leona's subservient fake attitude. My mind was preoccupied replaying our confrontation last night. The hurtful words dug deep into my heart. Once again lies, I had been played for a fool once again not seeing the mask of webbed deception. It was just convenient for him to take me off the shelf to play with me when he desired.

Maybe my feelings are out of proportion compared to the amount of our time together. Again, I jumped into a relationship without really getting to know the guy. The amount of time has been short, but my emotions run deep inside in places that had not been experienced in a long time. I felt deceived, that he did not tell me about their relationship. Internally feeling as a kidnapped victim, who fell in love with the kidnapper? A love filled with chaos and threats of life or death. Then in such a short period of time, the victim attached herself to the kidnapper, who would provide food, comfort and all the necessities in life. The victim tricked into love or just sex. Boy was I confused.

Apprehension prevailed about the men in the navy blue car, ever since my experience on the Kemah Bridge. The chauffeur seemed sincere enough even though he had a history with Dalton. Realistically, but not emotionally, I decided I was physically safe. Yes, I could breathe easy for a moment. It was a relief to be at Kennedy Space Center where no bad guys could infiltrate the place, it is protected like a fort. Yes I was out of harm's way.

I stared out the car window at the Shuttle on Launch PAD B with the back drop of brilliant cobalt blue filled the sky with billowy clouds. The Florida sunshine glimmered against the bright orange shuttle solid rocket boosters. The shuttle reminded me of the empire state building rising 36 stories on the top of a majestic mound as royal king on a golden throne.

A friend told me about the perfect job at the launch pad, it was called the bird watcher, who scared the woodpeckers away from the tiles by blowing a loud whistle. Secretly I wished for that job, this simple task preventing a multitude of problems such as birds pecking at the tiles which protected the shuttle from the heat during entry and descent. This simple task takes me away from the stress of auditing people who didn't want to be audited who sometimes called me names. Then I could be a part of every launch, not auditing the Space Software, but up close and personal with birds, who do not get angry or complain.

The view was breathtaking, exciting every inch of my body with goose bumps. The thought of the day's ahead working with an actual shuttle payload experiment made my goose bumps larger. Finally I would not be auditing the Space Software SQA Flight Readiness, but I would be on the team of an important research payload.

I decided silently, who cares about this guy? He's just an end to the means. I'm getting to do something most people only dream about and never have the opportunity. Yes this is fantastic. I watched Leona and Dalton whispering to each other. A twinge of pain stabbed my heart.

Finally Dalton turned to Susan, "Ken's company makes the Micro-Encapsulation Crystallization container. He will soon be here to take care of any problems with the equipment. Leona, Hardware Quality Assurance engineer, certifies the payload equipment is functioning correctly and provides the final safety signoff on the hardware certification that all is a go. I'm lucky to have two Quality Assurance Engineers helping me out this time, thank you ladies.

"The capsules will be filled with the ingredients that give life to this payload. Either Leona or you will fill the capsule while the other will perform the quality witnessing peer review. You two will work very closely together in order to assure the experiment's success."

I forced a smile, "Sounds great to me. I'm looking forward to learning what is needed to be done. I'm up for the challenge."

All of a sudden I remembered the mysterious note on the sail boat. Chills ran up my spine, but I managed to continue speaking, "I'm looking forward to seeing Ken again. He can give me an overview of the payload hardware. It's always good to understand how the entire system works."

Working on the experiment would have its negative side since I was stuck working with cold hearted Leona and strange Ken. Something was suspicious about both of them. I secretly swore to myself that I would get to the bottom of whatever it was happening.

Even though I felt hurt, confused I decided that I should begin planning what questions I needed to ask Leona to find out how she fit into the mystery. Did she have anything to do with Dalton and me being hunted like a wild animal. I retreated back to what was familiar, work, yes think like an auditor, plan your attack, forget about your hurt, and don't let Leona throw you a curve ball. Remember she comes from the same background, an auditor.

Why did Dr. Keller fear for Dalton's life? Who tried to kill us in the Bahamas? Who had killed Dr. Keller and his family? Why had Dalton not mentioned any of the mysterious incidents? He must truly be a rocket scientist, just focusing on his research and not on the chaos around him. Who stole the Top Security documentation from my home? I panicked with guilt about not disclosing the incident to Dalton. Should I? I just didn't know any answers to any of these questions. I remembered the note on the boat, *"Dr. Dalton Masters keep the MECS formula safe. This may be the beginning of life and death not as we know it. The future is in your hands. Your life may be in danger. Be careful."*

The words played over and over in my head like a broken recorder. I needed to think of something else. My thoughts turned to Leona.

I didn't care what Leona had told me, I still cared for Dalton even though we had only spent two wonderful days together. Our beautiful lovemaking made me feel warm inside, but then reality hit me between my eyes revealing the pain, unhappiness and chaos in my own life. I tried to make myself believe it just didn't matter about the intriguing Dr. Masters, but it wasn't true. Dear God, please let me concentrate on finding out what happened.

There was Leona sitting on her bed right before me. She was pretending I didn't exist. I built up enough nerve to ask my first question, "Leona, I was curious, where are you from?"

Leona hesitantly answered, "I'm from the Big Apple, New York City. I spent all my youth in the Bronx."

I had recalled many immigrants had settled in the Bronx. Majority of them were Jewish from various segments of international communities escaping persecution. But that situation existed in an earlier time before Leona's was born. Good times, great opportunities in America for all. It was a different era.

I appeared sincerely trying to win Leona's confidence, "Did your family immigrate to America?"

Leona looked very indignant and with a slight edge in her voice she said. "Yes, my grandparents immigrated to the U.S.A. settling in New York. I'm of Russian heritage."

"Oh how interesting. I would have never have guessed you were Russian. You are so pretty." I complimented Leona, once thinking all women in Russia looked like Khrushchev's wife.

"When your grandparents came to America what type of profession were they in?" I questioned.

"My grandmother was just a house wife, but my grandfather was a scientist." She proudly explained. She continued with reservation. "Great Grandpa did research in chemical warfare? He was very bright and apparently asked to participate in supplying the Germans with chemicals in World War I to destroy the Americans. He was a proud NAZI who believed in the supremacy Arian society. I don't know if he collaborated with the Germans, since he never got any credit for any of his research over the years. America was the answer for continuing his important research in the free country. The chemicals he used were documented in a journal I found as a little girl. I often pretended I was a famous scientist and master of the universe just like Hitler with the world at my finger tips, Leona, the ruler of all human-kind but this time forever."

Leona chided herself, "Oh, I'm just going on and on."

I complimented Leona, "How interesting. I would love to hear more about it. Wow, what a story. You must have been very proud of him. Your grandfather is an important part of history."

Leona smiled, "Yes he is and he will always be in my heart."

I thought I would never admit to having a killer grandfather who created chemical warfare for the Nazi party, which would destroy most of the Jewish Society. Apparently her Grandfather's chemical research had not interfered with Leona getting Top Security Clearance at KSC. This could only happen in America.

We had arrived at Kennedy Space Center before I knew it. I started to open the door, but someone opened it for me. It was Ken with a huge smile giving me a bear hug.

I politely said, "Hi Ken. I'm glad to see you." He motioned everyone to go inside a sterile building surrounded by barbed wire and security guards. The security guards checked everyone's identification by touching each badge and making sure everyone had proper credentials. NASA couldn't be too safe since 9/11.

The man at the desk sternly asked me, "Please complete the paper work before a temporary badge will be issued. We have already received permission from the Payload Director giving proper authorization." He motioned me to sit on the chair to have my picture taken. The flash went off and almost blinded me. It took no time at all to develop the print. The picture wasn't very flattering which actually made my look like a cartoon character. My hair looked bright yellow and my face white like a clown. It certainly wasn't a glamour shot.

Both Dalton and Leona cruelly began laughing at my picture. Leona commented, "You are perfect for the Saturday Morning Cartoons to play the dumb blond."

Dalton laughed with his lover. I defensively laughed back, but inside I was dying. I had to remember the importance of the mission and not let them get the best of me. Think of a witty comeback, "Leona your hair must be dyed red, since you really are a blond, a dumb blond. Aren't you? Well, guess what? I'm not." I turned and put my head up high with a big grin on my face. The good part about it I was telling the truth.

Ken left for the payload laboratory to begin checking out the hardware equipment.

"Security is extremely obvious," I said, "Look at the military armed guards carrying automatic weapons. How frightening! I should be thankful for their presence, remembering all the strange happenings during the past exhausting week."

Dalton commented, "Ever since 9-11 security is very tight, and for us it is especially a blessing. We don't have to worry about anyone on the base killing us. I've had enough of people shooting at us."

Standing outside the security building Dalton suddenly turned toward me embracing my stiff body. He gently lifted my chin softly kissing my lips.

I didn't respond back. I wanted to run away, I kept thinking what kind of sick game could he be playing? He had two lovers. I pulled away turning my back to him. I didn't want Dalton to see my tears streaming down my flushed face.

I watched Leona lead Dalton toward the car from my peripheral vision. I discreetly wiped tears from my face managing to take control of my emotions. I thought, "This is ridiculous, it must be hormones."

We climbed into the backseat of the car. Silently we headed toward the Aerospace building housing the payload laboratories, which held Dalton's experiment equipment. Dalton kept glancing over to me but I would not permit my eyes to meet his eyes. Never would I let him see me crying.

Chapter 15
The Laboratory

Upon arriving at the laboratory Dalton led the way through the couriers en route to his life's research. The Payload team entered into an icy cold room of stainless steel and glass. Signs were on the wall saying, "No Food or Drink allowed."

The laboratory was a white sterile room protected from germs and debris. It had two refrigerators, stainless steel tables with hard uncomfortable stools. It reminded me of an operating room, sterile, cold and barren.

They walked into the white room full of test tubes sealed in germ-free wrappings. Dalton began, "Each tube is to be filled with the correct amount of solution. The Micro-Encapsulation Crystallization consistency requires the exact proportion to be used in the experiment or it will fail. Leona I want you to mentor Susan. Please fill the tubes with the exact proportion of chemicals. This is very important step since the molecules will not mature unless the chemicals are precise. Each will perform quality control of the capsules."

Leona began lining up the hundred of tubes to begin the production line of the fragile research.

Dalton continued, "The secret is in the timing. The serum has to be put in the bottle right before the flight or the solution will lose its potency. It must be refrigerated immediately. Please handle each drop as if it's the most precious life force in the world."

Both Leona and I shook our heads simultaneously in agreement, as if we were the obedient Stepford Wives, "Yes, we will."

Dalton carefully explained the process. He pulled out a container with the glass test tubes. He emphasized, "We will work as a team. This is very meticulous work. It's the utmost importance that the measurements are precise and accurate. For example I want you to fill the first 5 test tubes with 3 milligrams marked 1, the second test tubes with 3 milligrams marked 2 and so forth. I will retrieve the Top Secret detailed procedures with the solution instructions for you to follow. Please guard this manual with your life. Remember the process has to be exact." His voice was stern and commanded complete control. There was no room for error. The calibration had to be perfect.

I stared in amazement. There were 2000 bottles of different chemicals to fill 20 trays of 100 test tubes.

I interrupted Dalton, "How long will this take us?"

Dalton said sternly, "From now through most of tomorrow. Once you begin you can't break the process. You cannot stop. I'll help you get started…The test tubes have to be refrigerated immediately. Leona has done this before so I can help you, but remember the ingredients must be accurate or the capsules will not create the valuable crystals. If the formula is not perfect the crystals will be deformed, irregular, and unusable. So young ladies, please take your time and be careful. I expect each capsule to be stamped, initialed and dated for the final quality check." He said dreamingly staring into my eyes.

For a moment I became disoriented. He was probably doing the same to Leona behind my back. I almost forgot where I was, what I was doing, and the malicious attack from Leona.

"What a womanizer? What a stupid fool I've been? How he has deceived me? Yes once again, another time but the same story, another man who wore a mask tricking to trust. Trusting what?" I grimaced.

Leona interrupted my thoughts by her obnoxious voice, "Dalton, I need your help, Sweetie. I must refresh myself of the details and ensure the process is followed correctly. Please could you check me out on the procedures, so we can begin?"

Her voice screeched and echoed. It sounded like someone standing on top of a mountain shouting repeatedly in my head. Even though I was not violent, I wished to show her something like a knuckle sandwich. Disappointed I shook my head and made a fist shaking it at them, as they walked away. All the while I watched the despicable Leona laughing and touching Dalton's arm. It hurt me to notice he didn't pull away from his dearest. My anxieties manifested, "Yes, I'm just second best. Leona is the one he wants, not me. She can have him on a silver platter."

I fumed inside, "It's not the time to be sad, but to be a Space enthusiast. I'm proud to be part of an experiment with Astronaut Dan Fletcher. The pride swelled in my heart acknowledging my hero since childhood, Astronaut Dan Fletcher. My hero is an Astronaut and Congressman. Leona's hero was a chemical warfare Grandfather. Each man having goals that would measure success from two different spectrums: space exploration using cancer research in comparison to chemical warfare for death. The talented men were catalyst of mankind's future, one a savior and the other a destroyer."

Unexpectedly I felt someone approaching from behind speaking vociferously, "Hi young lady." I jumped in surprise. I swung around facing Ken and my hero Astronaut Congressman Dan Fletcher. Dan Fletcher, the first American to orbit the Earth is making his triumphant returning to space as a Payload Specialist. He is now the oldest employed Astronaut.

*   *   *

Ken was schmoozing Fletcher laughing and making horrible jokes. He was smiling until he saw me. Then he gave a menacing frowned, "Why are you here?" He said roughly.

I found enough courage to respond, "I'm here to assist with the experiment. Dalton explained the project is delayed. My job is to execute quality control of Leona's test tube preparation."

Ken turned abruptly said, "I don't think you have the qualifications or the certification to do this type of work. You will put the mission in jeopardy." His voice trailed, when he noticed Dalton listening to his attack.

My face burned with embarrassment. I began rubbing my hands together in nervous gesture, but blasted him back, "She has twenty years experience working with the top rocket scientists at Space Software. She has never put any of the missions in jeopardy, and will not now. Her qualifications are impeccable."

Fletcher smiled at Susan, "Well young lady, I'm sure you have my safety in mind. I must admit I'm excited. If this experiment works I'll be like a new man. Not many people know this, but I've an inoperable cancer and if this doesn't work I won't be around too much longer anyway. So say a prayer for me, pretty lady."

"Yes I will, every day. God has a plan for you. I don't think he would let someone as special as you slip away." I said.

The Commander, Pilot Bob Rankin, Dr. Daryl McKnight and CheChee entered the room with an air of confidence. I was relieved they had not heard Ken's attack. Pilot Rankin shook my hand vigorously. "Hi young lady, I hear you came all the way from Houston to help us with the Payload. I just want to tell you as an Astronaut I always feel safe flying with the Space Software. It has never caused us a problem. Thank you for your expertise for a safe, on-time flight."

Dr. McKnight smiled with a boyish grin, "Hi! It's nice to see you have added a quality expert to your team." He squeezed my hand a little too long. His actions and words made me feel uncomfortable.

Instinctively his behavior made me feel creepy, but my excitement meeting my heroes overrode my anxieties, I felt thrilled, I couldn't contain myself, "I'm very pleased to meet all of you. I've read so much about the mission on the NASA website. Your credentials are impeccable. It's such a pleasure to work with you guys. Thank you so much for the opportunity."

Fletcher explained to Bob and Daryl, "Susan is a Space Software Quality Assurance engineer who has been on the program for 15 years and an added asset to our program and mission accomplishments. I'm proud to have her performing quality control on this valuable experiment and payload." He elevated his voice loud enough for Ken to hear. Ken still glared at me, but didn't say a word.

About that time Dalton held up the 5-inch thick procedure with both hands. He laid it down on the table in front of me, "Here are the Payload desk instructions. Do not deviate from one step of the process."

"Dalton" the Commander evaluated the black shiny ominous cylinder located in the corner, "Is this contraption for Fletcher's Payload experiment? Hmmm. It looks like a casket drilled with holes, with a heads up display, one who has an aircraft tracking screen filled with hieroglyphic diagrams."

"It's a little more complicated than that Commander. I'll explain it during our training." Dalton said. "Excuse me Gentlemen for a second, I need to instruct Susan and Leona. They will be working all night to make launch, the mixture has to be made at the last moment. The Payload is first, without the payload there is no experiment." Dalton bent over, brushing softly against me, so close I could feel the warmth of his body.

"Ladies please turn to Chapter 5. It has the solution amount for each ingredient in a matrix, with a step-by-step checklist. Remember it's very important you follow the process explicitly. The success of the molecule development depends on you two competent quality women. I'll oversee the production, but I expect perfection from the quality team."

I saw Ken scowling at me in the corner of his eyes. I had another chill run down my spine but quickly turned away. I began concentrating on the work at hand, as well as Leona. Soon we were engrossed in the task.

Dalton motioned the men to the black shiny cylinder. Fletcher, this capsule simulates a controlled environment. The cylinder prevents contamination, which will result in false readings. It is your home for the micro-crystals injections. These injections contain the medicine, which is administered into your veins traveling to the inoperable tumor. The key is the pure oxygen, which acts as a carrier and a catalyst. It allows your body to absorb the medicine. It actually triggers the chemical reaction to release the formula. Are you ready?"

Fletcher laughed, "What do I have to lose? My life is full with a wonderful wife, children, and everything I've ever dreamed as a child. What a ride it has been, but now I'm at the end of the track. I might as well go out with 1000 pounds of explosives under my butt, a real live bomb, in search of a cure."

He pointed upward, "Shoot me to the moon."

Dalton smiled in return, "You know Fletcher sometimes it's not the destination, but the journey. You have lived an exciting career and are going on a hell of a journey."

Dalton continued giving instructions to Dr. McKnight showing him the tubes leading to a huge cylinder of oxygen. "A shunt will be inserted into the chest arteries leading to the inoperable tumor. Multiple adhesive electrodes will be attached to monitor the vital signs, along with a blood test analyzer. Then Chechee will input the data into a software application, which monitors the digital measurement read out. Actually, the software application was developed by the Space Software Corporation. The information will be down-linked, so I can analyze the data. The information contains blood pressure, heart rate, and body temperature, percent of oxygen, PO2, uptake to the brain, vision, hearing, and arthritic pressure.

Furthermore, a CT Scan is built into the capsule. This process is called PCM, Pulse Code Modulation, which sends wave signals making a picture of the tumors. It will in return decode the information using a medical translator. Dr. McKnight, do you follow?"

Dr. McKnight with his twinkling blue eyes and boyish grin gave a huge smile, "Sure I do. This is the latest complex state-of-the-art equipment. What a dream! I never thought I would ever be a space doctor. Just call me Dr. Astronaut or is that Dr. Wilby, Dr. Kildare, or ER's good-looking George Clooney. Could you just pinch me?"

I felt nauseous to my stomach listening to his song and dance. He seemed like a real womanizer. All I could think of was revenge to Dalton, so I began flirting with the good doctor, "Come over here Dr. Mc Dreamy and I'll do the honors. Let me see if I can pinch an Irishman, Dr. McKnight even though you are not wearing green!"

Leona gave me a glaring stare, which cut through me like a knife. Surprised with Leona's reaction, I knew somehow a nerve had been struck.

Everyone began laughing hysterically, and Fletcher chimed into the conversation, "Dr. McKnight, over here, and I'll be happy to pinch you. You're kind of cute." Then Fletcher winked at me.

Fletcher composed himself and said seriously, "Now remember McKnight, I don't mind being a guinea pig, when my life is at stake. Let me tell you, I've been shot to the moon, and now I'm being used as guinea pig. It is all in the life of an Astronaut's career. This just happened to be my last flight, the last payload, so to speak."

Fletcher wrinkled his forehead and turned away from them. He gave a sigh. Dr. McKnight touched his arm and said, "I'll take very good care of the most valuable payload on the ship."

Everyone was silent. I thought, Fletcher is such nice kind man, so sweet. I felt sorrow deep in my heart, it was shame he has cancer. I knew Dalton would save him.

I began concentrating on the quality of the mixture of the secret chemicals. I witnessed the quality control of the test tubes being filled by Leona filling the test tubes. The checklist was done one step at a time. I stamped and initialed each activity upon completion.

Leona ignored me most of the time as I performed my job, except to harass me, "Can you go faster?"

I glared, "Leona, my work is an example of my reputation. I'll perform a quality job, as long as it takes."

In the background Ken kept asking Dalton questions about the formulas. "How does the chemicals in the formula interplay with Zero G?"

Dalton said, "It has to do with antigravity and the solution combining in Zero G environment. Your equipment harnesses the critical test tubes and provides sensors for their properties and development. In return the data is down linked to the Payload Laboratory."

He paused as he turned to us, "Remember, once you start, you can't stop until you are finished. It's a long and tedious job."

Leona responded, "Dalton I've done this so many times before, I can do it in the dark. I count drops like sheep."

I thought my eyes would cross observing Leona continuous motions. Leona meticulously used an eye droplet putting the exact amount of the formula into each of the capsule. She marked the test tube color coding them to the color associated with the number from the matrix.

Leona said snidely, "Susan, could you work harder? I told you once before, and I don't want to tell you again, you are not fast enough. I wish Dalton had not brought such an incompetent quality control representative."

My patience was running thin. "Leona you are just plain offensive. It doesn't matter how long quality takes. A mistake in this aerospace world causes life threatening situations. Safety is in our hands. Chill out or get out. I'll not take any more verbal abuse from you or you will have to do it all by yourself. We have a job to do, so just do it. Quietly that is."

Leona fiercely looked at me, but didn't say a word. Silence was golden to me. We would only stop momentarily for a potty break, plus a drink of water from the hallway fountain.

"Here you are girls. A tuna fish sandwich, a red delicious apple and of course things go better with coke." Dalton announced as he entered the room.

I barely ate the dried out sandwich. The crumbs stuck in my throat. Afterwards we cleaned our hands with antibacterial cleanser that smelled terrible. I made an awful face, "The cleanser reminds me of a hospital. I hate hospitals, sterile and unfeeling, almost like this lab."

Dalton ignored my comment, as Leona's hands gently scrubbed Dalton's hands back and forth with sensuous strokes, each finger one at a time. I thought how romantic, I think I'll get sick.

The time seemed to fly by as we worked hard into the night. I checked the clock and was surprised to see it was already 4 AM. Only 20 more test tubes to go. I concentrated determined to learn every step from Leona.

My stomach began aching. I tried to ignore the pains, but couldn't, "Leona, I've to take another potty break. Please wait for me to continue. We are in a good place to break."

When I returned scowling Leona was sitting impatiently tapping on the desk. I quickly said, "I'm back. Patience is a virtue, let's get started, so we can finish."

Slowly Leona picked up the eye dropper and began where she had left off. My time was lost in enthusiasm and concentration. Each test tube was made with perfection. I handled them as though it was a new born child. As a child we grow up so quickly, and the time passes as though it was a second, but the years had flown by. We finished the last 100th test tube with the remaining chemicals at 6 A.M the next morning.

I took a deep breath and exhaled. "Leona if I ever see another test tube," but I hesitated and recounted my words, "What a great experience. This is what it's all about, one drop at a time." A warm feeling came across my body, which was a combination of my tired bones and my exhilaration of the upcoming launch.

Leona approached Dalton first, "Dalton, can we go back to our quarters? It's 6:15 A.M. and we have been up for over 24 hours. Our work is done unless there is something else you want us to do. I'm so tired."

Dalton said adamantly, "We have to stack all the trays into refrigeration. It's very important, that the lids are secured airtight. Susan, please check them twice for quality control and ensure they are stamped and initialed. Leona you know what needs to be done. The sooner we get started, the sooner we can all leave."

I rechecked the lids verifying the stamps of approval, initials and the current date. Everyone in the lab joined in helping, even Ken began stacking all the trays in the huge horizontal refrigeration. I thought my inked covered fingers were going to fall off.

I noticed Ken was lingering behind and thought, "Wonder what he is up to? My gut feeling told me not only did I not like him, but he wasn't to be trusted."

Dalton caught me by the arm and whispered, "Well my sleeping beauty you need to get some sleep. Maybe a prince will wake you up with a kiss."

His eyes met mine as he traced my lips with his fingers. His touch felt so breathtaking I forgot my tiredness. Oh how confusing. Mother always told me to watch a man's actions and they would show the true self. I tried to remember this, but his words to Leona proved he was a player. A sharp stab went though my chest, deep into my delicate heart, and the anger bubbled inside, "Yes and that would be you, the frog."

Dalton joined in stacking the hundred test tubes trays into the refrigerator. Afterwards he put a pad lock on the refrigeration. "This will keep the tubes safe for the time being. We are all locked up Girls, time to get some shut eye and food, maybe not in that order."

I went to the ladies room and sat on the potty thinking. I was tired, but still felt like crying over my new found and lost love. Crying is not for a Software Quality Assurance engineer, who has to solve the Dr. Keller mystery.

It felt like I was so far away from my life in Houston, and the near death experience in the Bahamas. How did I end up at KSC working on the most important payload experiment of a life time? I didn't know how, but I knew I was part of something really big, a break through in science. How could a small town girl end up with famous Astronauts and a NASA rocket scientists?

Another question gnawed at me. How could Top Secret documentation be stolen from my home? What am I to do?

I finally walked outside getting into the back of the dark blue car with Dalton and Leona heading back to the Astronauts beach house. At that moment I was so tired I didn't care if I had to room with Leona. Just as long I could have a hot shower and get some sleep. I was too tired to be bothered.

Dalton said, "Time for breakfast."

Everyone looked at each other and said, "Let's go to the Moon Café."

Dalton grimaced, "If you two would like to go you can, but Susan and I must stay at the base."

Ken fumed and turned away seizing Leona's arm, "We will go get breakfast together, if that's how you feel. I need to get away from the base after all that work. Dalton you certainly are a slave driver. Why don't you lighten up and have some fun,"

Dalton responded angrily, "Ken as I said before and I do not want to repeat myself again. Listen and listen well, Susan and I are staying safe here at the cottage."

The driver dropped Dalton and me off in front of the cottage. Ken and Leona left us standing with their mouths wide open. We looked at each other in confusion. I finally broke the silence, "Help me understand, why did Ken act that way?"

Dalton replied, "That whole ordeal was ridiculous. It just doesn't matter, I'm just bushed. Let's go inside and fix breakfast. I'll make you an omelet to die for and will tantalize your taste buds."

My eyes got real big with fear, then Dalton noticed and corrected himself, "Let me rephrase that, I'll make a luscious omelet you will love."

I gave Dalton a huge smile and for a moment forgot about Leona. I began to relax saying, "I'll just bet you'll make me a broken egg shell omelet?"

"Oh no young lady, I'll let you watch my culinary creation. It has been said, I can compete against Emeril LeGasse. My alias name is Chef Masters, Chef Dalton Masters. I'm the master of omelet delight." He said laughing.

As we walked up the steps to the cottage I realized I had not taken time to look around last night. It was quaint and cozy romantic hideaway. The cottage had a porch that wrapped around the entire house like my deceased Aunt's house back in Rock Hill, S.C. It even had ceiling fans hanging above the rocking chairs along with a collection of wind chimes singing in the wind, just like when I was a little girl. I began twirling with the warm breeze caressing my body from the fresh salty spray from the ocean. The feeling was exhilarating even though I was exhausted.

Dalton went directly to the kitchen to prepare his masterpiece and I scoped out the inside of the house.

Inside, the walls were covered with pictures of Astronauts, girl friends, wives, families on one wall and the others decorated in various nautical hangings. One oil painting had tiny seahorses, fishes and other sea life under the water playfully swimming with graceful dolphins jumping above the water. The colors were vibrant of deep dark aqua marine water intermingling pink yellow green circling through the waves. It made me sad thinking of our short romantic stay in the Bahamas. Oh yes, I still wished I was in the Bahamas being courted instead as an alternative, a prisoner with a cruel roommate.

I smelled the delicious aromatic scent of bacon knowing it would be the best bacon I had ever eaten in my whole life. My mouth filled with saliva drooling down my dimply chin. I swiped the dripping wetness with my hand. The aroma led me into the kitchen where Dalton turned toward me, "Susan, could you please slice some mushrooms?"

"Sure. I will." I responded with no emotion in my voice while the record of Leona comments played in my head. The tenseness showed in my solemn face.

Dalton snuck up behind wrapping his arms intimately around my waist. He pulled my hair up and quietly kissed the nape of my neck.

My whole body froze thinking, "How am I going to protect my heart from this?"

Dalton turned me around staring directly in my eyes. "What's wrong with my beautiful Susan?"

Exhausted my eyes filled with water. Tears ran down my face when I blurted out furiously, "Leona said that you invited her to the Bahamas, not me and you two were lovers." I blurted out, "What does that make me? Dalton, I'm just being used by you. You are just like the rest of the men I've known, another user." Fatigue had taken over my rational behavior. I knew I sounded ridiculous, but I couldn't help myself.

"There, there." He said. "Leona exaggerated, "Let me see if I can straighten this out. First, I did invite her, but two it's not what you think. She has been my faithful quality assurance engineer, always working very hard and long hours. I thought she could use a break. Fortunately for me she couldn't make it, so it allowed me to invite you. Unfortunately, she does care for me, but the feeling is not mutual. I like her, but she is not my beautiful sensuous Susan. My Susan, who makes me overlook my life's work. I forget about everything except you. Yes Susan, you are my diversion. Thank you for coming into my life. I love you already. I can't bear for us to be separated. Even if you are in the other room, I want to touch you, to taste you, to feel you in my arms. The loneliness I feel inside is only when you are not near."

At that moment he lifted my chin, gently kissing my lips. The kiss was mixed with my salty tears and aromatic bacon. The kiss began slowly, erupting into a full blown out of control sensational kiss. We couldn't control our feelings. Dalton moved his hands down my back tracing every tense muscle from my shoulders to my waist. Explosions were going off in my head with pulsating excitement. Then I remembered the cameras positioned above us. I gently nudged Dalton, pointing up.

"Do you think they are enjoying the show?" Laughing happily as two little children, he wiped away my tears with tiny kisses. They magically covered my red face from embarrassment and sensual excitement. I took a deep breath trying to regain composure, "I'm famished."

Dalton asked, "Are you finished with the mushrooms? It's time to put them into the omelet, Mademoiselle."

"Yes I am." I responded as I handed Dalton the finely sliced mushrooms. Dalton carefully sautéed the mushrooms, as a gourmet chef prepared a superb meal for the Queen of England.

He licked his lips, "I really like my mushrooms soft and tender."

I couldn't help but to lick my lips in response, feeling tingly inside.

Dalton made the most delicious mushroom, red pepper, and cheese omelet. He put cinnamon in the coffee permeating the scent throughout the house. Both carried their food outside on a colorful sailboat tray. Each balanced the food in their laps as they sat on the porch looking at the ocean waves drifting to shore.

I exclaimed after the first delicious bite, "Darling you have out done yourself, every morsel is yummy. Each crumb produces a delectable taste bud explosion."

My thoughts were replaying Dalton's conversation, yes, he did want me. My mind sang silently, "Halleluiah, halleluiah, halleluiah, halleluiah."

Dalton asked, "You have the most beautiful smile in the world. Why are you smiling?"

"It's just because," I paused not telling him I've never been happier, "I'm so happy that you can make a scrumptious omelet to fill my empty stomach and alleviate my hunger pangs." We slowly finished eating our long awaited food, swinging back and forth matching the rhythm of the waves. We held hands listening to the crashing of the waves on the shore. The cottage was tranquil and peaceful, our secluded hide away far from the rest of the world.

Dalton persuasively asked, "It's so hot and I need to cool off before I go to sleep. Susan, let's go for a swim. I hear the ocean calling for us."

The food renewing my energy, "I'll go put on a suit." But before I could turn around, Dalton grabbed my hand pulling me off the porch toward the beach.

"You don't need one, darling" as he ran toward the water laughing like a little boy.

I thought this man is going to challenge me in every way. I shouted back, "Here I come ready or not. Last one in is a rotten something or another." I felt like a kid myself, so light on my feet and giddy inside. I forgot about being tired and exhausted. As I ran toward the seashore, I shed my clothes, so by the time I hit the water, I was completely naked. My nipples were hard standing erect against the warm salty water.

Dalton swam out beyond the breaking waves shouting, "Come over and join me my beautiful lady."

I took the plunge under the blue breaking waves swimming like a mermaid coming up taking a deep breath, "Where are you my Love?"

Dalton responded, "I'm here, my mermaid."

I swam over to him putting my arms around him gently pulling his body close. Surprised I could feel his manhood coming alive against me.

I whispered, "Well Mr. Confident man, what's this about? What about the cameras?"

"There are no cameras out here, unless they are underwater." He gave such a mischievous smile, kissing the tip of my nose. His hands touched every inch of my body. He squeezed my nipples between his fingers. Then his hands moved from my firm breasts to below my waist finding me smooth and shaved. He bestowed a smile of pleasure.

The moment was lost in time, oblivious of the blue glistening surroundings. I wanted to stay in his arms forever. I felt safe surrounded by the warm, silky water gently and passionately moving against our bodies. We fit together like a puzzle, each being the missing part we had searched for all of our lives. I was lost in the warmness of the sun, the water and his touch.

Dalton was the first to break the silence, as we clung to each other, feeling the comfort of our satisfied desires. "We had better get back to the cottage to get some sleep. More training is required at 1700. Also Leona and Ken will be returning soon from Cocoa Beach."

I poked out my bottom lip and pouted, "What a way to spoil a wonderful morning. No fair reminding me of work."

Dalton took my hand walking toward the breaking wave onto the beach. I almost lost my balance falling toward Dalton, but he automatically pulled me close kissing me gently.[6]

Reality hit when I saw in a distance the navy blue car coming. Fear struck, I scrambled to reach my clothes. Dalton was laughing so hard at my fear of getting caught in the buff. Then I remembered NASA probably had cameras on the beach, and I just died inside. Oh well, too late now, but I'm sure it certainly was a really big show for security. It probably wasn't the first time or the last time they witnessed nudity since Astronauts were known for their wild and naturist behavior.

The car stopped next to a grove of stately palm trees hiding me from Ken's and Leona's sight. Both seemed to be in better spirits as they got out of the car.

Leona called out to Dalton, "Hi guys, we had a delicious breakfast. Sorry you had to miss it. I do feel much better now."

Dalton grinned, "So did we, and a delightful swim. All of us need to get some sleep. At 1700 we will continue training and checking the test tubes. I have some tests to run calibrating the equipment for baseline measurements."

Instinctively, I knew Leona could tell things had changed between Dalton and me. I felt I had won a battle, a battle against all women, who selfishly sabotage blissful relationships. Why can't they just be happy for lovers? The whole world would be much better. No! People have to play games, especially women. The competition fills their life with hate, discontent, and in the end, no one is a winner.

Ken was up in Dalton's ear laughing and questioning him about the formula. I couldn't hear exactly what he was saying, but laughed silently.

---

[6] The poem "Wispy Clouds" is located in Susan's Poetry section.

He looked like he was French kissing his ear. Possibly he was cleaning his eardrum. I couldn't help but to chuckle softly out loud.

Overtiredness took over my body. I couldn't wait to enter the cottage and find the nearest shower. I scrambled up the stairs and entered the shower. I hurried to wash my blond curly locks and shave my hairy legs. All I could think of was the bed and sleep. I needed sleep desperately, and quit agonizing about Leona. I should have felt liberated by knowing the truth about the lying Leona, but I didn't. I collapsed into a sound sleep with thoughts of swimming with playful dolphins, which matched Dalton's playfulness.

It seemed like a very short time, when I was awakened with Dalton gently kissing my neck. "Time to get up my beautiful, one must work for a living. You have slept for eight hours."

I turned over giving him a passionate kiss. "My darling, I'm up are you?"

We both laughed and Dalton beamed, "Don't have time for that right now. I'll take a rain check after the flight."

I threw on some jeans and my favorite NASA gold and black sweatshirt for warmth, remembering the refrigerated cold lab. I certainly didn't plan on freezing all day and night again.

The kitchen smelled of bacon, making my stomach growl. When I walked through the kitchen door, Leona was sitting comfortably at the table drinking coffee. I automatically looked up to see her glare and snarl.

I sighed at Dalton's comment, "Eat as much as you can, since this will be another long night. Remember no food or drink in the Lab. We have a lot of work to do and not much time left to do it in. I want you guys to be well nourished."

"That won't be hard to do with this spread." My eyes consumed the mouth-watering buffet of cold cuts, heart of palm, artichoke hearts, black olives, salmon, cream cheese and chives, marinated mushrooms, eggs, sausage, Canadian bacon. It certainly was a gourmet feast.

"How delicious," I said picking up a heart of palm and eating it. Hungrily, I piled my plate with the tempting, delicious food. Quickly I poured a glass of water and a cup coffee, performing a balancing act heading toward the porch outside to eat.

I sat away from the others, feeling the need to get far away. I wanted space to reflect on all the activities of the last few days. I not only desired to eat my food in peace, but to evaluate NASA politics, the payload, and my new found payload position. The pressure was unbelievable, and I thought being the Software Quality Engineer for the Shuttle was stressful. If I make one mistake, then Dalton's experiment would be a failure. The payload responsibility was hanging over my head and shoulders. I began slowly eating the incredible food. I wondered how everything mysteriously appeared in the kitchen. Dalton sat down next to me, as I enjoyed the feast and the sound of the crashing waves.

My peaceful silence was over as he commented. "I am amazed at Fletcher's stamina and memory retention. He's like a steel trap, not forgetting one word I tell him in his training. He is truly a professional and a gentleman. Cancer must be incredible stress with death hanging over his head. The Micro-Encapsulation Crystallization capsules must work. I admire him so much. It amazes me that he can draw on continued strength with a positive attitude."

He paused, taking a deep breath, and then he went on with confidence, "What a roller coaster ride this has been my Susan. The last days have been dangerous and pressure-ridden. I do admire you in the way you have jumped right in working diligently, and performing a meticulous job.

I politely said, "Thank you. Dalton, this is the most excitement I've ever had in my life. It's the chance of a life time. People dream of working on a payload program like this. I just never thought my childhood dreams would come true, the dream, working in space exploration research."

He said, "I'm glad you are by my side. It makes all I do and accomplish worth while. Tonight, we will repeat the process. This event is to ensure the test tubes are the right mixture and consistency. After this is done the Astronauts will arrive at 1900 for another training session using the payload's operational procedures."

His self assured posture commanded a statue of leadership. I smiled,

"My confident rocket scientist. Did I ever tell you about the Rocket Scientist poem I wrote? Please don't take offense if you ever read it. It's just something I composed in a boring requirements meeting. Would you like to hear it?"

Dalton said, "Sure let's hear it. I promise I won't get too sensitive."

Large Foreheads

Have you ever seen a Rocket Scientist?
Strange words flow from this linguist
Using the square root and major modes
To determine the navigational loads

What is the common delineation?
Large Foreheads used for contemplation
Wide Space between hairline and brow
Explain their smart mind somehow

But yet one must remember gorillas have large foreheads too
Could this be the missing link? Could it be true?
Yes it must be what one would logically suspect
So I'll continue to research and inspect

Large Foreheads

Dalton laughed, "Well there you go, now that explains it all. The missing link, and to think it was just beneath my hairline. Do I resemble a gorilla with my large forehead or my receding hairline? You are full of surprises. Now we need to get on the road, before I ask for a banana."

I kidded, "Yes you do fit the description. You wouldn't say it, unless it was so."

Leona was standing behind us, listening. She rolled her eyes, "How silly. What a ridiculous poem."

I snapped back, "Poetry is personal and individual. Since you are not a rocket scientist, how would you know?"

Dalton retorted, "I liked it."

Leona huffed away. Again, we all piled into the navy blue car and headed back to Kennedy Space Center. Everyone's stomachs were satisfied from the huge feast, and I felt contented emotionally for the first time in many years.

Chapter 16
The Training

The team of Astronauts arrived at the laboratory, the handsome French Shuttle Pilot, Pierre Duvall, along with the smiling Payload Specialist, Chechee Ming, and the elite medical doctor, Dr. Daryl McKnight, the famous Commander, Bob Rankin and the honorable ex-Astronaut Congressman Dan Fletcher. I noticed Fletcher was already preoccupied examining the Payload's Operating Procedures (OPS).

Commander Rankin greeted Dalton with a handshake, "Hi Dalton! It's such an honor to see you again."

Dalton grinned from ear to ear with each handshake. "The honor is mine. I'm looking forward to working with my payload guardians."

There was huge admiration on both sides between scientist and the space travelers. I was thrilled to be a part of aerospace history. The atmosphere contrasted from my normal work with mounds of documentation to the pocket protector aeronautical engineers. The space software felt more real than ever before, knowing it would guide the ship and my new found friends into the depth of space research. I am now confronted with the responsibility of a successful flight up close and personal. The Software Quality Assurance Flight Readiness Audit Reports were completed prior to my leaving for vacation. Now another huge responsibility fell in my lap, the other end of the universal spectrum, space research of filling Dalton's secret mixture into test tubes. The liability, the heart of the payload experiment and the space software, is overwhelming knowing the consequences and the ramifications. If the software didn't work, then I am blamed for not finding the problem, and if the mixture is done incorrectly, then I am blamed for being careless in the mixture of the formula. I am in a no win situation, if either project is not successful, then the stakes are high. Dan Fletcher and the rest of the Astronauts are real people with faces, personalities, and now I'm a part of their NASA family.

Dalton began his instructions, "Susan, Please assist in the training tonight. Part of the training is correcting any anomalies in the documentation. The OPS Procedures anomalies must be captured on this discrepancy form and entered into the NASA Noncompliance system. Later I'll perform an evaluation determining the severity of the discrepancies which will be presented to the Quality Payload Control Board for disposition at 1400 tomorrow. You will represent the MECS experiment and answer their questions. You will be representing the MECS Payload program, and as such, you'll be my eyes and ears. Your words are my words. Please remember this." He said in a stern and serious voice.

"I will Dalton. I've represented the Space Software organization in many of Quality meetings. I understand the ramifications." I said with respect and professionalism. It was important I didn't mix personal with business. Never the two shall meet. The only problem, I can't quit thinking about the beach, our love, which made by body tingle all over. I don't listen to my own advice.

Dalton motioned to Dr. McKnight, "Please stand next to me to view the injection process. I will explain each step of the process. First I'm going to perform a simulation of the crystal injection using a guinea pig. A stint is placed into the main artery to open it enough to lodge a shunt. Next the Micro-Encapsulation Crystallization formula will be injected using a specialized hypodermic needle that only allows the liquid to flow slowly into the shunt. Let me demonstrate." Dr. McKnight paid close attention to Dalton as he performed the preparation and injection into the small black and white hairy creature.

"A blood test will be conducted daily before and after his injection, which provide valuable data to analyze Fletcher's cancer cells in his blood. Tonight, the first of our baseline data of his blood chemistry will be taken, before he has received the Micro-Encapsulation Crystallization modules. Other tests will provide insight into changes of his blood pressure, cholesterol, diabetes, white corpuscles, vision, hearing and arthritis pain. Here is the journal to capture the data and details of the process that will be inputted into an MECS application." He handed the journal to Dr. McKnight and Chechee to review.

Chechee had several questions. "Could you show me the MECS application? What is the norm for the tests?"

Dalton sat down in front of the computer with Chechee using the OPS procedure detailing the instructions to enter the information. They discussed entering and down-linking the information and data to and from the MECS application. Chechee nodded at the scientist reminding me of a spring-loaded doll with its head jiggling back and forth in the back of a moving car.

Dalton motioned to Fletcher, "Please enter the MECS experimental capsule. It is close accommodations, providing a safe controlled environment to perform the experiment. You will stay in the chamber for at least two hours at a time with the lid closed, this enables the pure oxygen to be pumped into the chamber without safety problems. This design ensures prevention of another Apollo One fire disaster with oxygen as the catalyst."

Fletcher said, "I agree with any safety measures for my protection. My only concern is the claustrophobic confined feeling of being trapped in the capsule that reminds me of a coffin. I guess I'd better get used to it if I want to get better. I'll try sleeping, that will make me forget the enclosed feeling." Fletcher slowly climbed into the chamber hesitating a moment looking directly into my eyes with sadness. For a moment I thought he would not continue with the program, but he laid down without any hesitation. Dalton slowly closed the lid of the bright shiny capsule. I thought this bright shiny capsule looked like a black coffin, no wonder Fletcher hesitated. He should remember the black coffin would bring back his life, not be a place for his death, but the death of cancer.

Dalton taught Chechee and Dr. McKnight how to mate the connectors. "These connectors are the same as an EKG with the electrodes being displayed on the capsule shield for monitoring. Let's do a check test of the simulated gages. The shield is a screen where the data is read and transferred to the MECS data application journal.

Dalton inquired, "Fletcher do you feel comfortable. Can you breathe?"

Fletcher calmly stated, "Yes I am. Breathing is normal."

Dalton explained, "Fletcher vital signs are taken upon entering the capsule, then immediately after an injection of the formula. His stay in the capsule is timed exactly for a two-hour duration starting after the closure and sealing of the lid. Then before he leaves the capsule his vital signs are taken. All this data will be analyzed and compared. It is necessary to follow the procedures. Please Susan, as soon as the Operational Procedures are finalized, please make copies for me, Dr. Daryl McKnight and Chechee."

"Yes I will." I couldn't help, but notice Dr. McKnight checking me out. He looked lustful with a devilish twinkle in his beautiful blue eyes, smooth face surrounded by blond wavy hair and not to mention his gorgeous physique. This man is a lady's man, always flirting with Leona and Chechee or any other woman who entered the laboratory. What else is new in this world? He is one more man for women to beware of his lecherous unprofessional behavior. Regardless I smiled to myself, he is definitely a cute boy. He can probably get away with this behavior his entire career."

Dalton told Fletcher, "We need to recheck the microcrystals. We'll be back in two hours and let you out. Just relax. This will become second nature in space." You could see Fletcher's anxious face. "Just kidding, you can get out now. You will spend enough capsule time in zero gravity."

Dalton opened the capsule and helped Fletcher out. He motioned for the group to enter the laboratory where Leona, Pierre, and Ken were rechecking test tubes and equipment.

Leona jumped in surprise as I stood close to her. She whined, "You scared the living day lights out of me. I had no idea you were beside me."

Dalton questioned, "Are you OK? Leona you are as white as a ghost."

Leona answered abruptly, "Sure I am, but next time tell Susan not to get so close."

Dalton and I both ignored her request. "Ken can you give an overview about the capsule you built. Let's go back into the MECS capsule room. I want to show everyone its capabilities. Fletcher has already tried out the comfort of the capsule."

Ken stated, "Thank you Dalton, I've been waiting for this moment. The equipment is ship-shape. It's designed just as stated in the requirements specifications. The back-up system is set to take over if there is a problem. Let me show you. The capsule is designed, not only as a controlled laboratory environment, but there's a CT Scanner, and an audiometer or testing Fletcher's hearing."

Ken interrupted his description of the capsule, "Would you be interested in a bit of trivia, as all of you are here at the same time?" With that, Ken had everybody's attention. "Now, Dalton, you know that CAT scan is short for "Computed Axial Tomography. It allows us to see slices of the human body to determine changes in Fletcher's anatomy during this experiment. It is extremely sensitive." He continued, "NASA's efforts to miniaturize equipment for the space program, has changed how we practice medicine. However, had it not been for the Beatles, and their music, in the 1960's and 70's, we couldn't do this experiment today."

At that moment, I tilted my head quizzically and asked with a quip, "Now that's a surprise, how did the Beatles have anything to do with the MECS Experiment?"

Ken continued his trivia education, "The first CT-Scanner, actually was called an "EMI Scanner", for the central research laboratories of EMI, best known in the early days of the British Invasion, as a recording company. In fact, the recording studios were renamed, in 1970, "The Abbey Road Studios". The massive profits generated by The Beatles' music provided principal funding for the first commercially viable CT-Scanner." Ken laughed, "And our parents thought they were just mop headed noise makers!"

With that, Ken continued with his explanation of the capsule. "Oxygen and nitrogen controls, here, give us access for selecting the right quantity of gas for the correct solution mixture, not unlike an anesthesiologist in the operating room. Its controls are next to the oxygen and nitrogen tanks. It is the state-of-the-art technology, or should I say out of this world technology."

Dalton, Dr. McKnight, Fletcher and Ken walked over to check the equipment. It reminded me of men kicking a set of new tires and checking their pressure. However, these weren't tires this time, but an experimental capsule headed directly to the far away Space Station.

I couldn't hear what they were saying, but felt Leona's glare, delivered out of pure jealousy.

Dalton abruptly inquired, "Why are red dots on these five bottles?"

Leona looked at the men and responded, "The micro-crystals formula in these bottles were questionable, so I placed a dot to analyze their composition in space. This will ensure quality of the other capsules."

Dalton removed one of the red dot test tubes placing the solution under a microscope to sample. "Curious, it has a small inconsistency in the tubes?"

"Leona, I need you to get rid of these samples. I know Susan will need to use the correct NASA Waste Contamination procedures, but get rid of them now, please."

Ken countered, "Dalton they're marked correctly. Why don't you allow these inconsistent formulas to fly as is, and see what type of crystals are created. Disposing of them may be a mistake. This could be of scientific benefit for mankind if they make better crystals."

His theory made Dalton's forehead to wrinkle, he hesitated momentarily thinking to himself, but soon agreed with Ken. "I'll allow the red dot test tubes to fly on the mission. What harm could it do? Just make sure they are kept in a separate area to keep any of the normal samples. We don't want any chance of cross-contamination with the abnormal formula."

I deliberated, "This seemed to counter the Space Software simulated tests requirements. If the formula is not the same then it should not be flown. This is definitely not the software world, where all tests are precise, there is no room for errors. Any inconsistency is documented and researched and mitigated immediately."

I thought, "I'm just suspicious of these people." They made me feel uncomfortable with their inconsistent rules that changed in a heartbeat. My hair was standing up on the back of my neck. This was not my world of constancy and the endless striving for excellence. I just hoped their desire to get anomalous red test tubes was justified and it was not linked with Dr. Keller's death.

Dalton interrupted my thoughts. "Let's get back to training. We have lots to do before the mission on Friday. It's already on top of us."

The team worked way into the night. Leona and I did turnover the experiment's equipment and test tubes to the assigned Ground Operations' Quality Assurance representatives. All the paper work was in order and quality stamped. It took Leona and I forever to document all the experiment's components with the proper sign offs. I felt like I was signing my life away.

I gave a sigh of relief, "Leona, now it's no longer our responsibility. Thank God. The stress of knowing Dalton's experiment is in our hands is too much responsibility for me to bear. If anything happens in this experiment, i.e. the red dot test tubes causing a problem, we could both be sent to "Club Fed". We can't afford to compromise with the least bit of data."

Leona looked confused, "Club Fed."

I returned, "Federal Prison."

Leona began laughing nervously, "Sure Susan. How would anyone ever blame a Quality Assurance person?"

"They would figure it out Leona. Whoever they are they would know. I'm tired, let's catch up with the others and see if we can leave?"

Leona and I walked into the lab, where Dalton was finishing up his last dissertation of the main details of the critical experiment.

I looked around and all the Astronauts were gathered around Dalton along with his faithful hardware partner, Ken.

Smiling, Chechee played a trick on Commander Bob. She placed a whoopee cushion under him as he sat down. The noise embarrassed the Commander, but everyone began laughing very hard. Fletcher, amused at their playfulness, joined in the fun. Serious Pierre and playboy Dr. McKnight took notes, reviewing the procedures while asking Dalton clarifying questions.

Fletcher took out a book that his grandchildren had given him. The name was, What To Do When Confronted By An Alien? He thumbed through the pictures of space creatures with green skin and big eyes.

I smiled, "This will be handy on the space station. You never know when an alien may be around, especially one with blonde wavy hair.

I began looking through the book when Dalton gave me a list of MECS discrepancies. He ordered, "Please enter the non-conformances into the database. I want to ensure each one is analyzed and dispositioned before flight."

I sighed, wanting to tell him I was too tired to touch a keyboard. Unfortunately, I knew it had to be done. Smiling with my last exhausted facial muscle, "What would you have done without me?"

Dalton face brightened up, moving uncomfortably close. For a moment I thought he was going to kiss me. His lips stopped dangerously near my lips saying, "Susan, I'm glad you are part of the MECS team. It's such a delight to have an extra set of hands with a cheerful and cooperative attitude."

The Astronauts chanted in agreement, "Susan you can work on the MECS team anytime. We need more quality people."

I noticed Ken and Leona didn't join in. They both had scowls on their faces. How ungrateful they appeared considering my hard work.

"Oh well, what sour pusses." I thought, "It just doesn't matter what they think. I would have liked to see Leona do all this work herself".

I feverously entered the data into the computer. Tomorrow I'll go to the control meeting to discuss the discrepancies the Astronauts reported. As I entered the data, I printed a copy of the listing for objective evidence.

I requested, "Dalton, we need to decide whether these issues are major, minor or just observations?"

"We will do that tonight, so just bring a copy with you, please, my

Susan." Dalton iterated.

Grinning, I fortunately had a printed copy in my satchel. I was happy, "He called me, my Susan."

After saying our "Good byes" to the Astronaut team, we traveled back to the Astronauts Cottage. I felt like a little girl with a new toy, really disgustingly happy to work directly on a Space Station payload. I wondered if anyone was noticing my joyous demeanor.

Dalton put his arms around my back and squeezed gently with his soft hands. "Nothing could be better than having you near me."

I shivered praying he didn't do this with all the girls and was not a player. Trust is still hard for me.

Upon entering the cottage I smelled the best aroma in the world. I followed the smell which let me to the kitchen to find a South American gentleman, a chef preparing fresh fish spiced with red ricotta and wrapped in banana leaves. Then I saw spinach, brown bean soup and rice. It would be dinner tonight. The smell made my mouth water. I politely asked, "Need any help? This reminds me of a meal I had in Belize."

The Chinese chef had been replaced with a short fat pleasant latin chef. He told me very abruptly "No help in the kitchen. Too many cooks spoil the food. This is my kitchen so stay out." Then he tipped his chef's hat to me and winked.

I got the message and walked outside onto the porch swing, sitting and swinging, admiring the crystal aqua blue ocean water. The waves were breaking in a pattern, which had a hypnotic sound that lulled me into a dream world. Soon I was sound asleep from exhaustion. In the dream I was peacefully snorkeling in a reef back in the Bahamas watching exotic fish, pirate fish, groupers surrounded by beautiful fan coral waving in the water's current. All of a sudden, and un-expectantly men in black diving skins came out of nowhere heading toward me at a fast pace. I was frightened and knew they were trying to harm me. Turning in all directions I chose to hide behind the sea fans and spiral coral. I was frantic.

I stayed very quiet not moving. Then one of the intruders grabbed me as I spun around, causing me to hit the coral with my bare skin. The cuts began to sting as I accidentally placed my hand on a black sea urchin, imbedding the spiny black quills into the delicate skin. Now I was in great agony and pain. Not being able to scream I fought back and pushed the man away. He was hit against the rock and all of a sudden an angry moray eel darted out. It attacked the man's face on his mouth and chin making it bleed profusely. I tried to identify the man but couldn't. He was struggling to remove the eel from it's hold. Now, another man approached me with a knife in hot pursuit of me. I was trying to swim as hard as I could, when I saw the man stop to check on his buddy. From behind a menacing shark swam toward them. The blood left a trail in the water showing the way for the shark's supper.

Frantic, I contemplated, "How can I get out of the coral reef?" It was like a puzzle, a maze and I didn't know which direction to proceed. You could look up and see where you needed to go, but under the water the search direction was lost. Which way do I need to go, please instincts be my guide. The sea was treacherous and the current was so strong I felt that I was going to be pushed against the coral again, causing more damage to my bare skin.

My eyes caught the shark feasting on the men and another one joined him. I felt like I would be next as more sharks gathered around. The school of sharks were ferocious and in an eating frenzy. They seem to be more interested in their recent catch than me. They blocked my way so I swam deeper and deeper into the reef.

All of a sudden I felt a tug at my arm. A shark had caught up and now was going to make me the next course. I began fighting ferociously hitting it on their nose. I wanted to scream, but I knew I would drown if I did. I struck again.

I felt my whole body shake, "Susan you were tossing about in the swing. Are you OK? What is wrong?" It was Dalton.

"I'm just fine. I was having a dream," I blushed from embarrassment.

"It must have been a bad dream at that. Susan I won't let anything happen to you." Dalton sympathized giving me a hug, "I will protect my Susan."

I commented, "Dalton something is strange. I don't know how I explain it, and I don't know what it is, but I still don't have a good feeling about the experiment. I don't like so many anomalies."

"Let's eat first and then we will go over the discrepancies. We can talk about it later in private. I know you're tired, and I don't want to discount your observation, but we still have a lot of work to do."

I got up, making my way to dinner. The succulent aroma made my dream fade away, and the anomalies, as Dalton led the way into the dining area. The meal's presentation was artistic but it did not keep me from thinking about the recent series of events. What clue did I miss? It was like analyzing a risk in the program. It had to have a symptom that leads you to a solution. Why did Dr. Keller and his family die?

The gnawing feeling of the unknown kept eating at me. Maybe I was missing the obvious.

After dinner, Dalton and I began dispositioning the discrepancies. The issues were just minor documentation errors with one major. After an hour of excruciating detail analysis, Dalton finally dispositioned the major error as "No Constraint to Flight" since it had no affect on the flight. Tomorrow in the newly assigned duty as Payload Discrepancy Report Chairman, I would be presenting to the Payload Board Chairman Configuration Control Panel.

Suddenly, I realized how tired my aching body felt. My eyes burned from looking at the voluminous data and my hands hurt from entering so much information. I laughed to myself shaking my hands at Dalton, "So much for the life of a computer geek. I'm going to sleep. I need my beauty rest to be able to keep up with your assignments and long working hours."

"Would you give me just a few more minutes of your time? Let's go out on the porch," he asked, guiding me with his hand.

We walked out sitting on the steps, watching the moonrise. It filled the sky with a red, fiery ball just barely sitting on the glimmering, sparkling ocean.

"I'm been thinking about your concerns. You may be on to something. Dr. Keller was a good friend of mine and he was trying to tell me about a research problem. We just didn't have time to get together before his untimely death. He was a good man and didn't deserve to die. He was the only other person who knew the complete formula of developing the micro crystals and the technology of the drug delivery system. I trusted him explicitly, even with my life. If I could find the person who killed him, I would strangle the monster with my own hands."

I interrupted, "This monster could be a woman."

"Who knows? I certainly don't." Dalton said.

"Dalton, how well do you know Ken and Leona? Have their actions changed recently?" I inquired.

"Well, business isn't going so well for Ken. He has been more agitated lately, but I think that's because his downward spiraling business. Well, to get anything done through the Payloads is an expensive endeavor. NASA wants more and more for their money, but they have so many rules and red tape. It's almost impossible to get things through the bureaucratic bullshit. No offense Susan, but Quality is a lot of number one-show stoppers. They put these policies in affect that make no sense, causing projects to go over their budget. I just hope they don't make the payload equipment go through Flight Certification for a fourth time. It would financially break Ken's company to perform a fourth inspection. He is hanging on with a hope and a prayer right now. I think he would sell everything he owned to keep his business afloat. I certainly help him as much as I can. He does love the Aerospace Industry and it would be a shame if he went bankrupt."

He paused, "Leona has always been a warm spot in my heart."

My heart sank as Dalton continued, "Both her parents are deceased now, but when her Dad died I stayed with him night and day at the hospital trying to manage his pain. He had pancreatic cancer, very excruciating, and terrifying. Oncology is my field, but she and her family needed a friend in the worst way. Maybe she misinterpreted my actions by doing so in the hospital. My intentions were only honorable. I've always considered her a little sister. All I wanted to do was help her and her family. I didn't see how my helping her could do any harm. I soon realized she is very naïve, always seeking a male attention, allowing her to be easily persuaded by men. She is so starved for attention, even now."

"Dalton I know you want to protect me, but I want you to keep your eyes and ears open for the both of us. Eventually I want us to have a normal relationship. Not having the chaos with us running forever from an unknown villain. I want to rest my weary bones." I gave a huge yawn. "I'm just so tired. Wake me up in the morning, so I can get an early start. I need to enter the remainder of the dispositions to make the meeting in time."

I turned away and began walking toward the cottage, when Dalton ran up behind me and tapped me on the shoulder. He gently twisted my head to meet his soft tender lips. I turned before he could kiss me and began walking away when Dalton pleaded, "Susan, please do not ever leave me without kissing me good night."

"I won't, my Darling, never again." I kissed him passionately which made every part of my body tremble. Glimpsing up I saw the most beautiful sunset with reds, oranges, yellows and bright pink. It reminded me of a backdrop from a Hudson Valley master's painting. I walked, tired and exhausted to the room which housed a woman who I never wanted to see again. Alone in the bed I laid thinking about the new found relationships who had taken me away from my safe software world and into a world of chaos. This world seemed so far away from all that was normal and predictable. I would never be the same again. Finally I drifted off to sleep snuggling into the silky sheet. As soon as I closed my eyes the sun was soon shining brightly into the small room.

Leona had rudely opened the blinds, and said, "It's time to get up. Can I tag along with you today? I want to see how the process is done with the Payload Configuration Control Panel."

I wanted to say, "No" but I couldn't quickly figure out the right words, since I was still half asleep. I wrinkled my forehead and in a meek voice, "Sure Leona, please remember that I'm on first and you'll be just an observer. The least said is the best. I can't give the chairman, Don, anything to use against us. He can stop the payload experiment and not let it fly. Sometimes it's just politics or whom you know, and since I don't know anyone, it's best I take the safe and cautious side. Let's hope the Chairman is in a good mood. I've heard stories. He may use us as an example of what not to do if he feels like it."

"I'll keep my mouth shut. I understand the ramifications. I want to fly more than you can ever know," said Leona. "I've just finished my shower and your number is next."

I didn't hesitate and jumped into the shower, quickly washing down the tiredness from yesterday. Then I knew the words to use at the panel. I was no longer afraid.

I dressed quickly grabbing a bagel and orange juice for breakfast. The breakfast of champions or at least something that would keep my stomach from growling. I was running toward the towncar, when Dalton ran out of the house calling to me. "Susan, please go to the lab when you two are finished. I've another surprise for you."

I turned, jumping up and down in excitement, "What is it Dalton. I want to know."

Dalton ran back to the house, "Darling, just wait and see. Patience is a virtue, trust me it's worth waiting for this one. "

As I entered the navy blue car Leona was waiting. We walked into the conference room together. The majority of the aerospace people attending were men, which was the usual in this industry. I started to sit on the chairs around the room when Don the chairman motioned for me to sit at the table. He had on glasses that were low on his nose and a smirk on his face that almost made you feel he could read your mind. I had never been asked to sit at the table. I thought he must know who I am and why I'm here. He motioned for the meeting to begin and asked me to discuss the major discrepancy that had found.

I began almost timidly and slowly continued with renewed confidence. "The heart analyzer signals are skipping beats intermittently. The anomaly has been preliminarily diagnosed as a possible hardware problem. The heart analyzer diagnostics are going to be run today by the subcontractor's personnel. They developed the hardware. They'll provide evidence of a possible wire broken inside the dial. If this is the case the proper tests will be performed and the problem will be corrected and certification will be performed again. It's a 1N critical category, meaning it's not a problem to fly and will not cause a safety issue if it's fixed."

Don studied the piece of paper and ran his hand down his face analyzing me in a studious manner. He tilted his head peeping over his glasses and asked, "If this doesn't work do you have a back up plan. Is there any type of alternative equipment?"

I looked him in the eyes and said, "No, there is no other equipment like it but it should not be a problem, as it will be fixed and certified today."

Don threw the paper on the table and said, "Susan, send me the certification as soon as possible. Make sure that it states the equipment is "Ready to Fly" with "No Constraint to Flight" and is signed and approved by Dalton Masters. He is fully accountable and responsible."

I continued presenting the other discrepancies one by one. Each being downgraded for flight by the close of the meeting but I was excited thinking about the surprise. I thought the meeting would never end. I had been stuck in the conference room for eight grueling hours while Leona just sat and watched my every move.

At the end of the meeting a stranger with a mustache came up to me while we were getting ready to leave. He said in a deep voice, "You did real well for a first timer. You caught Don on a good day. You just never know what he will pick on. Congratulations. Good Job."

I said, "Thanks. I'm just glad it's over and the payload mission will fly."

Anxiously I said, "Leona let's get back to the Payload lab to meet up with Dalton. He asked us both to come back. He has a surprise. I can't wait to see what the surprise is this time."

When they arrived at the lab, Dalton was just finishing up the MECS research experimental training with Fletcher and Dr. McKnight. "I'm glad you could join us ladies, could you come over here for a moment?"

He handed us blue and pink silk blindfolds. I looked at Leona with confusion. "Please ladies put the blindfolds over your eyes and let me show you the way. You will have to trust me. This will be the experience of a life time."

I felt the anticipated excitement run through my veins. I love surprises and wished Leona would not be a part of this surprise. Leona always was trying to make me feel bad. She had no right. She didn't know me and I wished she would disappear. Oh well, again I would have to be the actress pretending my emotions didn't really count. Often women can be jealous and play such games when it comes to men. I certainly was tired of playing games at my age. Dalton had explained to me what happened, but I questioned whether he was really telling me the truth. Men had always lied in the past, but perhaps he was different, or maybe he was just like all the rest. Perhaps he was just an opportunist taking advantage of my good nature and my sexual desires. I wish I could end the old record playing the same old message. "Stop," I said in my head and smiled demurely at Dalton, "Can you give us just a little bit of a hint? Pretty please, don't make us wear these blindfolds. If we're blindfolded we can't see what is happening."

"That's the plan. Sometimes Susan…just trust me. This will be a trip of a life time. I'm going to take you to a place you have never been before, to heights you have never felt. It's important you do not peak. Just have fun or it will spoil the surprise." He said, thinking Susan had refreshing, child like qualities.

"Put on the blindfolds, ladies," he commanded.

As I put on the blindfold, anticipated chills ran through my childlike soul. I felt exhilarated and free with tingly excitement. I giggled as he guided us to the navy blue towncar.

Leona said, "Oh please Susan, how childish you sound. Why don't you just grow up?"

"That's the point, Leona, to have fun just like you did as a child, experiencing life for the first time," Dalton chuckled in return, like a mischievous little boy while guiding us into the backseat of the car. I scooted against the window. I felt another person next to me. The smell of the strong nauseating cologne told me it was Leona. "Drat," I thought, "Leona was the last person I wanted to share this occurrence with and I certainly didn't want her to sit next to me, much less smell her cheap cologne."

Soon I heard Dalton's voice, "Leona move to the left on the seat." Then I felt the warmness and scent of my Dalton next to me. He discretely pressed his leg against mine causing a chill through my body.

I pressed my leg against his in return. I began to breath easier with the man I loved next to my side. He made me feel so exhilarated. The seating situation was much nicer, even though Leona was still in the car.

Dalton instructed the driver, "Please take us to our agreed destination."

The car began moving and Dalton took my hand and gently ran his fingertips at the nape of my neck and through my blonde curly hair. The sensation drove me wild with pleasure. I could hardly contain my desire to reach over and kiss him and touch him and to be touched by him. Being blindfolded my senses were sharpened, without my eyes, I was sexually aroused, when abruptly Dalton pronounced, "We are here, ladies. Do not take your blindfolds off unless I give you explicit instructions to do so."

I responded, "But Dalton." He took both our hands and guided us forward step by step. "Ladies, please step forward."

It seemed like an eternity before I was standing with my back leaning against a wall. I felt the sensation of an upward movement of us going up and up very slowly. I began to question Dalton, "Are we on the Empire State Building? Did you transport us to New York?" Then reality sat in, "No we have to be…"

Before I finished my sentence my Dalton commanded, "Ladies please step forward and you can take off your blind folds."

It took a moment before my eyes adjusted and I couldn't believe my eyes. We were on top of the launch pad with the Orbiter. "It's so beautiful up here. I can see the Atlantic Ocean, Cape Canaveral, all of KSC including the Vehicle Avionics Building (VAB). The Orbiter is so big and magnificent with the rocket boosters in their bright orange colors. The shuttle is a fine ship and so majestic." Then I spotted a young lady with the whistle. Unknowingly I asked, "What are you doing?"

The lady said, "My job is to keep the pesky woodpeckers away from the shuttles. This is a problem, you know, they like to peck away at the tiles."

I said, "Now I know what I want to do when I retire. Forget the Wal-

Mart greeter, I want to be the whistle blower at the top of the launch pad."

The lady explained, "It's really boring and it's either too hot or too cold."

I twirled around, "I love it up here." I noticed a cart like the ones they use in coal mines and amusement parks, "Can I take it for a ride?"

Dalton looked at me sternly, "It would be the last thing you do an Aerospace employee. It's an emergency exit system on a slide wire. The slide wire provides an escape route for the Astronauts aboard the space shuttle. Seven slide wires extend from the orbiter access arm level to the ground on the west side of the pad. It's on the orbiter access arm of the fixed service structure and can be used up to the final 30 seconds of countdown."

One 3-man basket with a flat bottom and netting all around is suspended from each wire and positioned for quick entry in an emergency situation. You can put four Astronauts aboard and then they have to cut the line with a knife that is attached to the basket. This is for quick escape with a 1,200-foot wire to the bunker west of the launch pad and being 195 feet up the basket can only hold 4 people. The only thing that stops you is a catch net and the drag chain at the end of the line. It certainly would be a ride of a life time."

I questioned, "In case of an emergency, would there be time for anyone to get in these baskets to arrive safely at the bottom?"

Dalton grimaced, "Let's hope it will never have to be tested in an emergency situation."

Dalton you are so wonderful and I spontaneously kissed him on the top of his bald shiny head.

He smiled at me. "Oops I'm sorry, not very professional of me." In the corner of my eye Leona angrily glared at them.

"We can look into the white room, but that's as far as we can go. This ship will be taking our Micro-Encapsulation Crystallization experiment. It's been many years of hard work. Thank goodness this is my last payload before I retire. Then I can live my dream, sailing in the Caribbean and throughout the Bahamas."

The trio watched the sunset sitting next to the bird lady and her whistle. The bright vibrant oranges, reds and yellows mixed with blue and white sunset was so brilliant I felt we were next to heaven. The sun looked like a ball of fire. No one spoke but absorbed the spiritual moment that was transpiring before them.

Soon Dalton said, "Looks like we need to go back and prepare for the big day."

I snickered, "Here Dalton put on the blindfold. It's your turn."

Dalton turned with a serious face, "Maybe next time" and he turned his back to us.

I smiled turning toward Dalton, "Tomorrow is the big day and I guess the fun and games are over. I'm ready to work at your command. Thank you so much for the surprise of my life. It's spectacular. I'll always remember this. It's the eighth wonder of the world."

When they got back to the cottage all three retired to their rooms. I tossed and turned thinking about the upcoming launch. I had never seen one and the thrill was too much for me to handle. I felt like a little kid waiting for Santa Claus. It took a long time before I fell asleep. Once asleep I began dreaming weird stuff. I felt that someone was sitting on my chest. I tried to wake up but couldn't. My voice wanted to scream at the top of my lungs but I felt salty tears streaming down my face. A hand touched my arm as I thrashed and fought back with all my strength.

In the back of my head I heard Dalton's voice faintly, "Susan wake up. It's just a bad dream. I'll protect you, no one will harm you."

I raised my trembling arms while Dalton held me close. "I had a bad dream, a dream that has reoccurred throughout my life. Someone kidnaps me. The Bahamas must have triggered this dream again. One day I hope it will disappear and never return."

Dalton tenderly kissed my lips, "Let's get through this mission and I'll take you away. Anywhere you want to go. The world is yours. We will get rid of your bad dream forever. It will be just the two of us together."

I looked up and smiled, "Oh Dalton I love you so."

"Get dressed. We have a launch. I've worked too long, too hard to miss the launch and to miss my payload, my Miss."

The morning's breakfast began with bagels and fresh fruit. We all hurried, taking a cup of coffee to go.

Enthusiasm was in the air. I felt like a little girl squirming between Leona and Dalton. I couldn't sit still. Ken was quiet in the front seat looking very serious. All were eager with anticipation of the coming days.

Chapter 17
The Launch

They arrived at the Mission Payload Support Building leaving the car quickly. Walking through the doors I noticed the KSC Employee Store with all the paraphernalia from caps to tee shirts. I wanted to buy a souvenir in remembrance of the flight but had no time to shop.

Everyone marched on the elevator in silence, not a word spoken. I could feel the electricity between our bodies surging. It was as though we had worked as a team all of our lives. The energy powerfully flowed between our bodies making a solid force for the success of the payload, Dalton's valuable experiment.

Dalton squeezed my hand discretely winking at me. We had designed a special communication. My body shivered with eagerness. I had never seen a launch but now was part of a payload team. All I could say was, "Wow" just simply "Wow." My childhood dreams had surpassed any hopes or wishes in just being a secretary on the space program.

I scanned the room. It had a huge window displaying the launching pad. There were four TV monitors situated at different locations. One was of the cockpit, where the Astronauts were being strapped on top of the main engines filled with hydrogen and oxygen and the two reusable Solid Rocket Boosters (SRBs). I thought to myself, they are sitting on top of three incredible large roman candles, the SRBs are dangerous bombs just ready to explode. They only had two minutes and eight seconds to turn them off if any liftoff problems arose. Another camera displayed the Launch Control center where the busy Mission Team was getting ready for launch. The third outside the launch pad recording any anomalies to the human man space-launch. The last was at the VIP viewing stands just outside the building that houses the Jupiter rocket exhibit. I noticed the space software technical Astronaut advisor, Doug, working the crowd in his flight suit. He was such an intelligent man who looked like my first cousin. I had always felt close to him knowing his philosophy of safety first before any politics.

The magnificent view of the space shuttle in the distance was incredible. Suddenly I heard everyone welcoming Dalton. They began showing him where the down-linked payload information would be downloaded. There were five computers situated in the room for easy access for the payload technical team.

In the corner of my eye Ken was pacing back and forth in an agitated manner. He really gave me the creeps the way he stooped over, staring at me with his piercing eyes. Dalton finally said, "Susan will you man this computer? I need you to monitor the condition codes of the data. Here are the discrepancy codes you'll track. Leona, please quality control her results."

I studied the condition codes, 0 is normal, and 9 designated as an anomaly. Codes 1-8 were within the payload boundary.

I heard Ken tell Dalton, "It's almost time for the 0500 launch."

The countdown clock began and the crowd became silent as the tension of the final countdown risks ripped the spirit of the final countdown. I hummed, "Proud to be an American". I busily scanned the monitors as I watched the shuttle, my friends in their flight suits, the clock ticking, and the crew/control chatter in the background.

The flight director announced the countdown, "T minus 30 seconds approaching the final countdown". Then I heard, "T minus 10, 9, 8 and all nominal 7, -6.6 seconds, main engine ignite". The room trembled as the engine kicked off in billowy fire with the enormous rise of water vapor with thousands of tons of water flooding the launch pad. "5, 4, 3", the vibration of the room at a mile and half away felt like a 6.5 earthquake on the Richter scale moving the ground uncontrollably under my feet. "2", I continued scanning the monitor, but wanted to look out the window at the launch as I heard "1, we have lift off."

At full throttle I couldn't believe the roar of the engine and the feeling of power, the thrill of the watching man's advancement once again in space. I was speechless as the white powdery exhaust trail moved across the sky. My mouth was wide open with enthusiasm and chills covered my arms and legs as the thunder vibrated through my body. The shuttle proceeded up hill with the morning sun guiding it like a giant beacon into the heavens.

The Space Software began its programmed roll maneuver to achieve a northeasterly track from KSC, heading toward a 51.6 degree inclination to the equator. The Space Software again did another maneuver roll to a heads up position, placing the shuttle on top of the external tank to improve communications between the shuttle and NASA's orbiting Tracking and Data Relay Satellite System. The shuttle completed the programmed roll maneuver positioning heads up and the wings level. The three liquid-fueled main engines throttled down to ease the vehicle's flight through the dense lower atmosphere. Then the main engines began throttling back up to about full thrust for the continued trek to space. The power, the majesty, the enormity of it all was overwhelming.

I watched the shuttle roll after the launch on the belly with the external tanks on the top. The SRB's powered the complicated, precision vehicle skyward and then jettisoned after depleting the propellant. I watched the beauty of the spiraling contrails against the awakening morning sun.

I heard, "Throttle up, now passing Madrid Spain. We have solid rocket-boosters separation at 27 seconds, the external tanks have separation after Main Engine Cutoff (MECO). Now proceeding to Orbit Maneuvering System (OMS) Burn and have achieved orbit. The Payload Bay Doors are opening." I knew that the payload bay doors opened to allow the heat to escape and to provide solar power.

The Astronauts began reconfiguring the General Purpose Computers (GPC) for Orbit and the Shuttle circled the earth with the initialization loads I-Loads configured to meet head on to the International Space Station. The coordinates had to place the shuttle in the precise orbit to mate with the Station. There was no room for error. Commander Bob Rankin acknowledged each phase of the launch. The crew had 2 days in orbit due to the size of the payload before they would meet up with the Station. Every forty-five minutes I observed the brilliant sunset and dazzling sunrise with the Astronauts. How wonderful for them to see the two most beautiful times in the day over and over again. I wished upon the North Star that one day I could join the Space Program and look down at the magnificent earth.

Chapter 18
The Payload

The next day the thrill of the launch diminished as I stared at the computer screen. My eyes were swollen and tired from monitoring the condition codes. My head began to hurt from the intensity and stress of the responsibility. I needed a break.

Dalton said, "Let's go to lunch Susan. Leona, please monitor the codes while we're gone. We won't be long."

Leona grumbled, "Sure Boss."

"Sounds good to me, I'm starving." I smiled trying to disguise the tension. We walked briskly next door to the government sterile cafeteria. It reminded me of an elementary school cafeteria with the tables lined up in rows. My nose detected the smell of a mixture of foods mixed with cleaning fluid permeating the air. At least it had multiple stations filled with tasty sandwiches, hot home cooked foods and crispy salads. I chose the hot food station realizing I needed veggies. My weak tired body, fried brain and burning red eyes needed nourishment and emotionally I needed to reconnect with my Dalton. It was our first private time since the shuttle take lift off.

I watched his every move as he slowly crossed the cafeteria and sat across from me. He moved like a young athlete crossing the finish line. He gave me a boyish smile, which melted every bone in my body, "What do you think of the launch so far?"

I said, "Awesome, I never imagined the crushing sensation vibrating through my body from the take off of the thunderous Shuttle.

It's unbelievable that a million pieces of integrated hardware and software travels through space as one extreme machine. On paper it seems feasible, but watching the enormous shuttle go into space is just amazing. No prettier sight ever. She is a beautiful lady."

Dalton commented enthusiastically, "I feel the same way after each launch, but I'm having lunch with the most beautiful lady on earth."

I said, "You make me blush. Thanks for asking me to lunch. I think I would die eating another NASA supplied sandwiches. All the excitement has made me ravenous. I'm now running on pure electrical energy. It's a high of all highs casting your eyes to the stars."

Dalton responded, "I've been watching you work hour after hour, just toiling away in high speed. I knew you needed a break, I certainly did. The sweat and toil is just beginning though. We haven't even begun the payload experiment. This is the most important payload in my life. It has to be a success for not only Fletcher, but for all cancer patients everywhere. The truth be known if it is not a success, NASA will cancel my program. They have already told me this will be my last payload if it's not. The funding will go elsewhere."

"Then your payload will be successful, a triumph for mankind. You can make it happen, Fletcher has the stay-alive attitude, which is half the battle. It's amazing how he learns so quickly for a man his age. We will have a happy ending, just like Cinderella where everyone lives happily ever after except for the mean old stepmother." I passionately spoke. "Fletcher will be cured of the awful disease and you'll be the catalyst to make it happen."

"Ok Cinderella, I'll ask my Fairy Godmother if I can make it happen, until then I'll keep my fingers crossed on my scientific ability." Dalton joked.

I snickered, "I'll turn you into a pumpkin if you make fun, a big fat one with fuzz all over it."

He stuck his tongue out at me like a little schoolboy. I burst out laughing, "Yes you are a little boy, a really cute boy."

Dalton rolled his eyes. They both finished eating their meals in record time. The hot cafeteria food tasted like a gourmet meal compared to the dried out NASA sandwiches. I said, "Let's go for a walk to get some exercise. Strolling around the KSC campus we spotted the enormous Vehicle Assembly Building (VAB). We entered the huge two-story garage where the vital Space Shuttle maintenance took place. The Astronauts trusted the mechanics would perform the needed repairs flawlessly. They are the space grease monkeys who had Astronaut lives in their hands and everyone else in the proximity.

We watched in awe as the cranes lifted the impressive orbiter, Atlantis, for needed repairs. We stood silently watching them securing the impressive Atlantis to begin the tedious job to remove the wiring and to replace it with new. It always frightening me if they fix one problem possibly 10 more may occur. That was always the chance.

A repair technician recognized Dalton, "Hi Dr. Masters, would you like a tour?"

I immediately answered for him, "Yes, absolutely."

Dalton smiled as we boarded the shuttle.

The NASA technician began giving us a full tour. "The splendid ship is the exact replica of the Discovery, which as you know is circling high above in space with the most important payload in the Shuttle history. The renowned Astronaut Dan Fletcher, your very own human payload, the first."

I recognized the heads up display in the cockpit. It's the instruments used by the pilot to maneuver the shuttle in space and on landing. I walked around the payload compartment thinking about Dalton's experiment. Several men were replacing damaged wires in the side panels. I turned around in disbelief. I never thought I would actually be onboard a real shuttle. We walked through the payload carrier just like the one that was carrying Dalton's precious cargo. I wanted to stay forever, but Dalton soon said, "We have to get back. I've a payload to check on."

Walking back a gentle breeze blew against my face. In the comfort of the wind, I never felt so relaxed and happy. It reminded me of the contentment of sailing on the open seas. I loved the feeling of freedom in the wind.

I finally broke the silence. "Dalton, thank you for taking me to places I've only dreamed about."

He said, "Thank you for making my dreams come true."

We walked silently back to the laboratory. As we entered the white room Leona gave me the mean evil eye. I felt coldness on my neck as the room became very cold, extremely frigid from her obvious hatred. I composed myself and said sweetly, "Leona would you like a break. I'll take over for you now."

Leona screeched, "It's about time you got back. I don't want to do all the work, while you are out playing."

I ignored her comments, turned my back, and returned passionately to the important work at hand.

The TV monitor displayed the shuttle approaching the Station. "How exciting, they are almost there." I watched as the French Astronaut, Specialist Pierre Duvall began using the Station docking procedures. The Space Software ran flawlessly.

"Now it's time to find out how well the payload will work." Dalton tensely whispered under his voice.

I heard his comment, "It will work Dalton, just as perfect as the Space Software docking the shuttle, which is the safest in the world with the least defects, just like your experiment is the top cancer technology available."

Ecstatic, Chechee, photographed the mating of the two space vehicles. Her happy, round face gleamed as the doors opened. The Station residents released the airlock smiling, and shaking everyone's hands, "Welcome to the Space Station home. It's home away from home."

She hugged everyone, "Thank you for your hospitality. I can't wait to get started on the work at hand."

After the welcoming introductions on the International Space Station, Commander Rankin ordered, "We will begin making preparation for the Payload experiments, especially for the Micro-Encapsulation Crystallization experiment. This is the first permanent experiment that will be housed on the Station. It will be used continuously for cancer research. Everyone, the Truss is ready for mate of the MECS payload capsule. Attach it to the test platform on the top extension of the ISS Trusses exposed to vacuum."

Commander Rankin continued, "Pierre, you can begin operating the shuttle robotic arm so we can remove the capsule from the payload area. Then proceed cautiously. Pass the capsule to the Canadian robotic arm for attachment to the underlying Truss. All components have to be fitted and installed within the next three hours. Chechee, please carefully deliver the containers of test tubes to the payload area after the connections are mated. Dr. McKnight, show our guests the Payload Configuration used to install the capsule."

All responded, "Roger." They independently began setting up the payload equipment as they had practiced during their training sessions with Dalton.

I watched Pierre as he nervously floated back and forth. I noticed his hands trembling uncontrollably. I thought, maybe he felt the enormous responsibility of maneuvering the Robotic Arm. This would make me tense with the world watching this historical installation. My hands would shake and tremble, too, under the pressure.

Unfortunately I was haunted about the death of Dr. Keller and his family, and if the circumstances, around which it happened, had anything to do with our near death experience in the Bahamas.

Dalton noticed me staring into space and asked, "Are you here or faraway on the Station?"

"I'm here, Dalton, just here. I am wondering about Fletcher, Dr. Keller and the Bahamas incident. Do you know what really happened to Dr. Keller?"

Dalton said seriously, "No I don't, but I wish I did. He was a close friend and the loss is still not real. He assisted me in the technology and we shared a lot of good times. His children were my godchildren. It's as though I lost a family member, but I can only focus on today, Susan. I just pray that all goes well with Fletcher. I have to trust he is safe under NASA's security protection. I rechecked everyone's security clearance and each has one, so we all should be out of harm's way. Not only that, they're personally dedicated to the space program. Susan, don't worry about the experiment or Fletcher, he's in very safe hands. I trust everyone explicitly. Protection is imbedded in the controlled MECS experiment, so Fletcher can return home cancer free."

"Yes Dalton, he will be cancer free, but something doesn't feel right. I just don't know what it is." Silently I agreed with him on one hand, but on the other I had an annoying feeling in the pit of my stomach. I couldn't put my finger on the problem, but I knew trouble existed.

I watched the Astronauts working diligently together. Their endless hours of training certainly worked to their advantage. I listened to the NASA channel as the spokesman gave a blow-by-blow description of the progress of their methodical steps mating the capsule.

He spoke to all mankind, "The capsule is now being maneuvered by Astronaut Pierre using the robotic arm to fasten the capsule to the Station. The capsule will provide a permanent new space home for cancer experiments. This technology is innovative, the leading edge of oncological technology. It has been developed by the foremost biological scientist Dalton Masters, Ph.D. He is our own NASA expert. Everyone, the capsule is now mated. Houston we have a successful first stage."

Everyone applauded as Pierre secured the capsule while the ISS residents held the valuable capsule in place.

The spokesman explained, "Nothing is simple in space. It's cumbersome and difficult to say the least. Pierre you did a fine job. Thanks to everyone who worked the robotic arm. Now the task of linking all the connectors to the capsule will take place."

Everyone in the Payload Laboratory quit performing their jobs, hanging onto every word the NASA spokesman spoke, "Now we will watch the Space Team fasten the oxygen and catheters to the capsule. I've been told it will be used for the injection of the tiny magical crystals called Micro-Encapsulation Crystallization of Drugs Delivery System leading to Fletcher's inoperable cancerous tumor. The electrode leads were fitted into the capsule. They were carefully positioned for each transmitter to the centralized body location for the consistent flow of medicine."

Fletcher anxiously watched with his hands crossed, listening to the NASA spokesman, "I've been told the release of oxygen is the trigger to dissolving the tiny crystals around the tumor, the menacing tumor invading his body, destroying Congressman Dan Fletcher's precious life."

His words vibrated in Fletcher's mind, lingering with hope on his face. His eyes gleamed with anticipation of spending the remaining time with his beautiful wife, four children and ten grandchildren. He felt bitter, life slipping away prematurely. He believed if anyone could save him, Dalton could with his space cure.

The commentator continued, "The micro-crystals have been growing in the test tubes for the last 1 1/2 days of orbiting the earth in the anti-gravity environment. They are slightly larger than your white blood cells. They can only be seen under a microscope and resemble bubbles."

Everyone watching the monitor felt encouraged, realizing the seriousness of his illness and the importance of finding a cure for cancer, not only for Fletcher but also for everyone.

I thought of the many bubble baths I had shared with my sister and brother as a child. It was amazing such tiny bubbles could change the world and free a human body of the ugly cancer that destroyed life without remorse.

I watched the whole operation intensely, since the data was not being generated. I could feel the excitement in the air.

Then the NASA spokesman closed his show, "Now this has been a long day for the Astronauts and the honorable Dr. Dalton Masters. Houston we have a successful installation and mating of the experimental Payload Capsule. Signing off until the experiment begins again at 0500."

Commander Rankin informed the crew, "OK guys, and its time for everyone to rest. We are 200 miles from home, straight up, and we have 400,000 miles to go on the trip. We have had a successful mating of the Payload Capsule with the Outer Truss. Yes, the first, a triumphant for the Payload Installation."

Grinning Chechee said, "First, I want to take a few more pictures of earth. It's so beautiful up here. It just makes me realize how small we are in this massive universe, just a mere speck."

Pierre said, "While you are checking out the specks, I need to double check all the capsule connections."

Dr. McKnight commented, "I'm tired and it's been a long trip, I need some shut eye. I'll do the quality peer check on all the connections after I wake up. Please excuse me lady and gentlemen." He gave his typical winning smile as he made his way to his sleeping compartment where he zipped himself into his small snuggly quarters hanging weightlessly in the air.

I said, "They will fall in love with him from afar. He will be the universal heartthrob. He looked very peaceful resting. How restful it must be to sleep in zero gravity? No aches, no pains from sleeping the wrong way. Of course there is no wrong way in space." It reminded me of how tired I was and I quickly began yawning loudly. "Dr. McKnight is so smooth on Earth, but even in Space he still has a certain charisma that will be charming millions of women."

Dalton laughed, "Of course I couldn't say about what a million women would want in a man, but we do have cots outside so you can sleep. This would be a good time before the payload data is down-linked. Please get some rest. I need everyone to be fresh and alert in the morning. 0500 will come early, just as the NASA spokesman had said, "0500.""

I sleepily stumbled out to the hall and found a cot, and threw myself immediately onto the bed. It was uncomfortable with bars protruding through the steel frame. Even with the discomfort I felt safe, knowing I could sleep without anyone hurting me. One, my Dalton was near for protection. Two, I was at Kennedy Space Center where no bad guys could find us. Exhausted I fell into a deep sleep. Soon I began to have happy dreams. I was a little girl running through a field of daffodils with the sun beaming on my face.[7]

---

[7] The poem "Field of Life" is located the Poetry section.

Day Number 1
The Payload Begins

Leona abruptly woke Susan, "It's your turn to man the computer. I'm not going to monitor the payload MECS data forever without any help."

"Oh I'm sorry Leona, I'll be right there. Give me a little time, I just have to wake up. I feel like I've been drugged." I sprinkled water on my exhausted face and headed for the eye straining tedious work. As I sat down at the computer I heard Dalton talking with the Astronauts. All were in good spirits.

He excitedly began managing the most important payload of his entire scientific career. He seemed as a little boy might, buying his first piece of candy in the corner store. He attempted to not show his mounting enthusiasm, but couldn't quite control his emotions. Trying to be really cool he said, ""Good Morning Space Travelers", in his best Robin Williams rendition, much like his "Good Morning, Vietnam". Hope everyone had a good nights rest. How's it hanging?"

Fletcher smiled, "Hanging? Doc, I'm just floating around. Pierre and Chechee are doing a fastidious job installing the capsule. Hey Doc, even if the MECS doesn't work, I want you to know how grateful I am for a chance to beat this ugly beast. This is the second time I've had this ride of a lifetime. Doc, I'm in it for the ride, however long it lasts."

The captivating Dr. McKnight appeared wearing his contagious grin. He floated into the white sterile laboratory. "Dr. Masters," he stated, "when I begin the MECS procedure, I would like you to monitor my performance. Foremost, I need feedback on the implementation plan. First, I'll insert the catheter into the sub-clavian vein at the anterior scalene muscle, before Fletcher enters the capsule. After his connection to the capsule and equipment, I'll use the MECS syringe to introduce 1 cc of the crystallized solution into the catheter. During the next ten days I'll sample his blood to monitor his progress. It's my understanding the capsule substitutes as a CT scanner to visualize the size of his tumor. Also, we will get an audiologic evaluation for measuring any improvements in his hearing. I'll measure his lung capacity with a new device for analyzing pulmonary function, by blowing out virtual computerized candles, intermittently it will measure his blood pressure, and the rest of his vital signs. I'll calculate the results three times a day at 7 AM, 2 PM and 8 PM and downlink the results to you for your analysis. I must admit this capability is unbelievable. Its possible Doctors' offices could install a similar capsule and have one stop medical shopping, the Space Approach. The patient would not have to waste their time scheduling appointments at the many different the medical specialized areas of expertise. It would be a patient's heaven. Do you have an estimate of when the MECS formula will reduce his tumor?"

Dalton explained, "It's my experimental hypothesis there should be an improvement each day. The numbers have already been downlinked showing the micro-crystals are ready for use to encapsulate the tumor. Then the weightlessness in the Zero-G environment will promote the perfect shape red blood cells. It will become a more efficient carrier to the target cancer site. The series of events are triggered by the increase of pure oxygen attached to the capsule. The downlinking of data then will be analyzed not only for Fletcher's safety, but to document a baseline of the results for future experiments."

Listening I said, "This event could change mankind's healthcare services and even extend life expectancy. It's totally mind-boggling. Dalton, thanks for letting me be a part of MECS Space history."

Dalton said, "Well my friend, it's not just history, but my life's work. It's what I've always wanted to do since college. It's helping cancer patients. That's how I got my fellowship in graduate school to pay for my degree. I was the only intern who volunteered to take over an oncology experiment. Look where it has taken me. I'm truly blessed."

"So am I," I said with my emotions on my shirtsleeve.

The payload specialists began engaging the connectors to Fletcher's body to perform the baseline physical. The scene reminded me of Frankenstein with the many wires attached to his fragile cancer ridden body. Dalton reminded me of the mad scientist with his wiry hair that stood at the top of his head. I finally looked at my watch, which read 0600. I realized I had overslept. Oops, no wonder Leona was so short and irritable. If she had felt so tired, why hadn't she gotten me up from my sleep? I believe she wanted to sabotage me for oversleeping and make me look bad in front of everyone.

Dalton began recording the events with his PA voice recorder, "Today is Sunday, February 6, 2005. All of Congressman Astronaut Dan Fletcher's vital signs are normal. Blood pressure 135 over 80, which is a little high for the subject, heartbeat irregular, temperature normal, and his breathing restricted with minimal wheezing. This is the usual vital signs for the patient."

He continued, "Loss of vision in the eyes due to pressure against the ocular nerve caused by the growing cancerous tumor and the right eye is 100/50 right eye and left eye 200/80. He is registering hearing loss due to years of flying as a test pilot. It's apparent that he has advancing osteo-arthritis. No changes in his medical diagnosis since take off. We will begin his treatment in a methodically process using the MECS Payload Medical Operating Procedure at 0800."

I asked, "Dalton what type of information do you need for MECS data collection?"

"I need accurate measurements of Fletcher's vital signs to analyze when the data is downlinked." Dalton requested.

"I can write a simple program that will graph the results identifying any differences sorted by the categorization of his vital signs." I explained.

"That would work just fine," he said as he began sorting out the preliminary data.

I immediately wrote an elementary Microsoft excel program to capture the basic vital sign data so Dalton could analyze. In just a few minutes I had created a draft set of graphic sheets inputting random numbers. "Dalton here is a sample report of the program I'm developing for the vital sign data. It will enable you to track the progress on a day to day timeframe so a comparison of Fletcher's baseline normal functions can be tracked to any changes. Is this something you would like to use?"

"This is great! Oh yes, Susan certainly amazes me with your expertise. Each time the data is downlinked, I want a report by date and time. Can you make that happen? Please make sure they are delivered to me promptly. Could you print the report in poster size? I want to be able to glance at the Fletcher's information at any given moment. Dr. McKnight I'm sure you'll confirm these numbers as we go along."

McKnight reputed, "Not only will I confirm the numbers, but I'll personally enter the numbers to be downlinked to the software application."

Chechee interrupted, "I'm assigned to enter the numbers. That is my job as Payload Specialist."

Dr. McKnight turned making eye contact in a manner that left no question of who was assuming the responsibility, "No I'll do it."

Dalton interrupted, "We will proceed as you two were trained. No changes to the job assignments. The process is critical and we will have no deviations. Chechee you will enter the data. Do you agree Susan?"

"I concur. It's advisable to have a peer review to assure that the data is correct." I said.

"McKnight you'll administer the drug delivery to Fletcher. You have enough to do without entering the numbers. Chechee shall enter the information." Dalton ordered.

Chechee accepted Dalton's instructions, "I'll do my best".

Dr. McKnight said, "I would never do anything to jeopardize the mission."

Out of nowhere Ken piped in, "Dalton, McKnight is the expert. He should enter the numbers."

Leona commented, "I'll verify, so Dr. McKnight can enter the numbers. I agree with Ken and Dr. McKnight."

I listened wondering what is wrong with these people. Why are they arguing about who enters the numbers?

Dalton firmly directed, "Chechee shall enter the numbers. McKnight, verify the numbers. Ken, please make sure the information transferred into the reports is accurate and correct. There is no room for mistakes, only perfection. This is a matter of life and death."

I thought, "These are the same words Keller had used, life and death." I shivered.

Day Number 2
The Payload Implementation

Everyone in the Lab watched McKnight meticulously implant the catheter into Fletcher's subclavian artery located in his chest. He grimaced from the discomfort as the tube entered his skin. "Hey Doc, can you be gentler. It's too early in the morning to inflict so much pain. I really feel you are taking advantage of my condition."

"So you can tell I'm really enjoying the look on your face, this will only hurt for a minute. Please stay still while I attach transducer connectors." Dr. McKnight chided.

I watched the monitor as the wires were connected to the transmitters. I began teasing, "Fletcher you look a futuristic I-Robot with connectors from your head to your toes."

Dalton kidded him, "No not a robot, but Frankenstein with all the wires and connectors?"

Fletcher chuckled, "Indeed I do, but please don't make me a Bride of Frankenstein. My wife would kill me if I started wearing dresses and jewelry."

Everyone began floating through the cabin moving their arms and legs back and forth like Frankenstein.

Chechee stopped playing and began downlinking the payload data from the Station. She imported the data into the database creating the base point of the nominal functions from Day 1 of the MECS experiment.

Out of the corner of my eyes I observed McKnight carefully removing the crystallized medicine from the tubes. During the long journey in orbit the precious drug had grown. He used a syringe to transfer the crystals with his steady surgeon's hands.

He inserted the valuable medicine into the catheter. Fletcher's forehead dripped with sweat as he grimaced.

Dalton, seeing his adverse reaction asked, "Any problems, Fletcher?"

Fletcher responded, "It feels so cold like someone has put dry ice inside me. I can feel it freezing as it travels through my veins heading toward my brain. It amazes me how quickly the circulatory system operates. The sensation is intense and it stings. I don't like this, but hey, the alternate isn't much fun either. I'll take a little pain and discomfort for another chance in life. Success is the only option I signed up for. Yes the sweet feeling of success."

I sympathized with this great man, who had made space history. Now again he was making history. His accomplishments were known throughout the world. But today his heart was heavy and the distress showed on his face. I could feel his hurt. It reminded me of my dear deceased stepfather. He had died of painful bone cancer. Just like Fletcher, he wanted to survive, not for himself, but for my Mother. He bravely fought his death to the bitter end and just like Fletcher who loved his wife beyond comprehension. My stepfather's heroic efforts of fighting the malignant cells were lost, but Fletcher has a chance to beat the ugly beast. I prayed to myself, "Please dear Lord, let Fletcher live. Let him live to spend another day with his wife and children. Give him a chance to lead the way for cancer survival."

I printed off the updated MECS Program Report and gave it to Dalton. He stopped to review the vital signs. Dalton questioned Fletcher again. "Fletcher, how do you feel?"

"Well I don't feel like dancing, but I'm getting a little more energy. Not enough to break dance, but it's a warm sensation throughout my body, tingly, just tingly. Actually after the shock of coldness, I feel quite warm inside."

Dalton gave the MECS Program Report back to me. "Please prepare the data categorizing the information by his primary functions."

Two hours later I produced the graph he corrected. It demonstrated nominal blood pressure, but his heart murmur showed a minimal improvement.

Dalton analyzed all the graphs from the MECS Program Report. He noticed a slight improvement, but didn't have time to analyze the data in detail.

Dalton was pleased with his first glance. He wondered if the numbers were actually showing improvement or was it just a fluke, "Fletcher that tingly feeling may be showing up in the numbers. I'm observing an improvement in the numbers, but this is just the beginning of the MECS's project. I'm going to keep you in the capsule for another two hours allowing your body to rest in a controlled environment. Dr. McKnight, please administer the antibiotics to prevent any rejection or infection from the catheter and drug. Dr. McKnight, please go ahead, I'll observe the procedure."

Dalton grinned from ear to ear. "Your MECS Program Report (MECPR) really helps me analyze the results in a glance. I'm so pleased with the second day of the experiment, only eight more days to go. I've regulated the formula with some secret ingredients that will do more than just cure the cancerous growth. Just you wait and see."

Ken and Leona overheard Dalton and nosed into the conversation. I noticed even in space McKnight and Pierre intently listened to Dalton's every word

Ken was the first to speak up. "Did you change the formula without anyone knowing it? What additional ingredients did you put in it Dalton?"

I could see the hair stand up on the back of Dalton's neck. "Ken the ingredients are top secret. I've repeatedly told you, you don't have a need to know and it will not be disclosed at this time. I have the formula documented and patented. End of conversation."

Dr. McKnight interrupted, "I'm the Flight Surgeon and I should know what is going into my patient's body."

Dalton said firmly, "This is my patient and I have full confidentiality agreement, written permission and formal sign off from Fletcher and NASA Administration to administer whatever drugs are required for the experiment. Do you understand? My patient understands and that's all I need to have. Dr. McKnight you are just the provider of service, since I'm not an Astronaut and can't be in space to perform the experiment. This is my payload and you and everyone else will follow my instructions. Does everyone understand?"

Every person acknowledged in silence except for Leona, "Dalton I understand. This is just like my Grandfather's formula. His formula is still worth a lot of money. My grandfather never got to implement his chemical warfare weapons methodology. You are getting to administer your experiment. I think this is great. Who cares what everyone else thinks?"

I looked at Leona and thought to myself. She is always trying to butter up to Dalton in some way or another. I looked at Leona suspiciously. I felt anger toward her or was it really just suspicion. I just didn't trust her.

The next two hours passed very quickly. Dalton told Fletcher, "It's time for you to get out of the capsule. It has been a total of four long hours and I know you want to stretch your stiff legs and body."

Dr. McKnight unhooked Fletcher's electrical leads except he didn't dare remove the catheter. It would remain in his body for the duration of the experiment. Fletcher pulled himself out of the capsule. "I feel so much better. I can't put my finger on it, but I do. Maybe the antigravity environment is making me giddy or maybe I got to much pure oxygen."

Dr. McKnight said, "Let me check your vital signs again." He called out the numbers while Chechee inputted the data to be downlinked. McKnight instructed Pierre to perform the Quality control to ensure the numbers were correct.

I converted the numbers into the MECS Program Report. The report would be published nationally and internationally on news stations and newspapers everywhere in the world. The report was printed on poster size paper as Dalton had requested. I couldn't believe that my name would now be known all over the world for a simple report with data that could change the world. How exciting.

When the Report returned it was labeled Day 1—Micro-Encapsulation Crystallization Delivery Experiment.

Dalton analyzed the results from the baseline and updated to the team, "There is a subtle difference in Fletcher's vital signs, improvement in his hearing, and his vision. After the next treatment we will do a CT scan and measure the tumor. The design of the capsule performs CT scan and for the record, gentlemen, the technology for the CT scan capsule is patented and classified, so don't ask any questions on how it works. I'm just getting a little aggravated about the many inquisitions about the top secret experiment."

I whispered to Dalton, "Why are all these people acting so weird? I feel like I'm in a bad movie, where no one knows the punch line. They keep on dancing around wanting to know more detail information about your patent and it's making me nervous. Do you think that one of them is involved in Dr. Keller's death? Do you think they want to steal the formula? Is the formula safe in space?"

Dalton sat back and observed me for a second, "You know I just don't know anymore. All I care about is Fletcher's safety and the success of the MECS delivery system. If it fails, then the Space Medical Exploration Program (SMEP) will be in jeopardy." He gave a big sigh and turned away from me, "All I care about is Fletcher, and the experiment."

He turned his back to me, shutting me out. My questions resounding in his agitation, which reverberated in the tone of his voice causing tenseness throughout the room.

"Dalton." Fletcher began talking, "I feel so wonderful. The antigravity makes the pain in my joints almost non-existent. I'm beginning to feel like a new man, no a newer man." At that time he pinched Chechee on her rosy cheeks."

Chechee laughed, "You certainly are acting like a young man, but behave yourself or your wife will see you are flirting with me."

The Payload staff laughed at full volume. I doubled up with laughter causing tears to run down my cheeks. Their laughter was exasperated by exhaustion and tension from the first 2 days of constant concentration of the program.

"Now it's time for a rest for everyone except Susan and Leona. I need to speak to both of you." Dalton said.

I turned toward Dalton and for a brief moment stopped analyzing the MECS information. He called, "Ladies, please come over here please."

"Here are the results for today," he said in a professional manner. "Fletcher's vital signs demonstrated a small improvement, but it's changing."

"Could this be a good day or do the vital signs change in space? How does the MECS work?" I inquired.

Dalton began explaining, "The answer to your questions is complex. Fletcher is in zero gravity and that does have an affect on his body. The blood system is a complicated in space. To pump blood vessels your body must compensate gravity by using numerous one-way check valves are located in the veins. These trap the blood with each beat of the heart. Then the entrapment allows the blood to travel back up to the heart. In 0G the one way check valves do not work as efficiently as on earth. The venus side returns blood to the heart and will be the location McKnight will insert the catheter below the Subclavian vein. The vein will pump the crystals to the tumor surrounding the cancer.

In space your body will respond the same as when your feet swell on earth, but without gravity fluid collects around the heart. It's almost like an overload, but you can urinate to get rid of the water. This result in changes to your blood volume to 88% compared to the amount it was at launch. Amazingly enough your body adapts to space just like it adapts to cold weather. It gets a new setting point to go by.

The oxygen attached to the capsule will trigger the micro crystals to release the treatment from the catheter. Now ladies that is how it works."

"Dalton, now I understand the importance to document any differences. I'll develop another application to generate controlled statistical analysis and build in the 88% capacity. This will provide configuration control ensuring the accuracy of the numbers. It will show the minute differences in Fletcher's vital signs." I thought to myself, I will make him proud.

Day Number 3 Through 4
Status Quo

Everyone was disappointed for the next couple of days. The tests showed no significant changes, but status quo. I diligently transferred the numbers into the metrics database. Unfortunately, the CT scan prints of the brain tumor recorded no progress.

It just didn't make sense. I laughed at Fletcher. He certainly was in unusually good spirits. He continued to tease Chechee like a little boy. He had infinite energy wanting to play.

Fletcher taunted her as he threw a bullet ball, "Let's play football, Chechee."

It floated directly above her head and Chechee jumped off the wall sideways catching it doing summersaults with the foot ball.

Her eyes crinkled laughing, "I got it. I'm the first woman Football Space Champion, out of this world"

I silently wished I were playing football in space with my heroes. The public enjoyed watching the playfulness of this older Astronaut. He had once again won their hearts. I admired the camaraderie and devotion of the Astronaut team. I could feel the love in their space family. Oh how I desired it was me drifting weightlessly between compartments with them.

The admiration of Dalton grew on ground and space. He proudly orchestrated his life's work, which was broadcasted live in space to all mankind. His name became a household word.

Daydreaming, I felt he was truly the most interesting, sexy and intelligent man I had ever met. My heart swelled with happiness and lust. I could still feel his touch and the softness of his kisses. He was such a wonderful lover, caring, gentle, and giving. He knew what I desired before I did. I wanted to be alone with him right now, but unhappily, I knew I had to wait until the mission was over. The sacrifices one must pay for the future of mankind.

I forced myself back into reality. I wondered when the Payload Report metrics would be available. Knowing the government it would be years. Yes, years with all their bureaucratic decisions. Unfortunately this would leave only a short span of my life left. I panicked. I felt the urgency of accomplishment before the mission was over. Time is passing fast. I entered the last quatrain of my life. The old age awareness grew knowing my days are numbered. My decreasing lifetime span left on earth is constantly a reminder to me and to all baby boomers. It is the number one dilemma and the topic of everyone. In magazines, television, the models are all beautiful, skinny and portraying the life style of the rich and incredibly young. Where could the justice lie that youth is given to the young? Yet we boomers have the money to travel and live life but often are too beset by illness and infirmity to enjoy it. Yes it is truly a dilemma.

Day Number 5
The Payload Test

On Day 5 another MECS Program Report is ready. I couldn't believe my eyes. The results are incredible. Excitedly I called to Dalton, "Come look at the report. The numbers demonstrated substantial improvement. It's unbelievable, his heart murmur is almost non-existence and his blood pressure is normal. See!"

Dalton's eyes got real large, "I need to confirm the numbers and verify the accuracy of the report. I'll hold any comments until I complete validation of the statistics. You know it may be a coincidence, since heart murmurs do come and go."

Fletcher drifted into the Payload Station room. I looked at his face. He looked significantly healthier. His face looked relaxed and it beamed with a happiness that glowed throughout the Station. His body language was of youth and his twinkling eyes showed a renewed happiness.

Not far behind him was Pierre. The two began throwing the football. Fletcher turned somersaults, smiling and making faces in front of the televised screen, "No pain, Dalton, no pain. I haven't felt this way in years. What do you have in that formula of yours? Did you find the 'Fountain of Youth'?"

Dalton laughed, "Of course if it's a Fountain of Youth, we shall all be rich, and you, Fletcher, shall live forever."

I evaluated Fletcher, his eyes didn't reflect any pain. I remembered before he had a Clint Eastwood look. The look Clint had before he was about to kill someone as Dirty Harry, eyes squinted with an intense expression. Now Fletcher reminded me of a little boy, a sweet little boy capturing everyone's heart. There is no sign of pain in his eyes.

Dalton interrupted my thoughts, "Fletcher let's run another CT tomorrow morning and measure the tumor. I want to evaluate any changes. Of course, I don't know how to evaluate your youthfulness you're displaying. I want to remind everyone, this is a cancer research experiment and not genealogy. I do observe outward physical changes, but I can't contribute that to the formula."

Pierre commented, "I'm excited for Fletcher, and he is acting like a new man." He said in his French accent and then requested, "I want some of what he's having." Everyone began laughing, as Pierre began pretending to have an orgasm.

I said, "We all would like some of that, Dalton can I be next? Maybe you can find a way to speed up a woman's metabolism after 40. I could finally lose weight. Also just think what you could do for menopausal women? I think you should formulate a research project for women's health. Females have so many problems that are blown off as hormonal and never fixed. Heart disease is the one number one killer, but heart research is always directed to men." I started to carry on when Dalton interrupted.

"Hold on Susan, let's get through this experiment before you get me into tackling the battles of menopausal women and the battle of the bulge."

He shivered, "That type of research could really be hazardous to my health."

I pretended to hit Dalton. "That's not fair to my gender."

Fletcher chuckled, "Well Dalton if the success rate for women is as good as I feel you would be more famous than Elvis Presley. The women would love you tenderly. Then again, the way I am feeling I might just respond the same way."

Pierre said, "Maybe I could be a part of this. I would love to meet some beautiful women."

Dr. McKnight floated by, "Did I miss something?"

I laughed, "Just the battle of the sexes." Then they all chuckled simultaneously.

Dalton became serious, "Dr. McKnight, please prepare more crystals for tomorrow morning and Fletcher for the capsule tomorrow morning. I want to run another CT scan and the standard test of his vital signs. Please analyze the reports. They show a gradual improvement. This is the midway point of the experiment. I want to re-examine the tumor's progress. I'm curious about improvements in his vital signs. Please perform an additional test of his hearing and vision. A full examination is in order at this time. So far I'm thrilled with the MECS experiment results."

"Dr. McKnight you are instrumental in the success. Thank you for all your assistance and competent work."

Fletcher exclaimed, "The crystals have magic in them. I can feel them working."

Day Number 6
The Payload Success

The next morning Fletcher entered the capsule to commence the additional testing of his hearing and eyes and the CT Scan. He could feel his heart pounding with anticipation. He knew they would test his eyes first.

Dr. McKnight said, "The ophthalmology equipment is imbedded in the capsule. Fletcher, the eye chart will be displayed on the glass portion of the capsule above your eyes. Stay perfectly still inside of the capsule. I'm going to use an electronic control to turn on the eye chart. An eye cover moves over your left eye first and then the chart illuminates on the glass cover of the capsule."

Fletcher exclaimed, "Do you want me to begin with the bottom line?" He began reading, "e G A u R S T".

Then the cover concealed his right eye. Once again he read the chart effortlessly and like an auctioneer, "Little e, big g, big a, little u, big R, S and T. Yes I can see. Yes sirree."

Chechee laughed in the background, "Fletcher you are nothing but a show off."

Dr. McKnight said, "Dalton no sign of cataracts, left eye is now 20/20 vision. Right eye is 20/20. Unthinkable, his baseline just 5 days ago was 100/50 right eye and left eye 200/80. I can't believe the drastic improvement."

I piped in jokingly, "Or is it you can't believe your eyes?"

Everyone laughed enthusiastically. Quickly Dalton commanded, "Let's execute the hearing test. McKnight, we will continue with the testing. As you know, Fletcher's hearing was damaged from years of flying. His baseline hearing test results are 45-75 decibels. This depicts a severe loss, probably from being a Pilot exposed to steady noise of the engines. This constant loud vibrating noise in his eardrums is similar to kids listening to loud Hip Hop music. Fletcher now has a relentless humming noise. Currently his emissions are not being sent to the cochlear and not responding to the photo-acoustic emissions. Fletcher, do you mind going through more tests?"

Fletcher eagerly responded, "Not if the results are this good."

Dalton said, "Let's get started. Fletcher please position the headset on your ears. They are attached on the side of the capsule. As I said before, the hearing test will be conducted in the capsule with McKnight using signals generated by the computer. Fletcher, raise your fingers on your right hand each time you hear a frequency. As a former military pilot, this should be old hat for you. The advantage is the capsule acts as the perfect sound free chamber. We can't even begin to duplicate this quality of hearing test on the Earth."

He raised his fingers to Dr. McKnight when he first heard the tone. Fletcher could hear the lowest frequencies, sounds he had not heard in years. McKnight monitored the computer as the software proceeded through the audiology exam.

Fletcher beamed, "I can tell you right now that my audible range has improved. I am hearing tones I have not heard in years. Gail, honey if you are watching you can't keep me from hearing your telephone conversations. You better watch out, Sweetie. I feel like a teenager. Yes, this is what the aging society needs. No stress on the bones. I can hear and see. I feel normal. Doc, I love this feeling. I love you."

As soon as Fletcher got out of the chamber he began playing with Dr. McKnight's stethoscope.

McKnight scolded him, "Let me tell you like I tell little kids and teenagers, if you break the equipment you'll have to work to replace it. Go sit in the corner of the Space Station away from everyone else until you can behave."

Fletcher hung his head like a kid and said, "OK. OK. I'll settle down. You are such a party crasher. Honestly, I feel like my body is changing inside. The constant pressure in my head is leaving. My eyes, ears and heart are running like a smoothly tuned '55 Chevy Bel-Air engine, just like they did 25 years ago on my last trip to space. I love it up here guys, I know this will be my last payload, and it's my best. I'm eternally grateful to everyone. Thank you Dalton and thank you Dr. McKnight."

Dr. Mc Knight interrupted, "The hearing test results show the decibels have improved to 25-35 and now he has just a high frequency loss. This is a significant improvement. His hair cells and cochlear in the inner ear must be rejuvenating themselves. This is unheard of and very exciting, Dalton. Fletcher, please return to the capsule and let me attach the connectors to perform the CT scan."

"Good," Dalton said, "I'm anxious to examine the results of the tumor size. My preliminary calculation after 5 days of treatment should show some type of transformation. Fletcher I've some questions. Have you had any nausea with the treatment?"

Fletcher quickly responded with hesitation, "No, I haven't, funny though, I can feel the coldness of the medicine going from the catheter to my head. It's sensitive, but not uncomfortable."

Dalton bantered, "Pain level from 1 to 10, with 1 being the least and 10 being the worst. Fletcher, what is your pain level during the treatment?"

Fletcher said, "Only about 5, no really bad discomfort."

Dalton inquired again, "Have you noticed any hair loss?"

Fletcher had this big smile on his face and said, "None whatsoever, but you know Dalton, it would take a lot to catch up with you."

Dalton laughed contagiously and ran his hand across his head, "Not fair, Fletcher you may enjoy having a smoothly shaven head. It has its attraction, but I'm pleased you haven't lost your sense of humor. This is good, real good."

Then he directed his response back to McKnight in a serious tone. "Of course, if Fletcher looses any hair, please bring it back so I can use it for a toupee."

They all began to laugh when Dalton, again, ran his hands over his pronounced baldhead.

I had the desire to touch his head, but I knew this was not the time or the place. I thought about the last time at the beach when I was in my lover's arms. What a splendid memory. I shivered.

Dalton noticed he had lost me again. Dr. Mc Knight turned on the CT scan by booting up a software program. The capsule had an arch built inside just inches over Fletcher's body. It began passing over his entire head, one increment at a time. The noise pounded loudly in Fletcher's ears.

After 20 to 30 minutes Dalton said, "Fletcher, continue to lay back and relax. We know you must be claustrophobic in this confined area, but we only have 5 more minutes remaining and 5 more days of experiments. Just think, 10 days of cancer treatments compared of months of chemotherapy with all the nasty side affects."

Each time, McKnight methodically analyzed the crystals in an x-ray diffraction microscope. He assured Dalton the crystals were perfectly created, each being flawless, each created naturally without the affects from Earth's gravitational pull. This requirement was documented in the Payload Operational procedures before the medicine could be injected into Fletcher's body. Dr. McKnight had checked this religiously.

The CT scan had concluded the day's session. Dr. McKnight and Dalton scanned the completed images. They were then down-linked.

He spoke firmly, "Susan, please run the MECS Program Report with the new information."

I ran the application, printing off an updated copy for Dalton to analyze. I handed it to Dalton.

Dalton reviewed the images with satisfaction. His face brightened, "Unbelievable, 80 percent shrinkage."

Dr. McKnight chimed in, "80 percent shrinkage with no side affects, mind-boggling."

Dalton tried to control his enthusiasm, "Yes, I'm delighted and extremely encouraged with the results. There is no sign of damage to the peripheral areas of his brain."

Fletcher piped in, "Well guys, I'm not fatigued, no hair loss, and no nausea. The best result of all is the significant tumor reduction. Not to appear too excited, but are we beating the ugly beast, Doc?"

Even Pierre and Ken grinned in acknowledgement.

Everyone at the International Space Station and the Payload Lab began to clap.

Pierre spoke first, "Dalton you'll win a Nobel Prize for this research. It's beyond, or should I say, where no other scientist has gone before."

Chechee picked up her camera taking pictures of everyone and their big smiles. "This is for my family album when I get back home. It's a momentous event in our Space Program." She continued to float around the crew, snapping one picture after the other.

Dalton commented, "Fletcher, please stay in the capsule, in the controlled environment, just for a few more moments for us to normalize your oxygen and nitrogen mixture. The tumor results are phenomenal. Gerontologist and oncologists will be able to take this data to study age related health problems of the elderly. We need to understand aging including bone and muscle loss, balance disorders and sleep disturbances. This could possibly help older people with a more productive and active lives and possibly reducing long-term care. Fletcher you are the catalyst, the catalyst for a healthier baby boomers era."

Fletcher rebutted, "I want to be the catalyst to keep, "Space Travel a Reality" and "Full Recovery of all Cancer Patients". I want my life back, that is, a normal productive pain free life again."

Dr. McKnight said, "The space program will continue to have more collaborative research efforts with Dalton, our very own space life scientist Doctor."

"I'm ready, able and getting old myself, so I really want to work on this project. As one would say, this could be really good for my own health." Dalton commented back.

I could see Fletcher relaxing in the capsule. He looked so peaceful. His vital sign data continued to be down-linked, which sustained progress. I printed off another report and pushed pinned it along side the others on the wall. I sat back down, contented, assessing the positive quantum leap on the fifth day.

Day Number 7
Payload Discrepancy

On the seventh day Dalton said, "Let's conduct another CT scan including his primary organs, complete blood count, and rhythm-tracing on the heart."

The data overflowed with positive and nominal results. I watched Dalton smile, which reached from ear to ear. He beamed, as I never had seen before.

I watched as Leona paced back and forth like an agitated cat. She seemed extremely jittery, hesitating momentarily before approaching me.

I asked politely, "Have you checked the data?"

Leona ferociously snapped, "Of course, I have. You made a huge mistake, Miss Favorite. You aren't as perfect as you would like Dalton or the world to think you are."

I cautiously responded, "Leona, please show me where any anomalies are located. The actual data is up-linked and my program then converts the numbers into the MECS Program Report. There should not be any anomalies, since this is the same program I've used forever on the Space Shuttle."

"Well your program is transposing numbers. I've written a Discrepancy Report. Here it is, DR 999999. You should be more careful how you write simple programs." Leona screeched.

I was dumbfounded. I died inside. Where did I make a simple mistake? What would this do to the MECS payload if the application is in error? Quality Assurance personnel are to be exemplary! I prided myself in being a perfectionist in every facet of my job. Quality is my business. I was mortified. My heart sank to the bottom of my feet. The world is watching the program results from my program.

I demanded, "Show me exactly what you are talking about."

Leona and I went to the computer and sat down revisiting the numbers.

Dalton heard the tension. He asked, "What is the problem Leona?"

My face went bright red with humiliation. I wanted to disappear into the floor. Now he was addressing Leona and not me anymore. I felt embarrassed.

"Let me show you the facts Dalton," as Leona swung her long stringy bleached hair hitting my face. "See the hexadecimal should have been a zero and instead it was a one. Just like the software application error in the MARS Climate Orbiter mission. Remember it exploded." She grinned smugly turning her back to me.

"Let's get back on target. Leona, please make corrections to the application now, review the code, run multiple tests to find any more anomalies. Don't just tell me the problem is in one place, but make sure it's fixed in every area. Then I want the reports rerun. I'll then re-analyze the data." Dalton requested with a long frustrated moan.

I re-ran the report with the new figures demonstrating Fletcher vital signs. They were not as good as previously shown.

I said confused, "Dalton, it counters the original degree of the shrinkage of the tumor, his hearing and sight. All numbers are significantly different."

Dalton immediately requested, "Leona, please schedule a Technical Monitoring Meeting with the Astronaut Team, NASA Technical Management, Payload Management and the Payload Team."

Leona smirked, "Of course Dalton I'll set it up immediately."

I silently left, going back to the Astronaut's Cottage. Tears streamed down my face as I put on my pajamas. All night long I tossed and turned. I went over the code in the simple program over and over in my head. Conversion of numbers was not new in the space program. If I had made the mistake I was not the first, only it was my error this time.

It just didn't make sense. When I awoke in the middle of the night and I gazed over at Leona. She looked very peaceful as she slept, just too peaceful.

I dreaded the next morning, but it came too soon. After breakfast we hurried to the conference room at the Technical Monitoring Board. The senior management attended and the board members sat tensely in their seats not saying a word. Their eyes followed Dalton's every move as he sat at the head of the table. He started the meeting clearing his throat, "Good Morning. First I'm required to discuss our safety exits if an emergency happens. If anyone needs assistance please ask the person next to you for help. The emergency exits are located to the right as you walk through the doors. Take the closest stairs which is the most expedient way to exit the building." He pointed at the exits. Please congregate across the street under the oak tree 100 yards away from the building.

He cleared his throat and held his head high, "I regret to say the reported progress is proven to have a faulty program. To be more precise, apparently there is an error in the algorithm that formulated the results. The interchange of hexadecimal caused a huge discrimination. Just one number was incorrectly entered into the program causing the numbers to be mathematically calculated erroneously. My team fixed the problem and re-calculated new numbers. In conclusion, it seems we have had a software anomaly caused by the coder."

Everyone in the room began to discuss the problem. It sounded like a rumbling earthquake in my head. I was mortified. My face was blood red and felt hot. My eyes swelled with tears. I could hear my heartbeat. It pounded so loud I thought everyone could hear. My career ended in this conference room and the whole aerospace industry knew of my mistake.

Still in the back of mind I couldn't understand how I had made such a mistake. It just didn't seem possible. Not that I am perfect, but it is the same program that I had used for the Avionics Software. The report had been used for previous missions, which had run flawlessly.

I was frozen with fear. I felt I couldn't move. How humiliating. I wanted to disappear and never reappear again. What could I do to redeem myself? Tears began to flow down my face and wiped them away with my hand. I valiantly worked to hold the tears back. My eyes burned. How could I have made such a mistake of that magnitude? My reputation was essentially now ruined. I knew Leona must have been glowing. My stomach is in knots.

Dalton came over and put his hand on my shoulder. He leaned down whispering into my ear, "Don't worry Susan, anyone can make a mistake. We are all just human." he paused, "not one person is responsible for this problem, certainly not you, and as a team we will have to perform damage control." He then resumed the meeting with the NASA Payload Technical Manager.

"As you can see by the new charts, Fletcher's vital functions are not improving, as we had previously thought. The numbers indicate a negative response to the MECS formula. The diagnostic tests will be reanalyzed. I would like to offer my apologies for the misinformation. There is a dichotomy between his behavior and the recomputed data. It seems we have what you might call a placebo effect. It may be Fletcher's desire for good health has his mind convinced that he is well, even though he's still a very sick man.

The Payload experiment has had a grave set back and we will continue our research, but keep in mind the prior results are now invalid.

I'll be holding another conference at a later date with the media. Hopefully this situation will be smoothed out and we will know exactly where we stand." Dalton explained.

I asked, "What do you plan to tell the media?"

Dalton said, "When the time comes we will inform them of the facts. Its apparent Fletcher appears to look and feel magnificent. This is a plus. I must admit this current state of events is puzzling."

I wanted to be left alone. I sighed, "Dalton, I would like to go back to the cottage and get some rest. I'm emotionally and physically exhausted." Secretly I just wanted to hide from all the media and the man I loved. He probably never wanted to be with me again.

I called for the navy blue car. I cried all the way back to the cottage until I could hardly breathe. The sobs were loud and uncontrollable.

The whole ordeal just didn't make sense to me. I had been doing this too long to make a careless error.

When I got back to the cottage it was empty. I wandered from room to room aimlessly. I had to take action, at least do something. I found my cell phone and called James Torry, who had written the Payload Avionics Software program that down-linked the vital signs.

"James, hi, this is Susan," I said in a meek voice.

Before I could say anything else, he interrupted me. "What happened with the program? I can't believe you made such a careless mistake."

His words felt like a brick hitting me between the eyes. I composed myself and responded, "James, I need your help. Could you get a copy of my program? It has been backed up from my Shuttle ID. Please run a comparison to the current file on the NASA system. Execute a checksum to show if there are any differences. I've a bad feeling about this Jim. If you tell me I made a mistake I'll accept the responsibility. If you decide to help me, please don't let anyone know you are doing this for me. I know everyone is talking about it and looking for a scapegoat."

James firmly said, "I'll help, because I believe you didn't make a mistake. You're right, the Big Dogs are in arms and they feel you have blemished their Avionics Software reputation. You're in a tough place right now. I'll lend a hand, but I can't promise anything. If anyone asks I will have to inform them of my dealings with you."

With all my strength, I courageously said, "Thank you for helping me. You are the only one I can trust. Call me with any results. James, data doesn't lie. I just need the whole story."

I felt comforted knowing James was doing something, anything. My body felt tense. I had to relax. I decided to escape to a long soothing hot bath. The smell of lavender bath bubbles in the hot water permeated throughout the steamy bathroom. I was mesmerized with the flickering light of the vanilla candles dancing throughout the small bathroom. I was hypnotized trying to figure out what happened. I placed a hot bath towel over my eyes.

I jumped when I heard Dalton's voice with a simultaneous knock on the door. Dalton commanded with no emotion and before I could respond he said, "I've a news conference in one hour. You will join me."

I gasped, "Why Dalton. I'm petrified at the very idea. I think I've caused enough disgrace. How could I face anyone?"

"Susan," he said firmly, "My whole team will accompany me. You are part of the team and you'll be by my side and the team's side."

"Is that an order?" I pleaded.

"Yes it is. The conference will be at the Payload Laboratory Room 966, two o'clock sharp." He ordered.

He turned from the door leaving my mouth wide open. I closed it when I began tasting the soapy bubbles. I was in a state of shock.

I lamented, "So much for relaxing." I ducked under the bubbly water trying to escape what I had just heard. I finally came up gasping for air. I knew I had no choice but to do what he ordered. I quickly dressed in the only black outfit I had brought for the long since notorious vacation. Black matched the sadness that bestowed me. I didn't want to wear any of my bright colored tropical vacation outfits.

I walked into the large warmly decorated kitchen. Leona leaned against the counter with her arms crossed. Her stare pierced through me. The constant glare burned through me while I slowly crossed the room to stand next to Dalton. It was even more uncomfortable with Ken leering at me while I passed. Their blame showed in their eyes.

Dalton noticed their ominous glances, "I want to remind everyone, that we're a team. We will stand as a united force. Remember it's united we stand. No more of these accusing glances and I will have no words of accusations. I'll not have it, you understand. What is done is done. We will talk to the media, who are after blood. Remember, no blame will be on one person, since anyone of us could have caught the anomaly, but none of us did. Did we?"

No one spoke a word. I didn't look up to see if they were still glaring at me. I just couldn't.

Dalton still exuded the same confidence I had seen when we first met. This, in itself, seemed ages ago, so much had happened. He discreetly squeezed my hand gently. My heart jumped with hope. I felt his energy streaming into my body giving me the strength I needed to confront the embarrassing situation.

I took a deep breath acknowledging the nightmare. I walked into maze without anyway out and nowhere to run from the shame, which grew insurmountable.

We all silently got into the car. I stared out the window with an empty feeling in my stomach and soul. I began playing an old tape of insecurity, "Failure, I'm just a failure. I can't do anything right."

I watched as the NASA leaders walked into the conference room with frowns on their faces. The room familiar with the Mission Patches hung on the bare walls in order of the launches. Dalton sat alone at the end of the massive mahogany 20-foot table. His serious face masked any emotion from the tension in the room. I wondered what he would say.

His dissertation began, "Press," he paused, "Medical Space Exploration is just that. Remember this is an experiment performed in space and as such, things happen that are not in our control. A problem with the data has been found. There were multiple factors affecting the data that caused the Payload Experiment to have a turn of events. There is a dichotomy in the numbers from Fletcher's experiment and the program providing the vital sign data has a miscalculation. One could say, 'Houston, we have a software problem.'"

My face flushed with humiliation. I wondered if anyone noticed besides the Payload Team. The time seemed to stand still and I thought the meeting would never end.

He continued, "Even though Fletcher seems the picture of health, his vital signs are not as we had hoped and the numbers are now showing negative results. We will continue with the Micro-Encapsulation Crystallization of Drugs Delivery System payload experiment. The press may ask questions at this time."

A skinny reporter with a mustache questioned Dalton unmercifully, "How did such a mistake happen?"

Dalton repeated, "It's an error in the Software Program."

"Who is responsible for the error?" He quizzed.

Dalton stood firm stating, "There is no one person at fault. I have a competent team and we work as a team."

"But someone had to create the program." He continued prodding Dalton.

Dalton didn't flinch, "As I stated before no one is at fault. This is not a witch-hunt. We are doing a formal investigation."

I could see Dalton's temples pulsing with frustration. He didn't loose his temper, but acted as a professional during the entire miserable meeting.

All of a sudden Leona squealed, "Well it doesn't take a Rocket Scientist to figure out, who the Software Expert is in the group."

Silence fell throughout the group and all eyes turned to me.

Dalton immediately spoke up, "Ladies and Gentlemen, no one person is at blame, this interview is over. I am the Payload Project Leader and bottom line I am responsible. We do not have any more information to disclose at this time."

On the way back to the cottage the team spoke not a word. Dalton, furious with Leona, broke the silence giving Leona a public evaluation, "Your behavior was unprofessional. I do not approve of your pointing fingers and giving blame. I'll directly hold you responsible for creating a rift in the Payload program. You will be dealt with later."

His words didn't relieve the humiliation and pain. I wished I could disappear from the face of the earth, but I couldn't and I had no other place to go. I was not allowed to go home and I couldn't leave KSC. Now, with all that has happened, I felt now my career had ended. The career I had worked so diligently for all these years. I was tired. We all were just tired, really tired.

Day Number 8
The Conflict

My cell phone rang waking me up from a restless sleep. My heart pounded with excitement. It was James. I quickly checked to see if Leona was still in bed. She was not.

"Susan, I've run the checksum for the comparison of the program. The results do not make sense. The program you wrote is flawless. There are no errors. Someone changed the code, therefore, manipulating the data. Someone is tampering with Fletcher's vital sign information."

I sat up in shock, "Oh my God. How can that be? The security is extremely tight."

James explained, "Many people have access to the program, Leona, Chechee, Bob, Pierre, Dr. McKnight, and even Dr. Dalton Masters."

I said, "But which one would do such a thing? How am I going to know who it is? I'll somehow set a trap. Can you prove my innocence, James?"

"Not really, since you also have had access to the data. Someone is trying to sabotage the program. Whoever it is wants to make this experiment look unsuccessful and put you at blame."

I said, "I have an idea. I'll need rest for tomorrow, so when I return to the Payload Evaluation Center I'll be alert to recheck the code. Thanks for the information. I want to get this person, whoever it may be."

Leona entered the room, "Who called?"

I smiled, trying to cover up my distain for her. An outsider would have thought I was talking to my best buddy, "A friend." Then I turned my back to nosy Leona, "I'm exhausted." I finally pretended to fall asleep. Silently, the question kept coming at me, "Why is this happening? Who would want to sabotage the MECS's experiment and harm my reputation?"

I noticed Leona tossing and turning in bed. Eventually she rose out of bed and stomped out of the room.

Dog-tired I turned over and fell sound asleep. I had to sleep on a solution to my mission.

Dalton returned to the Payload Lab to check the numbers of Fletcher's last MECS's treatment and observe him.

Fletcher was exercising on the lateral bicycle. Fletcher looked 10 years younger. His mannerisms made him seem many years younger than his actual age. He acted like a big kid and personally Dalton thought it refreshing. Dalton had not seen him act this way in 15 years. He was confused. Fletcher's vital signs didn't match his physical energy and behavior. It certainly is a dichotomy. He scratched his smooth baldhead, as Dr. McKnight and Pierre entered the Station Payload Lab.

"Good morning Gentlemen," Dalton began. "This is the last payload treatment we will be performing. Please administer the full range of tests. It will include a full CT imaging of his entire body. I want to measure the size of the tumor, and take his vital signs."

Fletcher grabbed a towel wiping off the sweat. He released his feet from the bicycle.

Dr. McKnight encouraged, "Fletcher this will be the last time you'll have to enter the capsule, your home away from home."

Fletcher grinned, "If this treatment makes me feel as good as the rest, I'll be eternally grateful. I don't understand why the numbers don't jibe, but bottom line is I feel terrific. I can't wait to see my wife, kids and grandkids. For the first time I have energy to keep up with them. My headaches have gone away and my muscles don't throb either. Thank you, Dr. Dalton Masters giving me the privilege to participate in this magical MECS experiment. You have made me feel young again.

Dr. McKnight said, "Fletcher it's time to get in the capsule. Let's get this show on the road. The whole world is waiting for the results."

As Fletcher climbed into the capsule, before Dr. McKnight closed the capsule lid Fletcher raised his hand with a thumbs up to Dalton.

Dalton smiled. He returned the thumbs up.

"Let's do the CT Scan first," Dalton requested.

The CT Scan began with a large knocking noise that was louder than usual. The CT Scan abruptly stopped. Everyone was starring at each other in disbelief. Dr. McKnight tried to reengage the CT but was unsuccessful. He checked all the lines and electrical cords including the oxygen tanks that hooked to the capsule. He couldn't find anything that was damaged.

"What's next Dalton?" Dr. McKnight inquired.

Dalton stated with frustration, "This is a mechanical problem. It will have to wait until the return home. Let's continue. We want to run the other tests. Since the Quality Assurance representatives are still asleep, I'll enter the numbers myself."

Dr. McKnight went over to the MECS capsule and administered the drug into Fletcher's catheter. He began releasing oxygen disbursing the medication traveling to Fletcher's brain tumor.

Fletcher grimaced, "This is certainly cold, like an icicle broken off a glacier. I've got the chills."

Dr. McKnight returned the MECS test tube to the refrigerator. He rechecked the capsule.

Dalton was busy evaluating the data from Chechee. All of a sudden Dalton observed Fletcher's irregular heartbeat and failing vital signs.

Dalton alarmed, shouted. "Doctor McKnight, what is happening up there? Check on Fletcher now. Get him out of the capsule immediately. He is in distress."

Dr. McKnight turned quickly screaming, "Fletcher is going into convulsions."

Fletcher could barely speak, "Please help me. Help me Dalton. The medicine feels different. I don't want to die."

Dalton felt helpless. The sweat beaded on his forehead and soaked his underarms. He observed Fletcher gasping for air. He couldn't help

Fletcher. He couldn't save him. He was witnessing the death of his lifelong research and cherished friend.

Dr. McKnight opened the capsule, slowly the lid rose. Dalton's muscles twitched, he wanted to help Dr. McKnight pull him out. The monitor showed Fletcher was barely breathing.

Suddenly Pierre took action and pulled Fletcher quickly out of the cold coffin-like capsule. Dr. McKnight got Fletcher out. He took Fletcher's pulse. He screamed, "No pulse! Get out of my way."

Dr. McKnight grabbed the defibrillator and began electrically stimulating Fletcher's heart. He stopped to check his heartbeat again. "No pulse!"

Pierre acted immediately. He began mouth-to-mouth resuscitation. Three continuous pumps, then one breath.

McKnight lowered his head to his chest. No beat. He put his cheek against Fletcher's mouth. No breath.

Tears flowed from Pierre's eyes as he breathed over and over Fletcher's open lips.

Dalton was the first to speak while Pierre frantically continued his resuscitation. Finally Dr. McKnight put a bottle of oxygen over his mouth.

From the Payload Room Dalton continued to monitor his life signs, "No change. Dr. McKnight, Pierre you can stop now. Fletcher is dead." Their efforts had been to no avail. The Congressman, Astronaut, Father, Grandfather and hell of a great person, was dead. It didn't seem real. It was the first time a person had ever died in outer space or in the International Space Station.

Everyone stood up in disbelief. The silence left a void in everyone's heart in the Payload room echoing from earth to space. You could hear a pin drop, until Chechee began crying uncontrollably.

Dalton was shocked beyond belief. "How could this have happened?" He wished it had been him.

I wanted to comfort him. I knew, he knew, they knew his research was finished. This death would make him unable to work in his field, the field he loved so much. It was not only the death of a friend, but also the death of his life's work. His MECS's experiment was no longer an option. Dalton kept looking at the numbers in disbelief. Now Fletcher was dead, had died in space and Dalton felt responsible.

Dalton noticed Pierre looking piqued, white from top to bottom. Dalton inquired, "Pierre, are you OK?"

Pierre said with tears rolling down his face, "Emotionally and physically I feel exhausted. I feel terrible."

Dalton exclaimed, "Check Pierre's blood pressure."

Dr. McKnight took his blood pressure monitor and told Dalton, "His blood pressure is elevated 240 over 130."

Dalton instructed Dr. McKnight, "Please give him nitro. He is having a heart attack. Dr. McKnight administered the medicine." Pierre appeared to be unconscious. He looked white and dead. Dr. McKnight gave Pierre the nitro and made him comfortable in the hospital bed in the Payload room.

Commander Bob Rankin stood at the door watching the whole operation. He said, "How is Pierre?"

Dr. McKnight answered, "Hopefully he will be OK. He is stabilized for now."

Bob commanded, "We will begin our Mishap Investigation Report immediately. No one touch anything. I would like everyone to leave the Payload Mission Room. I'll put Fletcher back in the capsule to preserve his body until we return to earth. I want every one to leave this area, now. That is an order."

Dr. McKnight interrupted, "I need to clean up some of the MECS test tubes, before I leave."

Commander Rankin ordered, "I'll do it for you." Bob began walking toward the capsule. He opened up the compartment to begin removing the oxygen from the capsule. His eyes spotted a suspicious attachment located on the oxygen line, which was another MECS test tube marked with a red dot.

He turned to question Dr. McKnight, but before he could speak Dr. McKnight launched across the compartment using his feet to push violently against the station bulkhead on to the Commander's back.

Dalton screamed to Bob, "Look out Commander. Dr. McKnight is acting crazy." Pierre was now asleep from the medicine that Dr. McKnight had administered.

Dalton yelled to everyone, "What in the hell is going on? Is this Space madness? McKnight!" Everyone stood dumbstruck as Dr. McKnight was trying to strangle Bob."

Chechee hit Dr. McKnight's back trying to get him dislodge his stranglehold on the Commander. Dr. McKnight fell backwards and Chechee's hand covered the front of his face. Dr. McKnight angrily bit Chechee's hand breaking the skin. Blood began floating around the cabin with red droplets dancing in space, as if to the Blue Danube waltz.

Chechee screamed in anguish and pain. His hold onto her hand was as strong as a Pit Bull dog.

Bob quickly thought and reacted quickly observing the surgical tubing tethered to the wall. He hit Dr. McKnight propelling the doctor, with Chechee in tow, over to the tubing. The Commander grabbed the surgical tubing, wrapping it around Dr. McKnight's neck. He began choking him with Dr. McKnight still biting Chechee's hand. When McKnight realized what was happening, he punched the Commander with his legs repelling him away and disconnecting the Commander's hold and releasing Chechee. Everyone began spinning throughout the chamber. It looked like an acrobatic act in space with tiny bubbles of blood floating around.

Dalton felt helpless watching the Commander and Chechee fighting for their lives. Dalton thought, "If only the Commander could get Dr. McKnight next to the tubing again he could possibly strangle Dr. McKnight."

He worried about Pierre. He looked dead. Dalton prayed Pierre wasn't dead. Who would land the Shuttle safely back on earth. Dr. McKnight would not want to be stranded in space forever. He loved himself and women too much not to return to earth where, now, he was either crazy or a madman. Why was he doing all this? He was a man who had everything money could buy, women, fast cars and notoriety.

It must not be about money, but power.

The Commander and Dr. McKnight fought like animals. Each of their punches was countered with another hit. It was like Yin and Yang. In Zero G they couldn't hurt each other with their blows. It was like two positive magnets repelling each other. It was almost seemed like an air dance instead of a fight.

Chechee watched in the corner trying to stop her hand from bleeding profusely. She applied pressure to the wound with a towel she found in a storage compartment.

The Commander screamed at the wild man Dr. McKnight, "You must be mad."

Dr. McKnight yelled back laughing, "No, I'm not mad. I'm the greatest scientist in the world and I'm going to be the richest and most powerful man alive. I've just completed the ultimate secret experiment. When I get back to earth, I will rule the world with my trial testing and newfound knowledge."

They continued to banter both verbally and physically. Once again the Commander saw his opportunity to position Dr. McKnight by backing him up against the wall. The Commander placed him next to the tethered surgical tubing. The Commander held onto the tubing, grabbing Dr. McKnight with all his strength. The Commander struggled to wrap the plastic tubing around Dr. McKnight's neck. This time he didn't let go when Dr. McKnight move violently, trying to set himself free. Bob continued to squeeze the line around Dr. McKnight's neck watching his face go from white to red. Time seemed to stand still and his heart stood still. The Commander's determined face was frozen with intensity and Dr. McKnight face had an air of surprise. It seemed like an eternity while Dalton watched Dr. McKnight gasped for breath. He struggled only one more time, but Bob knew not to let up pressure against Dr. McKnight's throat. Red welts rose on Dr. McKnight throat making a necklace of red welts. Dalton heard a deep menacing gurgling sound. He knew it came from Dr. McKnight's lip as the man went limp. Dalton knew Dr. McKnight was now dead, but Bob continued applying pressure.

Dalton finally interrupted, "Bob, please stop, Dr. McKnight is dead.

Get control of yourself Commander."

Bob turned to Dalton, "My God, what has happened up here? I now have two dead crew members." His face was pale with disbelief.

Dalton replied solemnly, "The whole world has just witnessed two tragic deaths in space. God help us."

Day Number 9
The Attack

I dreamed, peacefully, feeling exonerated from the nightmare of the personal assassination in front of the whole world. I wanted to tell Dalton, but first I had to reconfirm the data. Then I can announce someone had tampered with the software application software which manipulated the data. Suddenly I heard erratic breathing above me.

I froze. I peered through the sheets realizing someone was standing over my bed. Then I recognized Leona. Her wild eyes glared with long stringy untamed blond hair hanging in her face. She demanded in a penetrating voice, "Who were you talking with last night?"

The shrillness of her voice made my skin rise with chill bumps. She acted as wild animal, caged, pacing back and forth.

Instinctively, I told myself to be cautious, "Leona, are you OK? I told you before I was talking with a friend." Leona was a crazed madwoman. My fear barometer went up observing her fanatical behavior. Suddenly I felt helpless lying under the covers as this raving maniac paced. I began to panic.

Leona shrieked, "You ruined it all. You and your stupid software program giving instant results to the world. You have destroyed me and the man I love, Dr. Daryl McKnight. I have nothing to live for now. I'm going to wipe you out just like you shattered my whole life. Susan, Miss Perfect, you will not live another minute. I hate the ground you walk on and everything about you, Bitch."

Leona suddenly picked up a pillow and lunged toward me. Leona pounced on my bed pressing the pillow hard against my face. Before I could move she trapped me under the covers pinning my arms and body down. I was terrified. Struggling against the pressure, I couldn't breathe. It seemed like an eternity, but eventually I got one hand free. I blindly reached for the lamp next to my bed. I finally got a grip and violently hit Leona on the back of her head. I struck her again and again as I struggled to knock her out. I fought relentlessly without avail. Leona finally knocked the lamp from my hand. I heard a crash as it hit the floor. I knew it was the end.

Leona looked toward the noise. This briefly allowed her to release her hold allowing me to inhale one small precious breath of air. Leona realized what happened and forced the pillow securely against my face again. At that moment I knew I was going to die. It was all over. I didn't have the strength to fight back. This was unfair, just when I had found true happiness. All was going to be taken away from me by a crazy woman. I felt cheated praying, "God please save me."

As I was going into blackness into a deep sleep the weight of Leona was lifted from my body. Our bodies were torn apart as I frantically threw the pillow away from my face coughing for a breath. Dazed I sat up as I violently coughed seeing my rescuer, my hero, my love, Dalton.

Dalton harshly questioned Leona, "What in the hell are you doing Leona?"

Leona was mad. Her voice was wild and unrecognizable, "You are not a scientist. My grandfather was the true genius, the supreme scientist. Your experiment is nothing compared to his. His experiment worked superbly and yours didn't. You are nobody Dalton. You and your stupid girlfriend are nothing. I'm going to kill you both, just as you killed my beloved Daryl. Both of you will die just like Dr. Keller and his family. You know his suspicion destroyed him as will yours. Nothing can stop me."

Leona pulled out a gun hidden in her pants. She pointed straight at Dalton with her back to me. "I'm going to kill you, just like you killed Daryl."

I could barely breathe, coughing and gasping for air. With all of my strength I stood up and jumped off the bed onto Leona's back. My heart froze when I heard a loud explosion ringing in my ears. The gun had gone off. I cried, "Oh my God."

I dug my fingers into Leona's eyes while Leona swung me around trying to get me off her back. Leona screamed and fell to the floor dropping the gun. I held her down by sitting on top of her. Then I noticed Dalton leaning against the bedroom wall. My eyes filled with tears seeing the red crimson blood streaming down Dalton's shirt. Leona began fighting like the animal she had become. Tears flowed down my face, as I wildly hit at her.

Out of nowhere five Security Agents appeared in the bedroom pulling me off her back. They immediately secured Leona removing the gun and placing handcuffs on her hands behind her back.

Leona's eyes were mad, She began babbling loudly, "You've killed the man I love, destroyed my life's work, but you didn't stop my Grandfather's experiment from working. It can destroy the entire capitalist world, everyone who discounted him and his brilliant technology. Dalton, I've stolen your experiment, its technology and used it as the catalyst for a new revolution. I'll be rich with power….power…power…I want power. You can't stop me."

I rushed over to Dalton holding him close, "Oh my Darling, are you OK?" I placed a towel over his bloody wound and began applying pressure. Dark red blood covered him and me.

Dalton smirked, "You know, this relationship is hazardous to my now failing health and my faltering career." Then he lifted my chin, kissing me passionately.

My eyes filled with tears, "Dalton you'll be just fine, you, your health and career. You are my only love. Dalton, I love you so much."

A Security Agent interrupted the moment, "An ambulance will be here shortly, Sir."

While we were waiting, I said, "James Torry, the Chief Engineer, ran a checksum comparing the program. Dalton, he said the program wasn't wrong, it was tampered with, probably by Leona. Fletcher is doing just fine. You are curing his cancer. He will be returning to his family cancer free. I think Leona was in cahoots with Dr. McKnight. They are probably lovers. They wanted to be rich using your experiment. They even killed Dr. Keller and his family. Dr. Keller must have stumbled onto their plans, so they destroyed his family, the poor man. It's so sad, so many deaths and for what?"

In the distance an ambulance siren wailed. Dalton tightly held onto Susan, "Susan, I have to tell you, Fletcher is dead."

I screamed with tears running down my face, "Oh no! It can't be true. My hero is gone."

My thoughts were scrambled with sadness. Through the tears and sorrow it suddenly occurred to me. "They must have killed Fletcher using Leona's grandfather's chemicals. Is it possible the chemicals were dispersed by the pure oxygen intake triggering the micro crystallization delivery method? I believe ironically enough, two experiments were being performed at the same time, yours and her grandfather's experiment. Now, Fletcher is dead."

Dalton chimed in, "You are exactly right. It got real messy. Dr. McKnight tried to kill Commander Bob Rankin. He attacked him while he was isolating the payload area to investigate Fletcher's death. The fight was brutal. The Commander finally got the best of him. He strangled McKnight with tethered surgical tubing attached to the wall. Leona must have watched Dr. McKnight die."

"So much has happened, two deaths in space," I was shocked beyond belief.

Tears were streaming down my face as I mourned Fletcher's death. His cancer was gone and so was he. I finally said, "Let's go to the Doctor, Doctor. The orbiter has not landed and you have to get mended before it does. There are questions to be answered. The Investigation will be extremely long and tedious, and lots of paper work. Someone will have to tell Fletcher's family. I hope they didn't see this whole disaster on TV."

Dalton explained, "Their NASA buddy, their assigned Astronaut, will inform them. May God touch Fletcher's family. May they know he has a plan for them and for Fletcher."

Helping Dalton up, we walked toward the front door. Upon reaching the door, the ambulance arrived. Dalton walked to the back of the ambulance with me along his side.

The Emergency Medical Technicians (EMT) ordered, "Dr. Masters please lie down. We need to do our job." They began administering medical aid.

The EMT said, "You are a very lucky guy. The bullet went straight through. We'll wait for the diagnosis from the attending Flight Surgeon. You will have to be stabilized."

We rode to the hospital with the heaviness of our losses. The series of prior events had created a bond between us stronger than life itself. Life as I knew it before that day we went sailing on the Galveston Bay was gone forever. The world would be watching our every move. Dalton now had to re-analyze the results using the valid numbers in the un-tampered software application. Then he needed to publish exactly what happened to Congressman Fletcher. His research results would make a significant difference to the life of mankind.

I keep thinking about how Dr. McKnight had murdered Fletcher with Leona as an accomplice. Leona had already filled in the gap about her Great Grandfather, but how did they pull it off? They had fooled the top security organization in the world. Soon the Mishap Investigation would start. Hopefully it will reveal unknown answers to everyone. The whole process will be grueling. Day after day long meetings would be held. Dalton would be interrogated with a million questions. The whole incident would be lived over and over again. It was a necessary, but painful inquisition. I just hoped the death of Fletcher and Dr. McKnight would not be shown over and over again.

I turned to Dalton, "Did Leona become obsessed with proving her Grandfather's success using his chemical warfare methodology?"

Dalton grimaced, feeling discomfort from the gunshot wound, "All I know is that she continued to ask questions about the formula and how things worked. Leona is a very needy person, an easy picking for a charming man like Dr. McKnight. I've known him for a long time. He has had many women who had thrown themselves at him. After a while he would become tired of them, most likely bored, and then move to the next prey. Leona got caught up in his charismatic personality with the attention she desperately desired. She tried for the longest time to receive attention from me, but I was only interested in her as a little sister and a friend. She must have been desperate and lonely, going over the deep end. It's possible she will be tried in Florida for attempted murder, and possibly in Texas for the murder of Dr. Keller and his family. I'm not sure what the laws are in space, but she is an accomplice to Fletcher's death. It may fall under maritime laws rule or possibly the international law. Fortunately, Commander Bob Rankin took care of Dr. Mc Knight. He is dead, strangled to death. There will not be a need for any courts for him."

The Emergency Room was in chaos with the paparazzi taking pictures of our every move. I was thankful we didn't have to stay in the Emergency Room waiting area, the formalities of completing insurance were waived. He saw the "on-call" Doctor who read the x-rays. He said to us, "Dalton needs surgery for the torn ligaments and tendons in his left shoulder. The bullet shattered his clavicle when it ripped through his upper torso.

The doctor assured Dalton and Susan, "This is standard surgery, but it will take time to repair. I've called Dr. Burke, an Orthopedic Surgeon, to repair your collarbone. You are a very lucky man. The bullet just missed your heart. The anesthesiologist will be administering amnesia so you will not experience discomfort. Depending on what we find, your recovery will probably take six or more months to recuperate. Of course you'll have Physical Therapy to regain your normal range of motion of your left arm. Susan, will you please go to the surgical waiting room. I'll be out as soon as surgery is over to tell you the results. The surgery time should be approximately six to ten hours to repair the bone, muscles and possibly his lungs. I won't know until I get in there."

I leaned over the transporter bed and kissed him, "Dalton, please don't let anything happen to you. I want to see your sparkling brown eyes with that hint of devilish mischief."

Dalton pulled me down kissing me softly, "Every day of my life I want to see you before I go to sleep, Susan, and the first thing in the morning I want to feel your beautiful body next to me. I love you Susan. I want you to know if anything happens, I love you." Then he lost consciousness.

He didn't hear me say, "I love you more than life itself Dalton." I went to the waiting room with tears scorching my face. The photographers and news media began asking questions, "Can you tell me what happened?"

I kept repeating, "I can't answer any questions, you must talk to the Aerospace United Industry Public Relations Agent."

I sat in the corner trying to have some privacy and noticed Ken making his way through the crowd toward me. He sat next to me and fended the news reporters away. He put his arm around my shoulder comforting me the best he could. My opinion of Ken changed, he truly was Dalton's friend and now my friend. I reflected on me seeing the note on the boat, he was only trying to protect his friend. No words were spoken, as we patiently waited for the Doctor's arrival and the outcome of the complicated surgery. Time moved very slowly.

Three hours passed and no doctor. After 9 hours the doctor appeared and motioned for us to go into a private room. He began speaking very slowly. "The surgery was more extensive, than I first expected. The bullet had damaged more tendons and ligaments, because it entered diagonally and fractured his shoulder. We repaired the shoulder and the collarbone using plates and screws. Fortunately it didn't damage any vital nerves, vessels or his lungs. He has lost a significant amount of blood, which made it necessary to give him a unit of blood. He will be weak during his convalescence, but knowing him, he will bounce back fast. I hold you guys responsible to keep him down. He should be out of the recovery room in an hour."

Ken said, "Thank God he will be OK. Don't know what I would do without my buddy. He's the best friend I've ever had."

I felt a rush of relief knowing my Love would be OK, "Thank you doctor. I'm so grateful."

When the Nurse arrived, our four security agents were waiting to escort them to Dalton's hospital room. They informed us, "We will be with you night and day to ensure both your safety until the Mishap

Investigation is completed. Just pretend that we don't exist. You will stay again at the Astronauts Cottage. This time for your protection from the news reporters and anyone else that may have harmful intentions involved in this incident."

I was drained emotionally, "Yes, it's an incident, an incident that has caused so much pain and loss. Leona will go to trial for attempted murder on Dalton and me. Ken, I don't want to be involved in the murder trial or the Mishap Investigation or be any part of this incident. All I want to do is finish my vacation with the man I love."

Ken put his arm around me, "It will be OK, Susan. Just hang in there and you'll be in the Bahamas soon."

We entered Dalton's hospital room, exhausted and numb. I had bruises on my arm where Leona had hit me. The mirror confirmed the purple bruises on my face and the bald patch where Leona had pulled out my hair.

Ken observing my horror said, "Why don't you take a hot shower, while we wait for Dalton? It will make you feel better. I'll make sure no one comes into the bath room."

"Great idea, I need to wash off Leona's unpleasant smell and the awful taste in my mouth. Do you think someone could get me some decent clothes, a tooth brush and toothpaste? Oh no, the photographers must have had a field day." Mortified, I just remembered I was still in my silk PJs. I immediately headed for the shower. One of the nurses brought me some scrubs from the Operating Room.

I said, "Thank you. I'll bring them back as soon as I can. You have saved my day."

When I got out of the shower, I heard commotion and the flashes of cameras. They must be bringing Dalton to the room. I quickly threw on the scrubs and entered with soaking wet hair.

Dalton was a sight for sore eyes. He looked pasty white, but no worse for the wear. His eyes began to open saying quietly, "Even with wet hair, no make-up, you are just as beautiful as the first day I met you, even with the purple and yellow bruises."

I leaned over and kissed him with my wet cold dripping hair brushing against his face and down his cheeks.

Dalton shook his head, "I know I need a bath, but can it wait, with warm water, my precious?"

I laughed, "Of course. I'll give you a bath right now, if you wish."

Dalton smiled in return, "I'm not quite up to it, but I'll take a rain check. I'm so tired. I just want to sleep." He turned over and was fast asleep.

Day Number 10 Through 11
The Recovery

I stayed by his side while he slept. They had intravenous pain drugs keeping him in and out of consciousness, so he could mend. I felt as a mother would, nurturing a new born child. He looked so helpless. His moans made me realize the pain he was feeling and I felt them as well. The only time I left his side was to get nourishment. The hospital staff provided the best medical care possible. All were interested in his experiment and kept asking questions about the MECS Drug Delivery System. His research fellows visited his side while he slept. I still felt scared even though I knew we were safe.

I placed his hand over my heart with his eyes still closed deep in sleep. I felt safe to express my feelings, "Dalton we're one. You are the one I've been looking for all my life. The man I want to wake up next to me in the morning and the first one I want to see before I fall asleep. I love the way you make me see who I am and the way you believe in me."

His eyes opened abruptly with Dalton squeezing my hand, "How long have I been asleep?"

"It has been three long days. Your body needed to repair itself. Unfortunately the bullet did more damage than we first thought. I have been so worried. I'm so glad you are conscious." I said.

"I do feel better," he said as he tried to move his body. His face could not disguise the pain.

"Slow up big fellow that's why they make hospital beds with controls. I know you must be curious about the flight. It's almost time for their descent. I'll turn on the NASA Channel, so you can catch up with their progress." I said moving his bed up, so he could reposition himself to view the TV. Just as the TV came on the NASA commentator announced, "Dr. Dalton Masters is recovering in a nearby hospital. If everything goes as planned, he will be released Thursday. His physical wounds will heal, but the trauma of what happened on the Space Station will be with him and everyone forever. The question everyone is asking is why? Why would anyone want to hurt the heroic, kind, Astronaut Dan Fletcher? Talking about Astronauts, another important crew member of the shuttle, Pierre has fully recovered. The sad news is the crew has not determined why Pierre passed out, but more tests will be run upon his return. The shuttle is scheduled for landing on Friday, and Dr. Masters should return to the Payload Laboratory on the very same day. He is needed to continue the MECS research to figure out all the unanswered questions."

The station televised the crew making landing preparations. They somberly went over their checklists to ensure a safety departure. Chechee acted like a zombie, with her bandaged hand, in a trance. Her face was full of grief.

Dalton said, "Look at her face, she must be in shock. It's difficult for me to believe she watched the death of Fletcher and Dr. McKnight. Everyone will have adjustments with their space family destroyed in front of their eyes. Chechee loved Fletcher so much and they were truly playing like little kids. It saddens me to see Pierre, his whole demeanor has changed. They both will need counseling for a long time to come. Let's hope it will happen."

Pierre's head hung low as he put on his space suit. It seemed like an eternity. Commander Bob Rankin was solemn realizing leadership had its challenges and rewards. There were no smiles, happiness or laughter on the Shuttle and certainly no more football games.

The hospital staff all came up to give us a farewell. Dalton moved slowly into the wheel chair. He was anxious to leave the hospital and ready to get back to his research.

Day Number 12
The Shuttle Landing

We returned to the Astronaut Cottage to prepare for the long day in the lab. Dalton moved slower than usual, but his sense of humor and determination returned little by little. He had a mission to complete, to exonerate me from the accusations, reinstate my professional reputation and to continue his research. Early the next morning we were back in the navy blue car. The lab felt so familiar. I now didn't have anything to do but watch.

The screens gave a panoramic view of the Shuttle's undocking. The rendezvous with the Space Station had ended. Pierre released the latching dock adapter from the Space Station. The Shuttle backed away slowly distancing the ship from the Space Station. Pierre expertly maneuvered the orbiter into orbit below the station. The vehicle pointed backwards as Pierre fired the Orbital Maneuvering System (OMS) engines for 3 minutes. It eventually backed farther and farther away from the Space Station positioning the Shuttle in front of the massive home in space. The auto pilot software took over, while the flight crew configured the shuttle switches using a feed from the left Orbiter Maneuvering System (OMS) and aft right Reaction Control Subsystem (RCS) tank isolation.

If necessary Pierre could terminate the software sequence to inhibit the OMS-to-RCS gauging sequence, but the software performed flawlessly as the RCS jets turned the Shuttle forward. The RCS propellant tanks engaged ensuring proper operation during the entry mission phase. Pierre was thankful that everything worked per requirements. The crew settled in for their long dangerous flight home. They knew that re-entry and take off were the two most perilous time. As in all flying, if anything happened it would be during these two sequencing.

When they entered the atmosphere Bob took over the controls using the elevons (the flaps) and rudder (the tail) to begin landing the aircraft. I knew the egos of the Astronauts, once pilots they always are pilots, and as pilots they must land their ship. Bob soon had visual of the landing field and did a 270 degree turn to land the Shuttle without a glitch. All the time he talked with Capcom, the Astronaut Flight Capsule Communicator. "Well I almost see the blues of your eyes. I'm coming in for a landing, waiting for a good meal and something to drink." The Shuttle landed on the shiny steams of heat reflecting on the runway. The landing was perfect and the space software application performed flawlessly.

The Payload team watched from the Payload Laboratory located in the Astronauts' Building. It had only taken 40 minutes from the engines to fire to touchdown. It was a beautiful site, as the magnificent Shuttle came to a leisurely stop. All were silent knowing the inevitable, since the shuttle carried the precious merchandise, two deceased crewmembers, the psychopath Dr. McKnight and the honorable Astronaut-Congressman Dan Fletcher. This will be the first time NASA would have to carry the crew out in body bags. Both McKnight and Fletcher secured in their sleeping bags. I cried out, "Astronaut-Congressman Dan Fletcher and Astronaut Dr. Daryl McKnight would not be walking proudly from the ship. I'll always remember Fletcher. Dr. McKnight and Leona must have been as crazy, such a loss for all of them. I just don't understand."

Dalton said, "No one will ever understand."

Then the door opened to the Shuttle. It seemed like a million hours before the Commander solemnly walked out waving to the silent crowd. Chechee came forward with tears in her eyes, no smiles. Pierre lumbered out with the help of the landing crew, shaking his head as if to say to the American public, "I'm sorry." His movements were uncertain. The crowd silently saluted to the brave few as they left the ship. In the background played the patriotic song by John Phillips Sousa, "Stars, and Strips Forever". Everyone placed their hands over their heavy hearts.

The Shuttle had returned home landing like an eagle, proudly with the remaining three heroic Astronauts coming back to their majestic country.

Dalton's cell phone rang and his mouth opened wide in amazement. Everyone was surprised when he said, "Good afternoon, Mr. President."

The President spoke briefly, while everyone intently listened to every word. Dalton acknowledged his words, "Yes Sir. Thank you, Mr. President. I will. Don't you worry? I'll handle the situation."

Everyone looked at Dalton and curiously asked, "What did he say?"

"He wants to commend the Payload Experiment Team for their outstanding job performed during this crisis. He gave an order stating no one divulges any information of this incident, until the Mishap Investigation has been completed."

Everyone nodded in agreement. I said, "We will all follow our Space Core Ethics."

From the closed circuit television we watched as thousands of people lined the roads or any available site wanting to be part of history. The crowds emotions were visible, not a dry eye in the crowd. I finally broke down joining the world sobbing and releasing my pent up feelings.

Congressman Fletcher's devoted wife and family were seen in the crowd. They proudly stood in remembrance of their loving caring father and husband. They were not alone, Captain M.D. Van, USN, their buddy Astronaut, was by their side. He had his arm around Mrs. Fletcher, comforting her as best as he could. He had been a good man and a long close friend of Dalton. Fletcher wife's head was held high, but the immense sorrow showed in her eyes and actions. The body bags were carefully removed from their sleeping compartments by the local KSC security and carried out respectfully with admiration.

Finally this elegant, gentle lady broke down, when she saw her husband's body being removed. She wanted to run over to touch him one more time but instead she held her composure. Her courage was beyond everyone's belief, as she stood in silence, they put her husband in the ambulance.

No one was waiting for Daryl McKnight's return. His parents had long since died and his girlfriend, Leona, was now in jail. The many other women were nowhere to be seen. He was all alone in death.

The scene reminded me of what I would do without my new love, Dalton. He was part of me now. One day of sailing had become a life time of love. Even though Fletcher was at the end of his life, death knows no age difference in devotion. Losing life causes sorrow at any age. Life is so precious. With Dalton's experiment Fletcher would have been a winner in life. He should have lived another 10 to 15 years with his loving family. I hated the cliché', God does not give you more than you can handle. Who can handle death? Is his death right? Only God knows. Please God, let us celebrate his momentous life and the many people the Congressman touched, including mine, Dalton's, the crew and the many cancer victims, who will be saved from his courage.

Chapter 19
The Memorial

Two weeks later Dalton stood in front of the Johnson Space Center Astronaut's Building dressed in a black suit and his red shuttle tie. I held his hand wearing my plain silk black dress with a single string of pearls. We were surrounded by famous aerospace executives, Astronauts, and their families. The atmosphere reminded me of a family reunion with everyone hugging each other and comforting Fletcher's fragile wife, his children and grandchildren. The NASA family formed a bond of love and support.

Fletcher's wife hugged Dalton, "I know you were saving Fletcher from dying a horrible death of cancer. I am grateful for what you did, but please do not blame yourself for what happened. You had no control over the situation and had no way of knowing. He was happy up in space. I watch the video of him playing in space over and over. He had become a new man, rejuvenated. I hold you personally responsible for his renewed happiness and hope. Thank you for the time you gave him." She hugged him holding herself up. Her pain was felt throughout my body, I shivered in sadness.

Dalton held her close, "I wished I could make things different. He was certainly a good man and I feel very fortunate that I knew him for a short while."

The Astronaut families told stories about the times past, when all the Astronauts drove around in corvettes and were treated as celebrities. Today it was different. Most people don't realize the sacrifice each male and female Astronaut gives to their country, the United States of America.

I talked to the Challenger's Commander's wife. She was standing alone. Her face looked sad with grief. I approached her, "Hi. My name is Susan. I know this must bring back memories of hurt remembering the loss of your husband."

She solemnly responded, "The pain never goes away, no matter how long a time. I need to help Fletcher's wife and family any way I can. My husband gave his life to the program and now hers. We have been friends for many years, and she doesn't handle being without him, even when he was alive. I know it will be hard, but I'll be there until time makes her numb from the pain, the loss. It will just take days, weeks and years to start living again without him."

Tears came to my eyes and I squeezed her hand, "I understand." My eyes stung as the tears ran down my face. I turned away as Dalton touched my hand, so she could not see my grief.

I recognized a friend I hadn't seen in many years. It was Mike, ex-Astronaut and Boeing executive with his wife. I had once reported to him and would meet them at the local Mexican Restaurant. Then with a corporate change I no longer worked with him and he moved far away. Since then my organization had been bought and sold from one company to the next and I was shuffled from one management team to the other. It had been difficult adapting to the many corporate cultures, but I was a survivor. Most of the people I had worked with during that period had now left the aerospace industry.

My eyes continued swelling with tears as I thought of Fletcher's happiness and enthusiasm during his last days. Trying to shake the sadness I thought, "We must celebrate his life".

Before the Payload Team had left Florida, the Medical Examiner had notified us of the autopsy report. It had validated Fletcher's absence of the brain tumor. It seemed senseless he had died, proving Leona's grandfather's chemical warfare products could be disbursed using the micro crystallization process. These tiny invisible crystals could poison the whole world without anyone seeing it coming. They would be invisible in the atmosphere spreading with the wind and spreading death.

I felt I was part of a Greek Tragedy, "The Nonsense of a Hero's Death". Dalton interrupted my thoughts kissing me quickly on the lips.

At that time NASA security motioned the VIP entourage toward the door leading out into the courtyard where they watched the memorial. It was time to move.

Dalton gently tugged on my hand. I hesitated not wanting to go outside. The hurt and pain was too much for me to bear. Somehow I felt responsible.[8]

How could I have known Leona was mad? Now she is locked up in a maximum security prison without the possibility of parole. I felt pity toward her and anger. I would be dead if it wasn't for Dalton's intervention in the knick of time. Death would have been my fate and also my hero, Dalton.

I followed the crowd of VIPs into the courtyard. This was a dream come true to be sitting with my heroes, and the President of the United States. Only bittersweet was my circumstances.

I surveyed the massive audience. Thousands of NASA's employees, government workers poured into the area. To me it would now be called the Mourning Courtyard. This place where everyone paid tribute to Fletcher, the man, who first began his career in the Jupiter program, next, the Apollo Program, Shuttle Program, and last the Space Station Program. He gave his life, so many others would benefit from the cancer space research. Yes, the research was a success.

Dalton had told me Leona had added a variation of Potassium Cyanide, clear, odorless liquid, to the Micro Encapsulation Crystallization formula. McKnight dispersed the poison using Fletcher's oxygen. Would the public ever know what happened? The secret would probably end up tribal knowledge, only for the NASA family.

The President of the United States stood in the podium and spoke with exuberant pride, "Exploration and discovery is the base of the space

---

[8] The poem "The Sadness" is located in the Poetry section.

program, it's a choice, which Congressman Astronaut Dan Fletcher chose. He was a special person, a Congressman who served his community and the people, an Astronaut who went where no other mankind had gone, participating in research that will save human life, possibly your life or someone who you love. A family man dedicated to his family, the space program and the political foundation of our country. He was the best among us, sent forth into the unmapped darkness. When he left, we had prayed as a country the cancer research would save his life. It gave hope to other patients fighting inoperable cancer. Unfortunately corrupt villains had alternative plans, taking his life. He returned cancer free, but without life. The responsible parties will be punished with the strongest government judgment. I speak from my heart, heavy, that his family has to endure pain, suffering, with the greatest loss of all, an American hero. The NASA family and the world mourn. Into space he went in peace, but returned in harmony with God alongside of him. He provided medical research for all mankind, and all mankind we're in his debt. Forever, shall we remember the greatest gift of all, his life? Let us go today with thoughts of this brave man. Remember him as a good family man, a pioneer of space, and an exemplary example not only in the aerospace industry, but the world. Thank you Congressman, Astronaut Dan Fletcher, my friend, God speed you to the end of your journey and for all eternity."

My eyes scanned the congregation. Sadness overwhelmed everyone. Women and men were breaking down, mourning his untimely death. I glanced over to Dan's wife and family, who continued to hold their heads high as they stayed very close together.

Dalton and I were invited to the private congregation of the VIP personnel, who attended the memorial.

The closeness of this NASA family supporting each other today was incredible remembering all the past losses. Now I was a part of their community, a member of space exploration team.

Dalton was the center of attention. His expertise in cancer research and success was highly recognized throughout this elite community. Everyone was giving him attention that made him uncomfortable.

The women were aggressively surrounding him. I heard one woman say, "I have tickets to the Symphony for Saturday night, I would be honored if you escorted me."

Dalton smiled and graciously bowed away from the crowd. He finally seized my hand and said, "Let's leave. I'm getting claustrophobic."

We walked outside, and he turned, holding me close, kissing me like he had never done before. "After the Mishap Investigation will you accompany me to the Bahamas? I want to finish our short lived vacation? A sailboat is waiting for us to cruise the islands, without any interruptions from the news media, NASA headquarter or pushy women."

"Yes, I do too, my Darling. I can be packed in a moment or as one would say, in a heart beat."

Chapter 20
Mishap Investigation

The Mishap Investigation took place in Houston. Day-after-day, Dalton, along with the entire Payload crew attended the eight-hour meetings. Sometimes we were not given a break. First they concentrated on the topic "Breach of Security". How did it happen, and who was responsible? Did the Security Investigations policy need to change? This was a top security and safety environment, but it ended up not being so. Everyone was blaming different NASA government organizations. The accusations were hot and heavy with different departments blaming each other. I ignored the pettiness, and forced myself to complete the Mishap Report, describing the detailed design requirements of the software application. In addition I had to write a summary of the Payload Teams actions, which included Leona's activities, including the possibility of her adding new ingredients and possibly the potassium Cyanide into the capsules.

During the investigation, I was called up for interrogation. I fidgeted as I sat in the hard uncomfortable chair. The Security officer attached the lie detector on my arm. The NASA investigator questioned, "Did you have any involvement in the Chemical Warfare experiment?" Before I could answer he asked, "Did you see the formula being changed?" Again he questioned, "What accountability do you have to the corruption of the test tubes?"

So many questions to answer, "No, I have never had any involvement in any Chemical Warfare experiments. Yes, Leona had opportunity to contaminate the formula. She was left alone when I had to leave to go to the rest room or for something to drink and eat." Then I remember the red dots, "Oh yes, there were test tubes with red dots. These red dots were explained as anomalies and Leona said they might be better than the ones without the dots. Dr. Masters did not want them aboard, but the reasoning at the time made sense to everyone. Those test tubes possibly could have had the tainted chemicals." I was relieved that they administered a lie detector test. When this whole investigation is over everyone will know I had no involvement.

I cooperated with each probing question, as Dalton gave me strength to continue. All during the investigation his physical wounds mended slowly, but he was by my side and supporting me in every way. He stayed very close during the lie detector test. Even though I knew I was innocent, I was nervous and sweating. The interrogators were menacing and judging, before I even spoke. Thank God, the test proved negative. I knew I had not done anything wrong, but they made me feel guilty. I just wanted the nightmare to end and the violation of my privacy to end.

The forensic physicians had performed an autopsy on Fletcher. They had already concluded the honorable Congressman had no signs of the cancerous tumor but had documented it in the medical report. The cancer was gone. Dalton's delivery system and medicine had cured Fletcher's illness. It was the beginning for a cure of many people with a cancerous death sentence. His team would now begin working on a MECS Drug Implementation Plan with the Federal Drug Administration's blessing. This plan would institutionalize cancer victims with inoperable cancer to be administered with the precious micro crystallization formula. Dalton began creating a gravity designed capsule to create the micro crystals on Earth. He was very busy all day long, but every night he came home to me.

The Mishap Investigation continued for the next six months. There were times when I couldn't sleep at all. I would lay awake at night and remember the happiness in Fletcher's eyes. It was such a shame, and my dreams replayed his playfulness in space. Sometimes I would wake up gasping for air reliving Leona's hands choking the life out of me. I was miserable, which made Dalton miserable. I still felt guilty for ever removing the missing Top Secret documentation, but James had reported it to the company. When I would wake up in a cold sweat, he would comfort me with his love. He would stroke my hair, caressing my breasts softly with the touch that made me shiver. For a brief moment I would forget the interrogations and the many repetitive questions. The passionate love would relax me enough I could eventually fall asleep in his arms. He was my pillar of strength. I loved him more and more every day with my whole being. He was my salvation.

The Mishap Investigation committee continued to meet everyday. It was grueling with their security questions. "How did Leona and Dr. McKnight get the Chemical Warfare serum into the micro crystallization test tubes?" They even implied that I or Ken could be possibly involved since I helped fill them with the formula.

The big question, "Who was buying the Chemical Warfare formula and methodology? It was rumored of links to a foreign government, but no conclusive evidence was ever found. Many answers were not confirmed. James came to my defense with the program anomalies showing how the code had been change to imply that Fletcher's health was diminishing. He praised my work and my dedication to the Space Program. I was very thankful for his alliance, even though I knew I should have never removed the Top Secret documentation from the site.

Finally the results of the lie detector tests were published, which confirmed my innocence. The final report was finished with the details of Leona's and Dr. McKnight's involvement. It was available to the general public for everyone to read. We took a deep breath of relief.

The NASA Internal Mishap Investigation was over but the criminal investigation would be forthcoming. A court date had not been set. Leona would be tried for the murder of Dr. Keller, his family and Congressman Dan Fletcher.

Dalton and I didn't know when this would happen. Dalton smiled, "Susan, in three weeks, let's go sailing and finish our missed vacation."

Chapter 21
The SAIL

We walked hand and hand down to the yacht charter service dock. Dalton said, "There is our pristine ship, a 54-foot center cockpit Irwin."

I smiled, "Thank you Dalton for chartering a boat just like mine. I thought we would never get to finish our vacation. A lot has happened. I'm thrilled we're on our way to the Abacos, Bahamas. I need a vacation. Darling, can we call her the Naia II while we're sailing?"

"Yes we can. It has an electric winch, so you can pull me out of the water, of course if I fall overboard. Yes this is for easy cruising." Dalton joked.

I laughed, teasing him, "You have to be good to me onboard or I'll just sail by you. Then you will have to swim to shore, and you know it's a long way to shore." I leisurely walked down the companionway in surprise. "Wow! The salon is larger than my living room at home. It has a huge galley and it's completely stocked with my favorite wine, champagne and food. Dalton, you can cook for me any time, my man. I just love a man who can cook." I laughed happily.

Dalton said, "Yes I will, just call me any time you are hungry, especially for me." He kissed me passionately. "We should have enough food and water, my dear to last longer than the trip. It's provisioned with anything your heart desires including me. I'm already hungry for you." He said, as he reached over continuing kissing me on the neck.

I pulled away, and climbed onto the aft cabin's stateroom bed. Laughing I posed with my hand under my hair bending over showing my soft rounded cleavage.

"This is the best part of the boat. Come over here, Darling, it has a memory foam mattress, not just hard foam rubber. This is more comfortable than home. Let's try it out right now." I laughed and reached out for him.

Jumping back he said, "Don't get me started, you will have to wait. Susan, look at the full size bathtub in the head. We both can take a bath together, unbelievable. I wonder what size the water tanks that fill such a huge bathtub. At the price of 10 cents a gallon for water it will be a luxury for you my special lady. Every day will be a holiday. Maybe we should use the Champagne and celebrate."

I exclaimed, "How elegant!!!" peeping through the door.

Dalton looked at the navigation table and exclaimed, "I'm glad it has a HF single side band radio. I can keep communication with the Payload team."

I grimaced making a sad face, "Oh Dalton, how can you work while we're on vacation."

Dalton promised. "I'll work no more than two hours a day."

"If you don't, I'll entice you otherwise." I turned and ran up the companionway. I got behind the wheel and started the boat. The engine purred like a kitten. "We're ready to shove off, my Love."

Everyone on the dock waved to us, goodbye. I smiled and headed into the sun with the wind blowing softly in my hair as Dalton was busy adjusting the sails. In a distance I could see many sail boats and trawlers traveling to the exotic islands. I knew this was going to be the greatest vacation I had ever had.

We drifted from island to island, playing, staying, sleeping and eating whenever we wanted. We made love on deserted beaches in broad daylight surrounded by tall palm trees and tropical flowers blooming in the wild. He would stroke my hair and tease me. Dalton was the most loving and tender lover I had ever had. In the mornings he would water me down with the Solar Shower and caringly soap me from the bottom of my feet to the top of my head. He would gently wash my blond curly hair massaging my head with his strong fingers. I had never felt so loved. He was the most sensuous man I had ever met.

We would swim in the nude with the freedom of a mermaid finding time to tell each other our darkest secrets. He wanted to know everything about me, all my experiences in life. I found that it was a freedom, I had never experienced before, the naked body and the naked truth.

He heard the good times and the bad times I had had with men. He knew all my secret of how I had given my soul to my misguided true love and no hope for a functional healthy relationship. He could see deep into my thoughts, knowing me for me and the transparency felt good. My secrets, which always laid heavy on my heart, now known to this amazing man, not hidden anymore. Prior to Dalton, I never felt comfortable or trusted anyone to share my thoughts. Now I wasn't afraid to let Dalton become close and to my surprise even though he knew my secrets, he still loved me. It was the first time I was free of my demons I had carried since childhood. No longer did I feel abandoned, but a part of Dalton, a part that no other man had known.[9]

We had so many wonderful memories, both didn't want to return to reality. The next day on our direct course to Galveston, Texas, the single side band radio loudly announced, "CQ CQ CQ. This is Bronco 53, Whiskey broadcasting in the clear."

I jumped in surprise from the noise while Dalton answered, "Roger, roger. This is the Lady Naia II heading to home port toward Galveston."

I recognized the deep rusty voice and knew it was our friend Ken.

Dalton laughed, "Hey Buddy, you certainly won't leave a man alone even in the middle of the ocean."

Ken's voice exuded so much excitement that he was bubbling, "Dalton, sit down. I've some great news for you. You just earned the Nobel Prize for Medicine for the Micro Encapsulation Crystallization System Experiment. Your name is all over the news and newspapers world wide."

---

[9] The poem "Clear Blue Water" is located in the Poetry section.

Dalton screamed, "It's my life's dream." Then he began to laugh with joy. At that very moment a trio of dolphins jumped from the bow of the boat.

Ken said, "Hurry home, they want to have a Nobel Prize Reception in your honor in Washington DC. Even the President will attend. It's going to be grand ole' party. Then the Nobel Prize for Medicine will be given in Stockholm, Sweden December 10, on the anniversary of Alfred Nobel's death. It will be presented to you at the Stockholm's elegant Concert House by King Carl Gustaf XVI in front of a formally dressed audience. Dalton, the prize is $937,300. Can you believe it?"

Dalton replied, "I'm in heaven. Thank you my friend."

Dalton reached over and pulled me close to his body holding me securely.[10]

He kissed me passionately. "This is the happiest day of my life." He hesitated and looked deep into my eyes and abruptly said, "Will you marry me?"

The boat jogged separating us, I looked at him seriously saying,"You know my rule Dalton, that I have to know you for four seasons. This is just October and we have two more seasons to go."

Dalton had a solemn look on his face. I trimmed the sail using the winch as I smiled mischievously, "But you know my good Doctor, you won't have to wait that long." After I tied the line off on the cleat, I moved over next to him. I embraced him with all the passion I had stored in my soul, waiting for the right man, now to choose wisely this time. Silently I studied this man, this research scientist who had come into my life and changed it forever. As the sun went down on the western horizon, I softly said to Dalton, "Love is captured in the face of a sailor, as he sails the open seas searching for adventure, just like an Astronaut, who sails the wide open space searching for exploration. I see the love in your face, my sailor, my rocket scientist."

Dalton replied, "Take my hand and let me navigate us through life's journey, wherever it may take us, always together, my love."

---

[10] The poem "Holding Me" is located in the Poetry section.

Susan's Poetry

My thoughts were captured by the pen in the magic of my adventures. These adventures are words of the heart fashioned with the rhythms of life and soul.

Caribbean Music

Sensuous notes on thy body
Sounds of the torrid romance
Seek thy own soul totally free
Lost to the beat in a trance

Hearing music of the Caribbean
Dancing revived from years ago
Sway to the tropical rhythm
Make all wrong into right so

Passing ages through the years
Fading youth into tears
No longer should thy care
Left are all the fears

Touching the distance gone
Wishing the child to return
A kiss, a dance, a song
The love always will it burn

Listening to mysterious tones
Capturing the one heart
Sail away into the night wind blown
The future we will part

Sensuous notes on my body
Sounds of the torrid romance
Seek my own soul totally free
Lost in the beat of a trance

Music in the Caribbean, July 2000
(Chapter 1)

The Confident Man

Look deep, enter and see
What is it troubling me?
Could it be fear of being harmed?

Burning into the soul's alarm?
Searching for the one *Confident Man*
Taking a risk in giving both hands
A chance of reality into this life
Now possibly of being a good wife

Finding a *Confident Partner* in which to play
Full wind into sails each mysterious day
Removing the history of pain and sorrow
Far away to yesterday not in tomorrow

Playing with me and taking the part
A Man with Confidence of the heart
Confident is the *Man,* his knowledge of the plan
The future in us to believe, for hope in man

With The Confident Man (DM)
(Chapter 1)

The Touch

The sensation of the touch
The touch—making me come alive
Electrical impulses rush
Throbbing within my thighs

Gently over my body
Blinding to my senses

The Touch, the sensations
Awakening the desire
Leaving no contemplation
How can this go higher?

Gently over my body
Blinding to my senses

The touch, the hand
Crossing ecstasy with pleasure
Only oneness that can
Find a way to measure

Gently over my body
Blinding to my senses

The hands that touch
Breathlessly I say
The touch is so much
With you I lay

Gently over my body
Blinding to my senses

The Touch
(Chapter 9)

Safe Inside

The touch that links us together
Answers not questions
Making what was now forever
Wholeness in sanction
Reach for my hand always knowing
Sanction in Believing
In the look, the smile, the loving
Believing the searching
Every inch covered in kisses
Searching the ending
Beginning with the ecstasy
Safe inside resounding

Safe Inside
(Chapter 12)

The Mask

Take off the mask
Show me who you are
Don't make me ask
In truth to explore

Walk with me this day
Let us seek and play
In the warmth the sun
Make our life just fun

Hidden in the mask
Show me who you are
Speak the truth at last
Empty ever more

The warmth of your body
Blinding me to the real thee
The softness of your kiss
Touches lightly into bliss

Take off the mask
Show me who you are
Silence of your past
Secrets from the shore

Don't tell me your lies
Behind this disguise
In where our destiny goes
Child like giving as one knows

~continued~

Off is the mask
I know not who you are
Broken the trust
Empty hopes do soar

The Mask
(Chapter 13)

Wispy Clouds

The wispy clouds up above
The wind so softly upon thy face
Kisses returned, making love
Hearts together the challenging race

Watching the sunrise early in the morn
Playing on the rolling waves to shore
Being so gentle with each other born
Seeking our selves to be explored

Selecting shells along the way
Leaving foot prints in the sand
Taking the time for children's play
Kissing the salt from thy hand

Feeling thy body, the warmth, the sun
Laying together, side by side
Resting, caring, laughing just for fun
Nearing the blue liquid so wide

Swelling waves to the shore
Timing of the perfect dive
Sensing it must be more
Falling forward in the stride

The wispy clouds up above
The wind so softly upon thy face
Kisses entwined, making love
Sadly leaving this mystical place

With Wispy Clouds
(Chapter 14)

Love

Are you the love of my life?
Are you the one?
My dream, your dream, within all dreams
The once spoken words for this scene

I open my life to you
Redrawing the colors for us to see
Searching inside us for two
Playing, kissing in rapture of me

Are you the love of my life?
Did I meet you before?
Were you the one I hear calling?
Or was it my own voice speaking

Open thy strong arms
I softly feel your masculine part
Spoken are the charms
Revitalize the damaged heart

Are you the love of my life?
Will you always stay?
Will time be the lasting one?
Or the truth played until done

"Hello Love of My Life"
(Chapter 15)

Field of Life

Walk along the crooked path
Blue bells growing neatly
Singly one or two in math
Rolling together as to be
Flowing graceful shimmering sea
Into the field of life
The first step is hard to take
The second may even break
The beating pattern of my heart
Raising, falling swaying apart
Tender pedals falling to the ground
Circling in the air all around
Into the field of life
Sunshine caress by body
Touch my limb, my heart, my soul
Wrap your sweet rays into me
As if to say and to know
My thoughts on this crooked path
Seeking joyful peace not wrath
Into this field of life

Field of Life
(Chapter 18)

The Sadness

What was done in yesterday?
Can no longer be today
Plan for your tomorrow
Take away the sorrow

Take away the heavy sadness
Wipe the tears from your eyes
Erase those hideous lies
Find hope, love, sanctity, and rest

Hide away quickly to your haven
Hear the water shore sounds
Listen to tones around
Happiness nearing the next bend

Your child continues to grow
Always in your heart
Will stay safely a part
And will find a way to know

Forget the past silence
Return your voice
Seek to rejoice

With no more repentance
What was done in yesterday?
Can no longer be today
Plan for your tomorrow
Take away the sorrow

The Sadness
(Chapter 19)

Clear Blue Water

Deep in the clear blue water
Gliding just knowing the way
The sails and lines hard over
To venture in seas we play

From West Palm Beach to West End
Buying conch and lobster to sweet
Anchoring just in the sand
Boat slipping away while asleep

Deep in the clear blue water
Gliding just knowing the way
Salvaging a basket part
To take from yesterday

From West End to Great Sale
Dinghy to coral shore
Using the engine not the sail
Nothing there to explore

Deep in the clear blue water
Gliding just knowing the way
The sails and lines maneuver
To venture in seas we say

From Great Sale to Carter Cay
Exploring the shore of conch shells
Bohemians stingingly
Not waiting but taking quick sail

~continued~

Deep in the clear blue water
Gliding just knowing the way
Turtles and fishing as Dover
To peril in seas they play

From Carter Cay to the Fox Town
Having dinner at Ill Café
Playing and drinking Callick down
High seas in dinghy to May Day

Deep in the clear blue water
Gliding just knowing the way
Dolphins playing together
In the bow parting to play

From Fox Town in Spanish Cay
The rich and famous hide
Seeking all the privacy
Hide away from their demise

Snorkeling and fighting the current
Beautiful sunset at dinner
The touch, the kiss, the living spent
The peace in the days forever

Deep in the clear blue water
Gliding just knowing the way
The sails and lines hard over
To venture in seas we play

~continued~

Making the way back to Great Sale
Stopping at Mangrove Cay
A quick dip from the rail
Speedy return to West Palm Beach

Deep in the clear blue water
Gliding t knowing the way
Seeking home with sails hard over
The venture ending the play

In the Clear Blue Water
Abacos, Bahamas
(Chapter 20)

Holding Me

Hold me in your arms
Away from all harms
Dream of sailing away
Breathlessly for this day

A chance meeting
Love not seeking
Just to open the door
In walked you, no more

Hold me in your arms
With your simple charms
Never would I dream
Life could be serene

A chance meeting
A smile greeting
Reaching your hands
With no demands

Hold me in your arms
Feeling close, so warm
Taking me as no other
Never to be another

Holding Me
(Chapter 20)

Renné at the launch pad

Renné on the launch pad

Escape basket

Rocket booster

Renné at the shuttle

Renné VAB

Also available from PublishAmerica

PURPOSEFUL (NOT RANDOM) ACTS OF KINDNESS

Garie Thomas-Bass, BA, EX, CX
Dr. Kertia Thomas-Black, MD
Kirtis Thomas III, LLP LPC

Even though our book may not be considered politically correct, it is written with the hope that some ideas that used to be called "common sense" will again become the behavior of choice. There is one rule presented for each week of the year.

The fifty-two "suggestions" (or, as we say, "Finally using the brain that your mother gave you!!") presented within these pages are recognizable because everyone has had to experience the negative consequences that happen when someone does not remember to be neighborly in society. (For example: "Stop tossing your trash out the car window, knucklehead!!")

Paperback, 78 pages
6" x 9"
ISBN 1-4241-7958-0

Our hope is that each person will use in his/her life some of these straightforward and easily applied ideas after it is understood why they are important. Truthfully, these rediscovered actions will allow us to live together in society with as little confrontational stress as possible.

Available to all bookstores nationwide.
www.publishamerica.com

Also available from PublishAmerica

FREE AND WILD
By Gary Edward Haymes

Free and Wild is a fast-paced adventure novel written for young adults or anyone who has affection for horses. Part of the story is based in England during 1938 to 1945 during World War II. The turmoil caused by the Nazis includes surviving buzz bombs, bomber attacks, and airplane combat. Winston Churchill is in the story (his dialogue is authentic).

The story is loaded with inspiring, exciting activity. The textured plot combines intriguing characters in a compelling tale recreating history blended in with the sport of kings— thoroughbred horse racing. Prepare for horse brawls, gypsy advice, humor, and realistic battle scenes along with the most exciting sword duel you will ever experience. (Did you know that USA President Andrew Jackson survived one hundred sword grudge duels?)

Paperback, 197 pages
6" x 9"
ISBN 1-60813-790-2

To spice up the action we travel to the Sahara Desert. A boiling dusty sand and sagebrush-filled location. In the Sahara Desert, Captain Kirk and Whitey, his horse, battle hostile Arabs and Nazis, a factual World War II occurrence that few remember. During the Desert War both find love in strange places. An understanding of horse behavior, habits and psychology and other animal information is unified with a thrilling story from knowledge gained by the author, a published writer and stable owner who lives near the Fort Erie Racetrack, reputed to be the world's most beautiful racetrack, home of the premiere $500,000 Prince of Wales Stakes race. Thoroughbred racing and horse aficionados will glean horse motivations and gain insights to the racetrack from many pages of electrifying entertainment.